宏泰人壽投資長　廖瑞雄推薦

Here, I come! USA

留學達人英語通

洪子健 ◎著

不只教你怎麼做，還教你怎麼說
實用完整的留學生活指南

留學達人為你整理重點，告訴你 **4** 大 "撇步"！

step
①

step
②

step
③

step
④

出國前
申請、考試、行程
資訊樣樣不能少

留學中
食衣住行育樂+醫療，
你一定要知道

學成後
當地求職、面試、履歷
tips面面俱到

返國後
人脈維繫超重要

達人為你模擬情境對話、與你分享經驗、替你解決 "說不出" 的痛

d 作者序

　　我跟同年代的台灣學生一樣,從國中開始學英文,經歷六年背單字、學文法的台式英文教學,辛辛苦苦地上了大學。大學期間基本上是台灣經濟轉型為高科技的時期,也成就了當時的台灣奇蹟。家裡開始覺得是不是可以讓小孩出國念書?在大學畢業當兵退伍後,開始工作,也一邊補習托福準備出國念書。正好碰上台灣錢淹腳目、股市首度上萬點、台幣持續升值的年代。也就在 1989 年一美元兌換 25 台幣匯率之時,出國到德州農工大學念書。1991 拿到碩士,卻正好碰上美國經濟最差之時,也就繼續念博士。在學業中生下個男孩,後來在可以準備畢業之時,正好是美國與全世界的電腦起飛而網路業開始萌芽之際。也就在矽谷順利找到工作,而後也生下老二,女兒。但接下來也歷經了網路泡沫化,一開始公司沒受到影響,但是在後期營收也開始漸漸降低,因為兩家裡的親戚朋友都在台灣,而小孩的教育又可以經由實驗中學雙語部銜接,於 2004 年決定舉家回台灣。算算在德州六年、矽谷工作九年,在美國待了共計十五年。

　　回台後基本上還是在科技業任職,不過也找出時間,先在雅虎奇摩建立了個學習英文的部落格,因為奇摩部落格的關門,把它搬到了「隨意窩」:一個關於英文學習的部落格。後來發現台灣英文教育還是跟我國、高中時一樣的,專注在背單字、學文法,不重閱讀的學習方式。後來透過部落格有個機緣開始兼差教英文,加入了臉書,也建立了跟 TC 學英文的粉絲專頁,幾年之後決定從科技業退下來,專心致力於英文教學,只想改變台灣長期以填鴨的英文教學方式。

　　有幸承蒙倍斯特出版事業有限公司的邀請寫出這本書，裡面用中英文描述了出國留學所會碰到的問題與面對方法，其中有我或是朋友的親身經歷，也有我的一些看法，希望能對有興趣出國留學或遊學的朋友有所幫助。如果對本書有任何建議，還請到 FB 裡的跟 TC 學英文的粉絲專頁上留言，謝謝。

洪子健

推薦序

不見 TC，只見熱情

和 TC 是建中同學，算算也 30 年囉！

30 年前，初見他，就是渾身是勁，充滿熱情，任何話題他都能高談闊論，總有獨到的想法。說起來真該感謝當年的學風，讓我們除了讀書之外，對各種議題總是充滿的好奇，總想深入地探究，總想和同學分享各種新的發現。

30 年後，再見他，「鶴髮童顏」是第一印象，是個頭髮變白的留美科技學者，但不變的就是那大嗓門，不變的就是那充滿熱情的笑聲及生活態度，曾經，因短暫停車，停車場免收停車費，這位熱血中年竟自行解釋為：「停車場美眉說，帥哥免費」，這種率真。熱情的生活態度，其實是非常令人豔羨的！

這些年，TC 的熱情直指英文教學，更真切地說，那好像不是一種教學，他是在透過英文散播一種態度，他希望學習得過程是生活的，是自然的，是快樂的，那樣一切會變得更有趣。這有甚麼不一樣呢？這，讓「學英文」變成過程，「有趣」變成了目的，光這一點，就是個不平凡的成就。

這本書我也看了，令人驚訝的是，連我這樣的中年人，連我這樣沒準備留學的人，竟也十分受用，我想內容的流暢度應是主要的原因，從這裡，也可看出 TC 的用心。

我推薦這本書給大家，讓我們一起來閱讀 TC 的英文，一起來閱讀 TC 的熱情！

廖瑞雄

ⓓ 編者序

　　根據 2013 年「亞洲教育大調查」中的統計，美國是台灣留學生在選擇留學國家時的首選。而在同年 11 月份由美國國際教育協會的一項報告中指出，台灣留學生為美國國際學生中的第六大來源，相較於往年有下滑的趨勢，但是在學成後，留在美國工作的人數卻逐年增加。

　　本書一共分為四個部分，有出國前的準備事項、留學中所會遇到的食衣住行等的疑難雜症、留在國外找工作時所要知道的小撇步、還有返國後和同學好友的聯繫。所有的相關事項《留學達人英語通─美國篇》都有解析，每個章節內的對話以情境式呈現，讓您在遇到問題時，溝通上能更佳的流暢。還有達人的經驗分享，讓您在處裡留學的相關事務時能更加地得心應手。

　　《留學達人英語通─美國篇》是留學生活中不可或缺的生活指南。不僅僅適合想要留學，或是已經留學的同學們，也適合於想要一窺留學生活以及對英語有興趣的同學們 !!

　　　　　　　　　　　　　　　　　　　　倍斯特編輯部

目 次 Contents

Part I 出國前

Part II 留學中

Chapter 1 民以食為天

Chapter 2 怎麼穿比較好

Part I
出國前

 科系的選擇

1 主題對話

Michael Chen is talking to his girlfriend Judy Wang.
Michael Chen 跟他的女朋友 Judy Wang 聊到申請學校與科系。

Michael	I would like to major in Computer Science.	我想主修資訊科學。
Judy	I am shooting for Stanford. Are you considering it?	我想進史丹佛大學，你要不要考慮一下史丹佛？
Michael	It's going to be really tough for me to get into Master Program in Computer Science with Stanford University. I am applying UCLA and UCSD, since I have a better chance in getting in either one of them.	史丹佛的資訊碩士課程比較難進，我想申請 UCLA 和 UCSD，因為機會比較大。
Judy	You can choose other programs with Stanford. Graduate school life is tough, so I'd like to have you around in case I need any comforting. Don't you worry about the long distance relationship?	你可以選其他的科系啊，研究生生活蠻難熬的，我想要你隨時在我身邊，你難道不擔心遠距離戀愛嗎？

Michael	I know I can get into less popular programs, but it would be tougher for me to get a job after getting my degree. To be able to get a well-compensated job would make our life much easier later on. Also, with Facebook, we can stay in touch constantly, and we can talk on Skype as often as we like. I don't think it's going to be long distance at all.	我是可以申請一些比較不熱門的科系，但畢業後工作比較不好找，找個薪水較好的工作會讓我們未來的生活更好過。還有我們可以用 FB 保持聯繫，也可以隨時用 Skype 聊天，我相信這一點都不會像是遠距離戀愛。
Judy	I'd just like to have you around me if possible.	我只想盡可能地跟你待在一起啊！
Michael	How about you applying for UCLA and UCSD? Both business schools are great, as good as the Stanford one from what I heard. In this case, I can study Computer Science and at the same time you can get a good degree. More importantly, we can stay close together.	你要不要試試看 UCLA 和 UCSD？就我所知這兩個商學院都很棒，不比史丹佛差，這樣一來我可以主修資訊，同時你也可以拿到好學位，更重要的是我們可以待在一起。
Judy	Good idea. I'll check both schools and more than likely apply for them. It would be great for both of us.	好主意。我去查看看，並申請這兩個學校，這對我們而言是最棒的做法。

2 心情小語

💜 Choosing a major was not at all a problem for me. I got into Department of Electrical Engineering, National Sun, Yat-Sen University, after College Entrance Exam.It naturally became the major for my graduate study. To be honest with you, the fact that Electrical Engineering, especially Computer Engineering has been a hot field, helps my decision too. That being said, it is a major decision for most of the students since it would more than likely impact the life later on.

> 選擇科系對我而言不是什麼問題，大學聯考後，我上了中山大學電機系，很自然地在研究所主修電機。説實話，主要原因也是因為電機工程，尤其電腦工程，是個熱門領域，也因此強化了我的決定。對於大多數的學生而言，這會相對地影響日後的生活，自然是個重要決定。

💜 It's better for you to list the **options** and their **pros and cons** against each one of them. Obviously, you could easily get **torn** apart between interest and career. One thing for sureis that there is no perfect solution. Look deep down inside your heart and see if there is any interest, or better yet, passion, exists for the subjects you listed. Try to realize how strong the passion is. If you know what you want to do for the rest of your life, you may have found your answer. Besides passion, you need to consider the prospect career-wise. Is it easy to get a job? How much is the salary? Are you coming back or planning to stay in the US? Getting a degree could take two to four years, or even longer. How is the job market two to four years from now? You need to look ahead at least that far away from now. I know trying to predict the future is often tough, but without even considering it would be a **potential** risk, don't you think? Can you **legally** work in the US? More importantly, would you like to get a job there? If not, you have to choose a hot major, or a subject that is easy to get a job. Without the green card, it would be not easy for you to get a job in US. Even if you are planning to come back after getting the degree, you still need to consider a major that is easy to get a job domestically. It may sounds like a **cliché**, but you have to think about life after graduation. Making enough money to support your future family, or at the very least yourself, is a must, right? Of course, if you are interested in a hot field, then congratulations, you have the best of both worlds. Go for it, and work hard and study hard, knowing that you will enjoy a much better life later on.

最好是將你的選項及其優劣點列出來，很明顯的，你很容易就會在興趣與職業之間陷入天人交戰。你要先明白這件事沒有所謂的完美答案！問問自己，你的興趣甚至是熱誠是否有落在你所列出的科目當中？思考一下那份熱誠的強度有多少？如果你知道日後你想做什麼，你可能已經找到答案了！除了熱誠之外，你還需要考慮職業的未來遠景，是否容易找到工作？薪水多少？你會留在美國或是回國工作？拿個學位需要兩到四年，甚至更久，兩到四年後的工作狀況又是如何？你需要盡可能地展望未來。我知道試著要預測未來有點難度，但是完全不去考慮的話，會有潛在的風險，不是嗎？你是否能留在美國合法的工作？更重要的是，能不能找到工作？如果不行的話，選個熱門又容易找到工作的主修比較保險。沒有綠卡真的不容易找工作，就算你計畫在拿到學位後要回國，你還是要考慮國內的工作市場，這或許聽來是個陳腔濫調，但你確實需要考慮畢業後的生活，賺足夠的薪水來養家，最少也要能夠養活你自己，沒錯吧！當然如果你的興趣本就是個熱門領域，恭喜你，這是兩全其美，放手去做，努力工作，認真學習，我知道你日後將能享有更美好的生活！

3 單字與例句

option　*n.* 選擇

You need to check all options before making a decision.
在下決定前你需要檢驗所有的選擇。

pros and cons　利弊；優缺點

She balanced the pros and cons of this situation.
她權衡在這情勢下的利弊。

tear (tear, tore, torn)　*v.* 撕開、扯破

She was torn apart by the death of her child.
她因為小孩的死去而心碎。

potential　*adj.* 潛在的、可能的

We need to evaluate the potential risk before investing.
投資前需要評估所有可能的風險。

legally　*adv.* 合法地

Can we park the car legally here?
這裡可以合法停車嗎？

cliché　*n.* 陳腐的說法、陳詞濫調

The advertising world is full of cliché phrases and images.
廣告世界充滿了陳腔濫調的語言與圖像。

知識備忘錄

　　說到選擇科系，一般家長都會希望小孩挑一個穩當、風險小、容易找工作的主修。但是如果真沒有興趣，那未來只為了錢而工作，其實也不會是好事！話說回來，如果你只追求興趣，卻不考慮未來出路，萬一真的是找不到麵包，那只會更可悲！在選擇科系上面，你多半要面對興趣與現實的考量。我認為如果你沒有特別的興趣，或許穩當容易找到工作的主修會是風險比較小的選擇。如果你針對某些科目有興趣，甚至有熱情，那就需要仔細思考一下了。在許多勵志書裡還有網路上許多文章，要你不考慮風險而去追求理想，甚至舉出一些成功的例子來激勵人們。如果你就這麼毫不考慮地追夢，那你就是笨到了極點！說實話，如果摔慘了、夢碎了，這些所謂的勵志作家會幫你嗎？但是話說回來，我並不是要大家不去追求理想，只是先要仔細評估。例如你對文學有興趣想做個作家，那是不是先要評估一下，你是否真的有文學天分？就算有，是不是真的每個有文學天份的人，就會變成個成功的作家？至少在追夢前，是不是先看看幾位成功的作家，看他們是具備了那些要件？又是如何補足自己的缺陷？又是如何成功的？看著前人的經驗更會增加自己成功的機會，不是嗎？在仔細分析過後才來跨步朝自己的理想前進，是不是會更穩當、更有機會？

Part I

Unit 2 要到那兒去讀書

1 主題對話

Michael Chen is talking to his college professor Patrick Liu.
Michael Chen 正跟他的教授 Patrick Liu 聊天。

Michael	I'd like to major in Computer Science. Having several schools in mind, I'd like to know your opinion.	我想主修資訊科學，心裡已經有幾個學校了，但是我想聽聽你的意見。
Patrick	If I remember correctly, your GPA is pretty good, right?	如果我記得沒錯的話，你成績還不錯對吧！
Michael	It's 3.5, and my TOFEL iBT is 95.	我的學分平均是 3.5 我的托福是 95。
Patrick	How about GRE?	那 GRE 呢？
Michael	It's 1890.	1890。
Patrick	Pretty impressive, any particular schools in mind?	很不錯 想申請哪些學校？
Michael	I am thinking Stanford University, UC Berkeley, UCLA, University of Michigan, University of Texas, and Texas A&M.	史丹佛、加大柏克萊、洛杉磯、密西根大學、德州大學和德州農工大學。
Patrick	All of them are great schools. What are your **preferences**?	都是好學校。你喜歡哪一所？

Michael	I'd like to stay in the West, preferably California, but I know Stanford and UC Berkeley are long shots.	我想留在西部，最好是加州，不過我知道史丹佛和加大柏克萊不容易進。
Patrick	Worth a try, you never know. You have no chance if you don't apply.	值得一試啊！申請學校很難説，況且不申請就沒機會了。
Michael	How about University of Michigan? It is cold up there, though.	密西根大學呢？不過北邊真的很冷。
Patrick	Another great school. As for the weather, it isn't as bad as you think. There are heaters inside every building and housing. The only thing you have to worry about is the walk between them, and a puffer coat or a winter jacket can easily take care of that. Some people just don't like cold weather at all, though.	也是一個好學校，至於天氣情況沒你想像的差。室內都有暖氣，唯一要注意的是各個建築物間的走動，有一件羽絨外套或保暖夾克就可以了。不過有些人就是受不了冷天氣。
Michael	How about the two Texas schools? University of Texas does **rank** higher.	兩間德州學校呢？好像德州大學排名比較高。
Patrick	That is the **misconception** in Taiwan. Ranking isn't everything, especially for graduate schools. Both of them are great schools. You need to look at the professors there, choose the one that best suits your study. You know picking a good professor is way more important than picking the school itself.	這正是台灣的問題，排名不代表一切，尤其是研究所。兩所都是好學校。去研究一下，選一個最合乎你專長的教授。選個好教授遠比選學校重要多了。

Part I

Michael	Thanks, I'll do some research not only on the school, but also on the professors.	謝謝，我會多花點時間好好地看一下學校和教授。
Patrick	That's good, and let me know if you have further questions.	很好，有問題再找我。
Michael	Thanks for the talk. I really appreciate it.	感謝你給我的意見，對我幫助很大。
Patrick	Talk to you next time, bye.	下次再聊。
Michael	Bye.	再見。

2 心情小語

❤ We usually take ranking as one of the most important consideration while choosing a school, and underestimate a school if ranks lower, which cannot be more wrong. For most Chinese, if you can go to Harvard University, you'll never choose Princeton. When you can study in UC Berkeley, you'll never pick UCSD. It is ridiculous to take ranking as the sole consideration when picking a school. When considering a school, especially for graduate study, you need to pay more attention to the professors on their research topics, their publication and **academic reputation**. Choosing a good professor is way more important than picking a higher ranking school. You have to know, however, that the best academic and research professor is usually the toughest. You need to be well-prepared mentally and physically when you pick a professor like that. Once you get through the tough life and get a degree, however, that is the time you can enjoy the fruit after all the hard labor.

我們在選學校時往往把排名列為最重要的考慮因素。排名稍稍低一點的學校就覺得比較不好。這真的是錯得離譜！多數華人如果能去哈佛，就不會去普林斯頓；如果可以念加大柏克萊，就不會念加大聖地牙哥。選學校時只考慮排名真的很可笑！在考慮學校，尤其是研究所時，你更要看看教授的研究主題、著作與學術名聲。選個好教授遠比選個排名高的學校重要多了。不過你也要知道最棒的學術研究教授，往往也是最嚴格的教授。當你要選擇這類的教授時，生理上、心理上都要有所準備。不過等你熬過來拿到學位後，就是你享受辛苦得來的鮮美果實的時候了。

💙 Ranking isn't as important as most Chinese think, even if you are choosing a major for your undergraduate study. Most Americans really don't have any ideas of the ranking, except for schools in their own state. They do know the good schools, but not the exact ranking. Getting a good grade is usually more important. A higher GPA from a good school is as meaningful as, or even better than a lower GPA from a great school. When you are interviewed for a job, nobody will give you the job just because you got a degree from the top 10 school. You have to keep that in mind. Going to a school that is not among your preferred ones will not be the end of the world. Getting a good grade will compensate the difference in ranking. Study hard and get a good GPA is going to help you more down the road.

　　就算你選大學時，其實排名也不如華人想的那麼重要。多數美國人除了自己州裡的大學之外，對於其他學校的排名並沒有什麼概念。他們確實知道好學校，但對於確切的排名可說是一無所知。拿個好成績往往史重要。好學校高一點的成績，其實跟很棒學校低一點的成績一樣，甚至更好。在找工作時不會有人只因為你是前十名學校畢業的就給你工作。這需要謹記在心。好成績足以補足排名上的差別，認真念書拿到好成績，會在日後給你很大的幫助。

3 單字與例句

preference *n.* 喜好、偏愛

Do you have any preference for today's lunch, Chinese, Japanese, or American food?

今天的午餐你有什麼喜好，中式、日式還是美式食物？

rank *n.* 排名

The teacher ranked her student according to their grades.

老師根據學生的成績排名。

misconception *n.* 錯誤的觀念、概念

There is a misconception about you.

這裡有一個關於你的奇怪的誤會。

academic *adj.* 學校的、學術的、理論的

The professor is more interested in academic questions.

這教授對學術問題較有興趣。

reputation *n.* 名譽、名聲

This restaurant has a great reputation for customer service.

這餐廳就是出名在客戶服務。

知識備忘錄

　　說到選學校，華人多半以排名為主。說實話當年我也一樣！把電機系的排名找出來，就照著申請了。不過以我的情況，全家人連飛機都沒搭過，美國有幾個州？哪個州在哪裡？完全不知道，也難怪如此。好笑的是，有好幾個排名差一點的學校拒絕我，反而是其中一個排名最好收了我。在出國後慢慢發覺，其實老美不用說不在意排名，其實他們對排名真的是沒有 idea。他們只知道那些州裡有哪些好學校，不同州的學校排名他們真的不清楚，更不用說要細分到哪個科系了。在我畢業後找工作面試時，他們更在意的是學校的成績，只要是一般人觀念中的好學校，其實真的沒差別，排名差個十名、二十名、三十名真的沒人在意！更何況排名會根據不同的標準、不同的時間、不同的機構會有差異，有時還會有很大的差異。看看每年台灣所公布的所謂大學排名就知道了。真的差那麼多嗎？而且真的有心的話根據評審標準『做作業』，是很有可能讓排名前進，但是這有意義嗎？如果自己程度不是那麼好硬申請到名校，很可能只是自找麻煩，而以甚至念不下去也說不定。話說回來就算華人在意名校，其實也只有最後一個學歷算數而已。與其先找名校，不如在大學、碩士時也到個還可以的學校，適應環境之後也比較可以唸出好成績，幾年後再以好的成績申請到名校，這不是更好！

Part I

Unit 3 申請學校

1 主題對話

Michael Chen is talking to his college professor Patrick Liu for graduate school **application**.
Michael Chen 正跟他的教授 Patrick Liu 談到申請研究所。

Michael	I've decided on the colleges I want to apply for my master degree, and I'd like to check with you for the application process since you've done it before.	我已經決定要申請哪些學校，我想了解一下申請的程序，根據你過去的經驗來說。
Patrick	Sure, no problem, but it was a long time ago, and I am afraid that the process might be different now.	沒問題。只是那可是好久以前，現在恐怕都不太一樣了。
Michael	Still, your previous experience would certainly help.	我相信你的經驗應該還是會有幫助。
Patrick	The most important thing is to check the corresponding admission application web page of each college you are interested in. Just follow the instructions listed there.	最重要的是看一下你有興趣要申請的大學申請網頁，只要根據網頁上面所列出來的步驟就可以了。
Michael	Any documents needed generally?	一般需要哪些文件？

Part I

Patrick	You'll, more than likely, need to fill out the application form, and send in official **transcript** and copy of test scores. Also, you need to write an essay about yourself, and ask a few professors to write **recommendation** letters for you, and last but not the least, the application fee.	通常需要填好申請入學表，遞送大學成績單，各項考試成績，同時也要寫一篇自傳，也要請幾位教授幫你寫推薦信，還有就是繳交申請費用。
Michael	How should I pay the application fee?	我要怎麼繳費呢？
Patrick	The most convenient way to pay the fee is by credit card. For the transcript, you need to check our college web site for more details. Remember, the official transcript needs to be submitted directly from the college you attended.	最方便的就是用信用卡，至於成績單你要去我們大學網站看看怎麼申請？記得成績單要直接從學校裡寄出來。
Michael	How about the recommendation letters? Would you write one for me?	介紹信呢？你可以幫我寫一封嗎？
Patrick	Sure, you are one of my brightest students. It would be my pleasure.	沒問題。你是我的得意門生，這是我的榮幸。
Michael	I'll prepare the essay myself, but could you proof read it for me?	我會準備自傳，但是否能請你幫我看一下？
Patrick	Sure, remember to emphasize your passion you have, and the awards and competitions you have won. Just let them know you are the best candidate they can have.	沒問題。記得強調你的熱情，還有你曾贏過的獎項與比賽，也就是說，讓他們覺得你是最佳人選。

Michael	Thanks for all the information. I really appreciate it.	感謝你的資訊，對我幫助很大。
Patrick	Talk to you next time, bye.	下次再聊。
Michael	Bye.	再見。

2 心情小語

❤ Not that I am old, but when I was applying for schools, there was no internet in Taiwan, and internet in US was still in its infancy. Without emails and web sites, we needed to rely on regular mail for the whole application process. It certainly was time consuming with a sense of insecurity.

> 這可不是説我老了，我在申請學校時台灣還沒有網路，美國網路也還在嬰兒期。沒有電子郵件、沒有網站，全都要仰賴郵局郵件來進行申請，除了很花時間，也有份不安全感。

❤ The application process is a bit tedious but not complex. You just need to check and follow the web site instructions. Some of you may wonder why not just asks the overseas education consulting firm to help with the whole process. In my opinion, it is a waste of money. Nobody else in the world knows you better than you do. Only you can prepare the documents that best showcases you. However, it is better that you get somebody to check and proof read your essay to make sure that it is well-written. The most important point for the letter is to talk about your strength, to mention how you like the subject, and why you have the passion for it. Never, and I repeat, never talk about your shortcomings. In other words, don't be **modest** as the Chinese tradition tells you to. If you got awards, won some competitions, be sure to mention them. The purpose for the essay is to sell yourself to the college, to let them know you are the best candidate they can get.

整個申請過程有點繁瑣，但並不複雜，你只要查一下網路，跟著裡面的步驟就可以了。或許有些人會想委託留學代辦中心處理，在我看來那是浪費錢。沒人比你更認識你自己，只有你最清楚如何用文件來展現你自己。不過最好還是請人看一下你的自傳，來確認內容無誤。寫白傳時最重要的是談論你的長處、說明你為什麼喜歡這個主修、為什麼你有這熱誠。永遠，再次強調永遠，不要論及你的缺點！換句話說，不要遵循中國文化所強調的謙遜，如果你得到過獎項、贏過些競賽，盡量多提。自傳論文的目的是推銷你自己，讓學校知道你是最佳人選。

♥ As for the recommendation letters, from what I know, most Chinese professors would like you to prepare a **draft** for them to review, modify and sign on. You can search Google to get some samples. Based on that, you can write a good one. Again, do not talk about your weakness. For example, if you have less than a satisfying grade, do not give any explanation. Doing so would look like you are making excuses. Be sure to mention how you help professor on research, providing ideas, working on modeling, and collecting and analyzing data. Since the professor need to sign on it, check with the professor first for the things you are going to put on the letter. Getting a professor to work with you willingly is important.

　　至於介紹信，就我所知，多數的華人教授會希望你先提供草稿，讓他們編輯、更改、簽名。你可以先搜尋一些介紹信範例，根據範例寫出介紹信。再次強調，不要談論你的缺點，舉例來說如果你的成績不盡理想，不用提出任何解釋，這麼做可能只會讓人覺得你在尋找藉口。不如說明強調你如何幫助教授做研究、提供想法、尋求模式、蒐集並分析資料。因為需要教授簽名最好跟教授提一下你的想法，找一位願意幫助你的教授很重要。

❤ Please remember that getting in the school is only the first step, and the more important task is to work hard after you getting in. This is not only for your own good, but also to build credit for your school, and your professor. Good luck to your application.

> 　記得申請進入學校只是第一步，進入之後更要努力認真，這不只是幫助你自己，也是為你的學校、教授建立信用，祝你好運！

3 單字與例句

application　*n.* 申請

To open a bank account, you need to fill out the application first.
到銀行開戶需要先填好申請表格。

transcript　*n.* 成績單

As a new college graduate, you need to submit your transcript for the job application.
身為應屆大學畢業生，在找工作時你需要遞送成績單。

recommendation　*n.* 介紹

The company gives Michael a job based on his advisor's recommendation.
這家公司根據 Michael 指導教授的推薦聘任了他。

modest　*adj.* 謙虛、審慎、適度

Don't be so modest, your performance was wonderful.
不要這麼謙虛，你表演的真的很棒！

draft　*n.* 草稿、草圖

The novel differs quite a bit from the earlier drafts.
這小說跟原始草稿差別很大。

知識備忘錄

　　談到申請學校，比起現在，我那個時候連美國網路都是嬰兒期的時代可說是天差地遠了。在一個全家沒人搭過飛機、完全不知道美國有幾個州的家庭裡，也不知道為什麼，反正從沒想過要找代辦，就這麼一個人跌跌撞撞地把學校給申請好了。還記得那時候選了些學校，要求申請函的信就寄去了。多數都把相關表格和所需要的文件名單寄回來，還記得有幾個排名很高的學校，先寄給我個 preliminary application form，也就是簡化的申請表，只需要填入一些基本資料，諸如 GPA, 托福和 GRE 成績，不需要附上任何文件。把簡化表格寄出後，過沒多久就通知，謝謝再聯絡。其實這幾個學校有事先聲明因為申請人太多，需要初步審核；不過這樣也好，直接謝謝再聯絡，也確實省下我的一些時間。

　　在這個網路時代申請學校可簡單多了，到網站看一下有哪些表格需要填寫、有哪些成績需要寄出、有哪些文件需要準備，按表操課就可以了。如果說有要強調的，那就是千萬不要發揮中國人謙虛的美德！說實話，老美什麼優點沒有，就是有『自信』。一個謙虛的人跟一個有『自信』的人，以同樣的條件寫出來的介紹信與自傳，內容絕對會有很大的差別！記得介紹信和自傳是用來推銷你自己的，我沒有教你要說謊，我只是強調你要有『自信』！有自信、雄赳赳、氣昂昂的推銷自己就對了。

Unit 4 考試準備

1 主題對話

David Hsu is talking to Michael Chen for TOEFL iBT and GRE preparation.

David Hsu 和 Michael Chen 談到 TOEFL iBT 以及 GRE 的準備。

David	I'd like to take GRE and TOFEL iBT. Do you have any advice for me?	我想考 GRE 和 TOFEL iBT，你有什麼建議嗎？
Michael	They are two different kinds of exams with different purposes, so you need to prepare each one differently.	這可是兩種目的不同、不一樣的考試，所以準備的方法也不一樣。
David	I only know GRE is for graduate school application, and TOEFL is basically an English test. Also, I heard GRE test format just changed recently, right?	我只知道 GRE 是給研究所學生的，而托福基本上就是測試英文能力，而且聽說最近 GRE 改形式了對吧！
Michael	Yes, while TOEFL is just a test for you to show that if your English is good enough to study in an English speaking country, GRE is set up for student to show their capability for graduate school. Educational Testing Service (ETS) completely changed GRE test in August 2011. Unfortunately for you, I took the old format.	托福是用來顯示你是否有足夠的英文能力在英語系國家念書，而 GRE 則是測試學生是否有能力念研究所，ETS 在 2011 年八月改變了 GRE 的測試形式，不幸的是，我考的是舊的格式。

David	You can still help me, though. How do I prepare for the two tests?	你的經驗還是能幫到我，我該怎麼準備這兩個考試呢？
Michael	For GRE, since it's a tougher and more difficult test for r egular Chinese students, I would suggest you to go to one of the cram schools. As for TOEFL, especially iBT, it can really test your English capability, so the better way to prepare for it is reading, reading and more reading.	GRE 一般對於華人學生而言比較難，也比較難準備，我會建議你到補習班上課。至於托福，尤其是 iBT，較能測出你的英文實力，所以最好的準備方式就是讀英文、多讀英文、加強讀英文。
David	How about the speaking and writing sections for TOEFL? I am really nervous about these two parts.	那口語和寫作呢？我最擔心的就是這兩部分。
Michael	Just watch more American TV shows and repeat what you heard. Simply pretend that you are a **parrot**. As for writing, just read more. If you find some sentences interesting, just memorize it.	多看美國電視影集，看的時候跟著你所聽到的唸出來，把自己當成是隻鸚鵡。至於寫作還是要先多讀，如果看到一些你喜歡的句子多念幾次，把它背下來。
David	Thanks for your suggestion. I'll try my best and keep my fingers crossed.	謝謝你的建議。我會盡力的，希望我有好運。
Michael	Sure thing, talk to you next time.	沒問題下次再聊。
David	Bye.	再見。

❷ 心情小語

❤ When I took the TOEFL and GRE tests, it was before the internet age. Needless to say, both of them were pen and paper tests. It's way different from the new ones taken with a computer.

> 我考托福和 tests 時網路還沒成形，不用說兩種都是紙筆測驗，跟現在用電腦考試可說是天差地遠。

❤ For the GRE test, it is basically design for whoever wants to go to a graduate school, so it is basically a test for US college graduates, which makes it a lot tougher for Taiwanese students. I would suggest you to go to a cram school for the preparation. As for TOEFL, straight from ETS, "The TOEFL iBT test measures your ability to use and understand English at the university level. And it **evaluates** how well you combine your listening, reading, speaking and writing skills to perform academic tasks."It's basically a test designed for students whose first language is not English, which makes it easier for us in terms of English. Thus, I'll talk more about TOEFL here.

> 以 GRE 而言，基本上是用來測試想上研究所的學生，所以設計上是個給美國大學畢業生的考試，當然對台灣學生而言就比較難。我會建議到補習班補習比較好！至於托福，以下是 ETS 官方的說明：『TOEFL iBT 測試你對大學程度英文的了解與使用能力，同時評估你在執行學術工作上綜合聽、說、讀、寫的能力』。托福基本上是用來測試非英語母語學生的英文能力，比起 GRE 要簡單多了，因此我會多談一些托福。

❤ Even though the test format is different, the basic idea is still the same, except that speaking and writing are now part of the TOEFL test. For reading and listening, I have to **emphasize** that in order to have a better score, when you are listening to English news or reading in English article, Chinese language is not allowed in your brain. You have to train yourself for this, and it isn't as difficult as you think. When you are trying to prepare for listening comprehension, read the sentence out loud first. Make sure you understand what you are reading, and then close your eyes, listen to the conversation. If you have any problems understanding the whole paragraph, try one sentence at a time. If there are five sentences in the paragraph, try to understand each of them one by one. After that, you need to listen to the whole paragraph and try to make sense of it. For reading **comprehension**, there is no way other thanreading. Pick the topics you are interested in, and choose related articles on the web for your reading pleasure.

除了說與寫也成為測試的一部分以外，托福就算測驗方式不同，基本的理念是一樣的。講到聽和讀，如果想要有好成績，那麼不管是聽或讀的時候，腦袋裡只能有英文，不能有任何中文！這需要訓練，但是沒有你想像中的難。練習聽力時記得先把句子大聲地唸出來，確認你了解你所唸的，然後閉上眼睛聽，如果你無法了解整段話，先一句、一句的試，如果這段裡有五句話，一句一句的分開聽懂，當然最後還是要試著把五句一口氣都聽懂。而說到閱讀，只有一個方法：多讀、多讀、再多讀。在網路上選你喜歡的主題文章來讀，才會有樂趣。

❤ Now comes the tough parts of speaking and writing. When you are listening, try to repeat what you heard like what a parrot would do. When you are reading, just memorize the sentences that impress you the most. Mimic the good oral and written English is the best way to improve your English in a short amount of time.

再來要講到最難的說與寫了！在你聽的時候，記得重述你聽到的句子，就像隻鸚鵡一樣。當你閱讀的時候，如果看到讓你印象深刻的句子，就背下來！要在短期內學好口語英文和英文寫作能力，模仿是最好的方法。

❤ Finally, happy preparing for the tests, and good luck.

　　最後，好好準備考試！祝你好運！

 **單字與例句**

parrot　*n.* 鸚鵡

You need to talk like a parrot and repeat what you heard in order to learn English.
學英文要像隻鸚鵡，重述你所聽到的。

evaluate　*v.* 評估、估價

You need to evaluate all the options before making the final decision.
你需要評估所有的選項，然後才做決定。

emphasize　*v.* 著重、強調

Using all kinds of gestures, he emphasized what he was saying.
他以各種手勢強調他所說的言論。

comprehension　*n.* 了解、理解力

The problem is so complex that it is beyond our comprehension.
這問題複雜到讓我們難以理解。

知識備忘錄

　　自己本身是教英文的，講到準備考試可有話説了。一直以來，在台灣教英文，都把重心放在背單字、教文法上面。我就針對這兩點提出我的看法和建議。大家都背過單字，一禮拜五十個、一百個單字的背。想想什麼時候真的把這五十個、一百個單字記下來了？就算記下來了一個月後、幾個月後呢？如果你有注意的話，這本書裡所有的單字都有例句。硬背單字不如多唸例句，把例句唸到有FU、對例句裡的單字有FU，自然而然地就會把單字記下來了。碰到新的單字最重要的是要會唸，如果不知道單字怎麼唸，簡單，線上字典都有發音，知道嗎？線上字典最大的好處不是解釋中文意思而是發音，跟著唸，把單字唸出來，唸單字而後唸例句才是王道。

　　講到文法台灣最喜歡的就是把文法規則弄成公式，拜託！又不是學數學、學物理，語文是活的，哪能套公式！就算要學文法也是要從例句開始，我常跟學生講：唸例句，叫他們在老師教文法規則時不要去管公式，低下頭唸例句就對了！把例句唸個十遍、二十遍更好，説實話不管是單字還是文法，把例句多念幾遍、唸到有FU，不管是什麼單字。文法自然而然的就學起來了。更棒的是：還很難忘記！唸文章尤其是唸自己有興趣的文章，效果更好、更棒，網路裡多的是各式各樣的文章，找你有興趣的文章來多唸、多讀就對了！

Part I

訂機票

1 主題對話

Michael is talking to a travel agent, Tina, to order airplane tickets.
Michael Chen 跟旅行社員工 Tina 在電話裡訂票。

Tina	ABC Travel, this is Tina. How may I help you?	ABC Travel 我是 Tina，有什麼需要幫忙的？
Michael	I'd like to **purchase** a couple of tickets to Los Angeles.	我想買兩張到洛杉磯的機票。
Tina	When will you be leaving, and any particular airline in mind?	何時出發？想找哪家航空公司？
Michael	I am leaving on August 8th, and I prefer China Airline. I am a **Dynasty Flyer**.	八月八號搭機，我想搭華航。我是華夏會員。
Tina	OK, let me see. You want coach class, right? Any preferred arrival time, and is it one way or round trip?	好的，請稍等。你要經濟艙對吧？想什麼時候抵達？是單程還是來回？
Michael	Coach, please, and I would like to arrive at night. It's better for my **jet lag**. One way ticket, please.	經濟艙。我想晚上到，對時差比較好；單程，謝謝！
Tina	You'll be leaving at 23:50, August 8th, and arriving at 19:15 the same day, LA time.	八月八號 23:50 起飛，在同一天 19:15 洛杉磯時間抵達。
Michael	Sounds good. How much is it?	好的。價錢是？

Tina	It's NTD $26,000 for one ticket, so it's NTD $52,000 for two. How are you going to pay for it?	一張票台幣 $26,000 兩張是台幣 $52,000，要怎麼付款？
Michael	Credit card, and my card number is 1234 5678 0123 4567.	信用卡，號碼是 1234 5678 0123 4567。
Tina	Thanks. One moment, please.	謝謝，請稍等。
Tina	Would you like to reserve seats now?	想現在就劃位嗎？
Michael	Sure, I prefer the window seat.	當然。我喜歡靠窗。
Tina	Since you are traveling in party of two, how about taking a window seat and an **aisle** seat?	既然你買兩張，何不一個靠窗、一個靠走道？
Michael	Wouldn't that make the seats separated?	那兩個位置不是分開了嗎？
Tina	Yes, but if the flight is not too crowded, you might have an empty middle seat.	是的，不過飛機沒有很多人的話，你們中間的座位可能就會是空的。
Michael	What if the flight is near capacity?	如果航班客滿呢？
Tina	In that case, you can always exchange the aisle seat with the middle seat passenger. You have nothing to lose, right?	那你可以和中間的乘客換靠走道的位置，這樣不會造成您任何的損失。
Michael	Great idea, why didn't I think of that before? Thanks for the suggestion.	好主意。我怎麼沒想到過，謝謝你的建議。
Tina	My pleasure. Your reservation is done and the fare is charged to your credit card. Is there any other thing I can help?	我的榮幸。票劃好了，已從您的信用卡支付款項，還有需要我的地方嗎？

Part I

| Michael | No, and thanks for your great service. | 沒有了。謝謝你。 |
| Tina | My pleasure, bye. | 我的榮幸，再見。 |

2 心情小語

❤ Compared to the time when I was purchasing airline tickets, it is easier, more convenient, and especially cheaper now. Back at the day without internet, we had to buy tickets through travel agents. We could only pay what the agent says without any way of knowing how much the price really is.

> 比起當年我在買赴美機票，現在可是更簡單、更方便而且更便宜了！在那個沒有網際網路的時代，買票一定要透過旅行社，只能按照旅行社所説的付錢，買機票完全不知道實際的價格是多少。

❤ I can still remember the day I had to go to US first in order to get the ticket to College Station, Texas, for my wife and myself. Basically, I was flying to a college town, where ordinary tourist would not go. Thus, I did not go to **traditional** travel agent, but instead, I went to US first Furthermore, since Easterwood Airport at College Station was, and still is, not a big airport, there are only about 10 flights to and from Houston or Dallas each day. It took quite a long time for the travel agent to find the suitable flight route for us. I still remember we went to Portland, Oregon first, and then took another connecting flight to Dallas, and finally arrived College Station with the final flight. Starting from CKS Airport, The whole trip took more than 24 hours, including the connection time. It surely was a long and tiring trip. It was even worse because we don't know what the real price was, and if there is any other cheaper or faster alternatives. Everything is under travel agent's control, and we had no choice but to take whatever the agent offered.

> 為了去德州卡城（又稱大學城），我還記得我必須先到美國，再買轉乘機票。基本上，大學城鎮是個一般旅客不會去的地方，因此我只能放棄熟悉的旅行社，自行找人代訂機票。。卡城的 Easterwood 機場不大，每天往返休士頓和達拉斯的班機只有十班左右，所以我在美國花了一些時間才找到合適的航班。我還記得先飛到波特蘭，轉機到達拉斯最後才飛到卡城。從中正機場起飛開始，包含等機、轉機時間整個旅程超過 24 小時！真的很長很累，更糟的是完全不知道實際的機票價格多少？有沒有更便宜或是更少時間的行程可供選擇？一切完全以旅行社為主，我們只能接受旅行社所提供的建議。

Now, with a click of a mouse, we can set our options, look at the **routes**, compare the price, and then decide on the budget allowed best scenario to purchase the tickets. It couldn't be more user-friendly than that. We now have full control of where we want to go, how we can get there, and how much money we want to pay for it. All thanks to the convenience of internet.

> 現在滑鼠一點，我們可以設定選項、看看各種行程、比較價格才來決定預算容許下的最好行程，這可真是便宜又好用。感謝便利的網路，我們可以全程控制到哪裡去？怎麼去？付多少錢？

3 單字與例句

purchase *v.* 購買

We need to purchase new suits for the graduation party.
為了畢業舞會，我們需要買些新衣服。

dynasty *n.* 王朝、朝代

Tang Dynasty ruled China for 276 years.
唐朝統治中國共 276 年。

jet lag 時差

I had serious jet lag after that last trip overseas.
上次的海外旅程我有嚴重的時差。

aisle *n.* 走道

Accompanied by her father, the bride walked down the aisle.
在父親的伴隨下，新娘沿著長廊走。

traditional *adj.* 傳統的、慣例的

Traditional Chinese medicine is getting more popular these days.
傳統中藥最近越來越受歡迎。

route *n.* 路線、路程

This is the shortest route from here to downtown.
這是從這裡到市區的最短路線。

知識備忘錄

　　現在訂機票可真是方便多了！上網後起點、終點選定，網站自動把所有可能選項列出來，日期、票價、行程一次搞定，相關的情形第二部分都說得差不多了，在此我就簡單把當年第一次搭飛機而且是一趟超過 24 小時的行程大致描述一下吧！

　　當時爸媽一起到機場送機，我和老婆帶著三大袋行李到中正機場，在兩個家族裡我們都是第一次搭飛機，期待、緊張、興奮之情溢於言表，因為需要轉機、轉航空公司，行李一事還特別緊張的問航空公司會不會有問題？服務人員一再保證下才稍稍放心。最後終於搭上飛機，開始這個超長旅程。

　　在飛機上即將抵達美國時，空服人員拿出美國出入境 I-94 表格要我們填寫。一看裡面的美國地址當場傻眼，哪來的地址來填啊！還好詢問空姐後知道直接填上學校就對了。進到海關時一開始有點緊張，尤其前面幾位裡有一個人不知為什麼被另外帶到別的地方！輪到我時只問了去哪裡？幹什麼？為什麼帶了近三萬美金？簡單回答後就蓋章了。當時我只說了念碩士的錢一次帶足，就直接蓋章通過了。後來我才知道一次帶這麼多美金並不常見。另外我想說一聲，當年可是台灣錢淹腳目的時代，再加上 25 塊台幣就可以換 1 塊美金，以華人而言這並不是大問題。

　　當時在等轉機到達拉斯時，等了好一陣子才上飛機，最後一趟轉到卡城的九人座小飛機，完全坐滿，當時就感覺行李根本沒地方放，果不其然，行李要一兩天以後才會到。當然還有一些事情，不過年代久遠，也都忘了，只是還記得那第一次，也是最後一次超過 24 小時的超長航班，還好以後再也沒搭過了。

Unit 6　安排接機

1 主題對話

Michael is talking to Steve Chang for airport pick up arrangement.
Michael Chen 跟 Steve Chang 在電話中討論接機事宜。

Michael	May I speak to Steve Chang?	麻煩請 Steve Chang 聽電話？
Steve	This is he speaking.	我就是。
Michael	I am a new student, and I will be arriving on August 8th. Could you please **arrange** someone to pick us up at the airport?	我是個新學生，將在八月八號抵達，能否請你安排接機事宜？
Steve	Sure, what is the flight number and when exactly are you arriving?	當然。航班號碼是？何時會抵達？
Michael	The flight number is 209, arriving at 7:30 PM. I have no idea how much time the custom checking would take, so no idea about the best time to pick us up.	209 航班，7:30 到達，不過我不知道海關檢查需要多久，所以也不知道最好的接機時間。
Steve	Us? How many people are traveling with you, and how many bags of luggage? Don't worry about the best pick up time; we would take care of it.	我們？連你有幾位？有幾袋行李？我們知道接機時間，你不用擔心。

Michael	Two, including me, and four bags of luggage.	包含我,共兩位,四袋行李。
Steve	OK, let me check with Taiwanese Student Association, and see if anyone is **available** at that time slot. Do you have any email account?	好,讓我跟台灣同學會聯絡一下,看看誰有空。有沒有電子郵件帳號?
Michael	My email is michael@gmail.com.	帳 號 是 michael@gmail.com。
Steve	Good, I'll email you once I have somebody for you.	好的,一有消息我會 email 給你。
Steve	How much should I pay for it?	我該付多少錢?
Michael	You don't need to pay for it usually, just be **polite**. It is more **courteous** of you, however, to prepare some gas money.	通常是不需要,但一定要有禮貌。最好準備一點油錢。
Steve	Thanks for the suggestion.	謝謝你的建議。
Michael	Anything else?	還有其他事嗎?
Steve	No thanks.	沒有了,謝謝。
Michael	Give me a day or two, and I'll get back to you through email.	給我一兩天時間,我會以 email 聯絡你。

Part I

② 心情小語

❤ I still remember the day I talked to Chinese Student Association (CSA), Texas A&M University for the pick up at the airport. By the way, yes, the name is Chinese Student Association. Because it was registered a long time ago when there was no students from China. Later on students from Mainland China could not use the same name for their organization, and they had to use other names such as China Club. If I remember correctly, they eventually decided on the name of "Chinese Students and Scholars Association."

> 我還記得當年打電話給中國同學會安排接機事宜的情形。順道一提，沒錯，名字是中國同學會，因為這名稱是在很久以前還沒有大陸同學時就登記了，後來的大陸同學沒法用這個名字，只能用像 China Club 這樣的名稱！如果我沒記錯，後來他們用了中國學生學者聯誼會。

❤ Before calling the CSA, I got in contact with another single female student who was also going to Texas A&M. I learned that she easily got someone to pick her up at the airport. Traveling as a couple, however, it takes a bit longer to find someone for us. Eventually, we did get a couple to pick us up at the Easterwood Airport. Later on, we found out a little secret. Since Texas A&M is a **predominately** Engineering school, there are many more male graduate students than female ones. Thus, a single female student has the **privilege** of easily getting someone to pick her up. The year I came to Texas, two single female students were married to the guys who picked them up, including the girl I mentioned earlier. It's just like the old Chinese saying, "a single string ties the couple thousands of miles apart together." Still, we not only got the pick up service from that young couple, but also one week of free stays at their apartment. They were actually Chinese Malaysian, truly a great couple, and it was fun to be with them. The best thing is that they gave us rides when we needed it. That continued until we bought a car. We insisted on giving some money in return to what they had done for us. They refused the money, but allowed us to treat them at at a local restaurant. The only thing they asked us was to do the same thing for other students next year. As promised, we sure picked up another couple from Taiwan from the airport next year, as requested by the Malaysican couple.

Part I

> 在打電話給中國同學會之前，我和另一位也是去德州農工大學的單身女孩連絡上。聽說她很快就找到人接機，我們夫妻則花了一點時間才找到人到 Easterwood 機場接機。後來發現一個小秘密，因為德州農工大學基本上以工學院著名，男研究生比女研究生多多了！所以單身女孩很容易找到人接機，我去德州農工大學念書的那年，有兩位女士後來就嫁給了當初接他們的男士，包含前面提到的那位。這可真是命中註定，千里姻緣一線牽。我和妻子當然就沒有那份特權，但最後還是找到一對夫妻幫忙，他們還提供了一星期的免費住宿。他們是馬來西亞的僑生，很棒的一對夫妻，和他們在一起也很有趣。更棒的是在我們買車前，他們還開車接送我們。後來我們堅持給一點錢表達謝意，但他們拒絕了，只讓我們在餐廳請他們吃一頓飯，並希望我們來年也能如此接待其他同學。第二年，我們理所當然的接待了另一對來自台灣的學生，以相同的方式，報答了這對馬來西亞僑生的款待。

3 單字與例句

arrange　*v.* 整理、布置

We need to arrange transportation and accommodation for the trip next week.
我們需要安排下禮拜旅遊的交通與住宿。

available　*adj.* 有空的

Are you available this afternoon? I'd like to talk to you.
下午有空嗎？我想跟你談談。

polite　*adj.* 客氣的、有禮貌的

It was polite of you to hold the door for the group.
幫整群人撐著門，你真的很有禮貌。

courteous　*adj.* 謙恭的、有禮貌的

The customer service representatives should have a courteous manner.
客服代表應該要有有禮貌的態度。

predominately　*adv.* 佔優勢的、顯著的

Understandably, the student body of Air Force Academy is predominantly male.
可想而知，空軍官校學生多數是男生。

privilege　*n.* 特權、恩典

As an ambassador, he enjoys the diplomatic privilege.
身為一位大使，他享有外交特權。

知識備忘錄

　　還記得當初打電話跟德州農工大學中國同學會聯絡安排接機，真的很感謝他們的幫忙，在超過二十幾小時的漫長旅程後，能夠有人到機場接機。當時要到卡城基本上有兩種方式，一是搭飛機到當地機場，或者是搭飛機到休士頓，然後安排同學開將近 90 分鐘的車去接機。而後者幾乎是單身女孩的特權，因為我們是夫妻檔，所以一開始就知道要搭飛機直接到卡城。

　　當時接待我們的是一對馬來西亞僑生，據說先生還是位貴族，他們真的很幫忙，到處帶著我們去買傢俱、腳踏車，和各式各樣的用品。想起腳踏車還記得 Walmart 裡面所有的腳踏車都要買回去後自行組裝。單身女生比較簡單，只要說哪一台，自然會有人義務服務。而男士們只能自行處理，當時連簡單的桌椅組裝都不會，腳踏車哪會啊！更何況萬一組裝不好可能會有大問題，只好找了幾個男士，一起找一位熱心的老學生，在他幫忙裝車時，在旁邊觀摩、學習，最後才順利的把腳踏車裝好。為此我們還特地都買了一模一樣的車，差點弄得 Walmart 缺貨，勸我們要不要買其他車款。我們只能硬著頭皮，說我們就是喜歡這個款式。當時聽老學生的話，立刻買了學英文的利器：電視！我們一樣到 Walmart 買了最便宜的三洋電視，讓人意外的是，這個電視竟然陪了我們十幾年！從德州搬到加州從來沒壞過，後來真的只是因為老舊，才依依不捨地換了新的。沒想到最便宜的電視機卻最耐用。說真的，要學好英文，最重要的還真是要多看電視上的英文電影和影集。

Part I

Part II
留學中

校園餐館

1 主題對話

Michael is talking to Nancy for campus dining plan options.
Michael Chen 跟 Nancy 在電話中討論學校餐廳用餐選項。

Michael	I am a new student here, and I'd like to know the **various** dining plan options.	我是個新學生，想知道各種餐飲方案。
Nancy	Sure, we have different choices for you. How many meals per week are you looking for, and do you need a more **flexible** meal plan?	沒問題。我們有各種選擇，一個禮拜大概需要幾餐？你需要比較有彈性的方案嗎？
Michael	I have no idea. Could you describe the more popular ones?	我不清楚，能不能介紹一些比較受歡迎的方案？
Nancy	For students who prefer flexibility, I would recommend **Premier** 19. It offers a preset number of meals at the beginning of each semester. Unused meals carry over from week to week and can be used during the same semester for extra meals and snacks for you, your friends, or your family. All meals, however, must be used by the end of the semester.	對於需要彈性的學生我會推薦 Premier 19，每學期固定提供設定好的餐數，每個星期沒使用的餐點可以順延到下個星期，而且你的朋友、家人都可以用來訂購餐點、點心。不過所有的餐點必須在同一個學期內使用完畢。
Michael	Good, how much is it?	好的。那價錢呢？
Nancy	If you choose 19 meals per week, it would cost you $199.	如果你選擇每周 19 餐就是 199 美元。

Michael	That is over my **budget**. Do you have any more **affordable** ones?	這超出我的預算，有沒有便宜一點的？
Nancy	Gold 19 is our most cost-effective plan. It provides breakfast, lunch, and dinner, Monday through Friday, as well as for brunch and dinner on Saturday and Sunday. However, unlike the Premier 19, unused meals do not carry over from week to week.	Gold 19 是我們最實惠的方案，週一到週五提供早餐、中餐和晚餐，週六週日提供早午餐和晚餐。但是跟 Premier 19 不同的是，沒有使用的餐點不能順延到下周。
Michael	Sounds good, and how much is it?	還不錯。那價錢呢？
Nancy	If you choose 19 meals per week, it would cost you $149.	如果你選擇一周 19 餐，價格是 149 美元。
Michael	Good, how do I pay for it?	好的。那我要怎麼付款？
Nancy	When you are registering for the semester, just pick the meal plan best suitable to you. The cost would be included in your total tuition and fee payment.	在你註冊時只要選擇最適合你的方案，相關的價格會自動算到你的學雜費裡。
Michael	Thanks, you are a great help. Nice talking to you.	謝謝你的幫忙。很高興跟你談話。
Nancy	Me too, bye.	我也是，再見。

Part II

❷ 心情小語

Going to Texas for graduate study with my wife, I was one of the lucky ones that didn't need to worry about everyday meal. I really didn't have a lot of experience dining inside or even outside the school. However, I do have some experience from my friends to share with you.

> 　帶著老婆一起到德州念研究所，我很幸運的不必為每日三餐擔心。講起學校甚至校外餐廳，我還真沒什麼經驗。不過我朋友的一些經驗倒可以和大家分享。

♥ Unless your college locates in one of the few cities with a good amount of Chinese population, like New York or Los Angles, chances are that it would be hard to find a decent Asian restaurant, let alone Chinese ones, around the campus. Almost all colleges offer some kind of meal plans for their students, which usually consist of a preset number of meals in a week. During that week, you can choose to go to any on-campus restaurants to have your meals. Depends on the plan and the cost, you can or cannot carry over the unused ones. Some other plans work like a debit card. Usually your student ID works as the card, to which you can **deposit** some money. Going to any restaurants, you simply swipe your ID and the proper amount of money would be **deducted** from your account. Once the account is nearly empty, simply recharge it. You would have the highest flexibility, but at the same time it comes with higher price. Just go to the school website and search for "meal plan", and you should be able to get all the options and corresponding detail information.

> 　除非你的學校位於很多華人的大城市，例如紐約或洛杉磯，你應該很難找到亞洲餐廳，更不用說中餐了！但幾乎所有的大學都有各種餐飲方案供學生選擇，通常就是一星期吃幾餐，根據不同方案和價錢，沒吃的餐點有些可以延用，有些則不行。有些方案就像現金卡，通常就是用你的學生證，可以儲值，到餐廳用餐時只要刷卡，就直接從裡面扣除，等沒錢了再儲值，選擇性很高，但價錢也比較貴。你可以到學校網站搜尋「meal plan」，就可以得到所有的選項和相關資訊。

The problem with campus meal plan is that American restaurants offer pretty much just salad, sandwich, fried chicken, hamburger, pizza and maybe **spaghetti** or lasagna. Honestly, these are not the choices for us. Worst of all, some of them provide a buffet style eating environment, which make you want to consume as much food as you can. One of my friends joined a campus meal plan with all you can eat option. It sure is a great way to gain weight. If I remember correctly, he gained some 20 pounds in one semester.

> 校內餐飲方案的問題是，一般美式餐廳就是沙拉、三明治、炸雞、漢堡、披薩，或是義大利麵和千層麵，老實說對華人而言選擇不多；更慘的是往往會有吃到飽的餐廳，結果讓你真的多吃、吃到飽。我有位朋友加入學校吃到飽的方案，真的很容易變胖，如果我沒記錯，他一學期增加了 20 幾磅！

If you do find a Chinese restaurant, it is more likely to be American Chinese food, which comes with only two flavors- sweet and sour. It is not Chinese at all, even if they call it Chinese food. Unless of course, if you are in New York or Los Angles, you may find real Chinese restaurants.

> 如果你在校內發現中國餐廳，很可能是美式中餐，滋味沒有別的，就是甜和酸。就算美國人稱之為中餐，但一點也不像中國食物，除非你在紐約或是洛杉磯，才能找到真正的中國餐廳！

3 單字與例句

various *adj.* 各種各樣的

Here at ABC Travel, we have various tour packages for you to choose from.
我們 ABC 旅遊公司提供各種各樣的旅遊行程給你選擇。

Chapter 1

flexible　*adj.* 有彈性的、可彎曲的

The new computer program has to be more flexible to meet the needs of all clients.
新的電腦程式需要有更大的彈性，來符合所客戶的需要。

premier　*adj.* 首要的、首位的

Alishan is the premier tourist attraction in Taiwan.
阿里山是台灣最吸引遊客的景點。

budget　*n.* 預算

We try to keep our monthly budget under $800.
我們常試著把每月預算控制在 800 以下。

affordable　*adj.* 負擔得起的

This car is too expansive. I need a more affordable one.
這車太貴了我需要便宜一點的。

deposit　*n.* 放下、放置、存款、訂金

You need to pay a deposit to reserve the seats.
要保留座位你需要付訂金。

deduct　*v.* 扣除、減除

The deposit will be deducted from the total payment.
訂金會從總款項裡扣除下來。

spaghetti　*n.* 義大利麵 lasagna: 千層麵

Of all the Italian dishes, I love spaghetti and lasagna the most.
在所有的義大利菜裡，我最喜歡義大利麵和千層麵。

知識備忘錄

　　在德州念書，校內外的餐廳有所謂的 Tex-Mex，顧名思義 Tex-Mex 指的就是 Texan and Mexican。這種餐點就是混合了德州和墨西哥口味的飲食，德州一般被歸為 South 或是 Southwest，以德州人而言 Tex-Mex 就是 Tex-Mex，是獨一無二的，但是對一些距離德州比較遠的美國人來說，Tex-Mex 其實就算是 Southwestern cuisine。

　　說實話以華人觀點，實在是吃不出 Tex-Mex 和 Mexican food 有什麼差別？進了餐廳都會先上一份 Nachos 加上 salsa dipping 算是餐前點心，主餐一般點的是 Fajita，也就是牛肉、豬肉或雞肉，或有時是蝦子，配上洋蔥、青椒、紅椒或黃椒、起司和番茄、豆子炒過後，和米飯放在鐵盤上，夾在 taco 或是 tortilla 裡當主餐，配上 sour cream salsa（包含 green salsa 和 red salsa）。在德州的幾個南邊大城像是 Houston（休士頓）、San Antonio（聖安東尼）、Austin（奧斯汀）都很普遍，當然我所在的卡城也不例外。還記得灣區有家餐廳就直接把 tortilla 的機器放在餐廳正中間，客人可以看到一片一片的 tortilla 做出來，我的兩個小孩很喜歡到那家餐廳吃飯，尤其要坐到機器旁邊就是要看到 tortilla 做出來才高興！

　　說到這裡難免想起當時在美式足球季節，尤其是大學比賽時，和學校裡的一群朋友聚在一起看球，一邊以 nachos 當點心，一邊吶喊加油的情景。還真讓人懷念。

Part II

Chapter 1

Unit 8 餐館

1 主題對話

Michael is talking to Tony on where to go for lunch.
Michael 跟 Tony 討論到哪兒吃午餐。

Michael	Hi, Tony. Want to grab a bite?	Hi, Tony. 一起吃飯？
Tony	Sure, What do you have in mind?	當然，到哪兒？
Michael	How about burgers?	漢堡如何？
Tony	I have it yesterday already, and I'd like to try something else.	昨天吃過了想吃點別的。
Michael	How about a quick sandwich at the Subway?	簡單的三明治 Subway 如何？
Tony	I had sandwich for breakfast. How about Chinese food for today?	早上才吃過。吃個中國菜好嗎？
Michael	Sure, let's go.	走吧。

In a local Chinese restaurant, （在當地的中國菜餐廳）

Waiter	Welcome to Golden China, how many people?	歡迎到 Golden China, 請問幾位？
Michael	Two.	兩位。
Waiter	How about the **booth** seats by the window?	靠窗的沙發座位可以嗎？
Michael	Okay.	Okay。

| Waiter | Here is the menu for you. Please take a look and I'll be back with water. | 這裡是菜單，請先看一下，水馬上來。 |

A while later,（一會兒後）

Waiter	Here is the water. Are you ready to order?	水來了，可以點餐了嗎？
Tony	I'd like to have General Tso's Chicken with steamed rice.	我要左宗棠雞和白飯。
Michael	I'll have Broccoli Beef with fried rice.	我要花椰牛肉和炒飯。
Waiter	Any soups?	什麼湯？
Tony	I'll have spicy and sour soup.	我要酸辣湯。
Michael	Egg drop soup for me.	蛋花湯。
Waiter	Anything else?	還有嗎？
Both	No, thanks.	沒了，謝謝。
Waiter	I'll be back with your orders.	餐點等會兒就上。

Part II

20 minutes later,（20 分鐘後）

Waiter	Here are the fortune cookies, and the bill. May I take your plates?	幸運餅乾和賬單，餐盤可以收了嗎？
Both	Sure.	沒問題。
Michael	Let's go Dutch this time.	這次平分好了。
Tony	Sure.	沒問題。

At the checkout counter,（收銀台）

| Clerk | The total is 18.80 with tax. | 含稅總共是 18.80。 |

Michael	Here's 20.	20 給你。
Clerk	(gives out the receipt) 18.80, (gives out two dimes), 19, (gives out one dollar), and 20. Thanks and please come again.	18.80,（給了兩毛）, 19,（又給了一塊）, 20，謝謝歡迎再次光臨。
Both	We sure will.	一定。

2 心情小語

♥ Living in College Station, there aren't too many choices eating out, at least from Chinese/Taiwanese point of view. Besides traditional fast food like burgers, fried chickens, pizzas and sea food, there are BBQ, steakhouses, Mexican food, and a few casual restaurants. Of course, there are some Chinese ones, but they are really American Chinese style.

> 以華人的觀點，在卡城外出吃飯，實在也沒太多的選擇。除了傳統的速食漢堡、炸雞、披薩和海鮮，還有 BBQ、牛排、墨西哥餐。另外還有一些比較休閒性的餐廳。當然也有一些中式餐廳，不過基本上是美式中餐。

♥ We ate in those Chinese restaurants a few times, and never really enjoyed it. The dishes were mostly sweet and sour and prepared with **cornstarch**. I learned later that American like sweet and sour, and they don't **favor** spicy hot. That's why spicy and sour soup is sometimes named sweet and sour soup.

> 我們在那些美式中餐廳吃過幾次，還真不怎麼樣。多數的餐點都是甜酸味再加些勾芡（糖醋）。後來得知美國人喜歡糖醋，不太喜歡辣，也因為這樣，有時候酸辣湯被稱為糖醋湯。

♥ First, let's talk about the word "hot". The problem with "hot" is that it can be hot-hot or **spicy**-hot. When you say the soup is hot, is it hot-hot or spicy-hot? To avoid confusion, American use spicy hot or spicy to portray spicy hot. In my opinion, using spicy and sour soup is way clearer and less confusing than using hot and sour soup. From here on, I'll use spicy and sour soup for 酸辣湯 .

> 　　首先聊聊「hot」這個字，「hot」這個字的問題是，在美語裡它可能是燙或是辣。當你說這湯很 hot 到底是燙還是辣？為了避免誤解，美國人會用 spicy hot 或只用 spicy 來表示辣。在我看來，用 spicy and sour soup 比起用 hot and sour soup 更明白、也更清楚。從這裡開始我會用 spicy and sour soup，來表達酸辣湯的意思。

♥ Traditionally, American don't really like hot and spicy for soup. Thus, the real spicy and sour soup would not be **appealing** to Americans at all. The rest of the **flavors** and **ingredients**, however, really match American taste. Thus, American Chinese restaurant cooks keep the sour flavor and all the other ingredients but reduce the spicy taste as much as possible. If you go to that kind of restaurants and try the spicy and sour soup, you would know what I mean. It only has the sour without spicy taste. In this case, some owners just simply rename the soup to sweet and sour soup. My guess is that "sour soup" doesn't sound good at all, so they just added the word sweet to the name, even though the soup itself isn't really that sweet. Therefore, the name sweet and sour soup sometimes replaces spicy and sour soup. This is just IMHO (in my **humble** opinion), not necessarily the right one.

Part II

Chapter 1

　　傳統上，美國人不喜歡辣味的湯，所以他們對真正的酸辣湯不太有興趣。但酸辣湯裡其他的味道和食材卻符合美國人口味，因此有些中餐廳的廚師就保留了酸味和其他食材，但是降低了辣味，甚至盡可能的不加辣。如果你去過那些美式中餐廳嚐過酸辣湯，你就明白我的意思，只有酸味沒有辣味！在這情況下，有些老闆就直接把名字改成：sweet and sour soup（糖醋湯）。我猜因為酸湯這個名字聽起來不對，所以把甜加到名字裡，雖然湯並不怎麼甜。所以 sweet and sour soup 就取代成為酸辣湯的英文名字了！不過這只是我個人淺見，不見得一定是對的。

3 單字與例句

booth　*n.* 攤位、座位

He went into the telephone booth and made the call.
他進到電話亭打電話。

cornstarch　*n.* 玉米粉（美國人用來勾芡）

The cook used some cornstarch to thicken the soup.
廚師用玉米粉來做濃湯。

appeal　*v.* 呼籲、懇求、有吸引力

The mayor appeals to the citizens to stay calm.
市長呼籲市民保持冷靜

humble　*adj.* 謙遜的、謙恭的

In spite of all the great achievements, he remains humble.
就算擁有這麼多的成就，他還是很謙虛。

在美國德州留學期間，外出飲食的機會實在不多，前兩年沒有獎學金，更少外食。還記得慶祝生日時，最多就是到 Golden Corral 吃一頓 buffet，卡城的中餐廳吃了幾次感覺都不怎麼樣。當然也有幾次開車到休士頓買些中國東西，順便小打一下牙祭，比起卡城，休士頓的中餐好多了，可是跟灣區一比，可真是天差地遠。還記得第一次到永和超市買個便當，發現天底下竟然有這麼好吃又便宜的便當！別人就不說了，連自己一兩年後，都不敢相信竟然那簡單的便當會讓自己回味無窮。

在這裡不提一下卡城的餐廳好像也不對！說起來卡城有兩家餐廳不得不提，一家是 Freebirds。那次是個美國朋友帶我去的，他說來到卡城一定要吃 Freebirds 的 burrito，他點了個 monster burrito。我呢，也在他推薦下，也來個 monster burrito，看到時當場傻眼！想知道多大嗎？重 1.5 公斤！其實還有更大的 super monster，一個 burrito 重量三公斤！另一家是 Tom's BBQ，也是另一個美國朋友推薦，一定要試試它的 "Tom's Famous Aggie Special"。其實就是選你喜歡的 BBQ 烤肉、一塊起司、醃黃瓜、一顆洋蔥和麵包全部放在一張紙上，特別的是餐具就是一把刀，其他叉子什麼都沒有！我都還記得那洋蔥真的很甜，不會嗆。最後我想幫卡城的中餐廳講一下好話，因為他們基本上都是作美國人生意，只要你先跟老闆說一聲，廚師還是會準備道地的中餐。還記得當時找到工作搬到加州前，特地請老闆準備了一桌請好朋友吃飯，那頓飯確實是中餐原味，好吃！

Chapter 1

Unit 9　自己煮

1　主題對話

Judy Wang is visiting Michael Chen and they are preparing some dishes for tonight's potluck with their friends Steve Chang and Tony Huang.

Judy Wang 來找 Michael Chen，他們正在準備今晚跟朋友 Steve Chang 和 Tony Huang「各出一菜」的聚會中所要的餐點。

Michael	What do you have in mind for tonight's dishes?	今晚你準備了什麼餐點？
Judy	I'd like to prepare **broccoli** beef and cheese cakes for dessert.	我想準備花椰菜炒牛肉，還有起司蛋糕當點心。
Michael	Do we have **cauliflower**? I believe Steve and Tony had enough broccoli lately.	有白花菜嗎？我相信 Steve 和 Tony 最近應該已經吃了不少花椰菜了。
Judy	Sure, I can use cauliflower instead. The cheese cake for dessert should be fine with them, right?	有啊，我可以用白花菜，那起司蛋糕當點心應該沒問題吧！
Michael	Homemade cheese cake sure beats the supermarket one. I am wondering what kind of dishes they would bring for the **potluck**.	手工起司蛋糕絕對比超市買的讚！我在想他們會帶來什麼菜？
Judy	We'll see.	待會兒就知道了。

Later that night, Steve and Tony are at the door.（當晚，Steve 和 Tony 到了。）

Michael	Welcome! Please come in.	歡迎請進。
Steve	Here is my dish, lemon chicken.	我今晚的餐點，檸檬雞。
Tony	Here is mine, spicy and sour soup. I prepared it at home. I guarantee it would taste a lot better and more **authentic** than the restaurant ones.	我的是自己做的，保證比餐廳的更好吃也更道地的酸辣湯。
Michael	Smells good. Let me put them on the table.	好香啊，我來把它們放到餐桌上。
Judy	Are you ready for dinner? I sure am hungry.	可以上桌了嗎？我還真餓了。
Steve and Tony	Let's eat.	開始吧！

Part II

A while later（一陣子後）

Judy	Here comes the dessert, homemade cheese cakes.	甜點來了，我自己做的起司蛋糕。
Steve	Yummy, I'll have one.	好棒，我來一個。
Tony	Me too.	我也要。
Steve	Having potluck and watching football with my best friends. Can anything be better than this?	跟好朋吃飯，一起看足球，還有比這更棒的事嗎？
Michael	I love it too.	我也很喜歡。
Tony	Let's plan for the next one. How about next month, my place?	那就來計劃下一次吧，下個月在我家如何？
All	Deal.	說定了！

Chapter 1

② 心情小語

♥ For students living overseas, there is nothing better than getting together for a meal. We usually had potlucks when there are important football games, especially the ones involving our school and its archrival –t.u. (for those who have no idea, we refer to University of Texas as t.u., little t and little u). Since this topic is more related to home cooking, I'll leave the sport part for later section.

> 　　對於海外學生來説，沒什麼比找機會和朋友聚在一起更棒的事了！如果有重要的美式足球賽事，尤其是對上我們學校的死敵 t.u. 時，（我們把本校的世仇德州大學寫作 t.u.，小寫 t 和小寫 u）。我們通常會舉辦 potlucks。但因為這個章節的題目是自炊，我就把運動留到後面再談。

♥ The word potluck literally means pot luck. Basically, each participant prepares a pot of food, and everybody goes to a place, usually someone's house, to enjoy the meal. The word potluck means you don't know your luck until you open all the pots. It's a great way for friends to get together, enjoy a meal and have some quality time.

> 　　Potluck 的意思真的就是：pot 和 luck 這兩個單字合在一起。基本上，每個人準備一道食物到一個地方，通常是朋友的家裡，來享受餐點。potluck 的意思是，在你打開所有的容器後，你才會知道你的運氣好不好。這是個讓大家聚在一起享用餐點的好方式。

♥ Besides potlucks, we usually ate at home with my wife preparing the meals. For the first few months after arriving US, there was one little problem: my wife didn't really cook before we got married and came to US. That means my wife never really cooked before. To be fair to her, that would be the general case for most girls in Taiwan, right? In Texas, there's one **vegetable** that we had no problem **identifying: cabbages**. For the first few months, the only vegetable we had for lunch and supper is, of course,, cabbages. There's one more vegetable that I recognized in supermarket: **spinach**. I tried to tell her there's spinach, but she just **ignored** it. I thought maybe she docsn't like it, and I stopped mentioning it. A few months later, while joining a potluck at a friend's apartment, there was a dish of spinach on the table. She looked at it and said it looks familiar. It is similar to something she had in Taiwan. After tasting it, she said it is indeed the vegetable she enjoyed in Taiwan. Then I told her that I had mentioned it several times in the past. It's good to have more than one kind of vegetables on the table.

Part II

> 　　除了 potlucks，我們在家通常是由我妻子準備餐點。剛到美國後的前幾個月我們面臨一個小問題，就是我妻子在婚前不太煮飯，婚後到美國也不擅長開伙。不過平心而論，很多女生都是這樣對吧！到德州後只有一種蔬菜我們能一眼就認出來：甘藍菜。開始幾個月時，我們每天午餐和晚餐當然也就只吃的到甘藍菜。在超市裡我還認出了另一種蔬菜：菠菜。有幾次我提醒妻子有菠菜，卻沒什麼反應，我當時想或許她不喜歡菠菜，也就不再提了。幾個月後參加朋友辦的 potluck 時，桌上擺了一盤菠菜，她一看就說這好像是一種台灣看過的菜，吃過後她更確認是她喜歡的菠菜，我才和她說，我已經提過好幾次了。好消息是，我們桌上從此有第二種蔬菜上桌。

❤ There is one more vegetable I need to talk about: **water spinach**. At first, someone brought it into Collage Station and planted the root. All you need to do is to cut the stem, and it would grow back. When people eventually knew the secret, everyone started to plant their own water spinach. It's lucky for us to be able to choose from more kinds of vegetables.

還有一種菜我要講一下，那就是空心菜。一開始有人把空心菜帶來卡城，種下去以後，只要拔菜莖就好，反正它會再長回來。但消息傳開後，大家都開始種空心菜，於是我們也就有更多種選擇了。

3 單字與例句

broccoli *n.* 西蘭花、青花菜、花椰菜　**cauliflower** *n.* 白花菜

Broccoli and cauliflower can help us fight cancers.
青花菜和白花菜能幫助我們對抗癌症。

potluck *n.* （每人各帶菜餚共享的）餐會

We really enjoy the monthly gathering of potluck.
我們很喜歡每個月的聚餐。

authentic *adj.* 可信的、可靠的、正統的

This dish tastes like authentic Chinese food.
這盤菜嚐起來就像是正港的中國菜。

cabbage *n.* 甘藍菜

Cabbage is one of the most popular vegetable in the world.
甘藍菜是一種世界上受歡迎的蔬菜。

spinach *n.* 菠菜

The spinach from the garden is really fresh and delicious.
菜園里的菠菜新鮮又好吃。

知識備忘錄

　　雖然説老婆跟著我去德州留學，讓我在吃的方面省下不少功夫，但之後也沒有機會品嘗到傳統的中式美食了。尤其在偏遠的德州小鎮，不要説臭豆腐、肉圓一類的小吃，就連個台式麵包都沒什麼機會吃到。這時候老學生的妻子們就有機會展現功力了！還記得同學中有位麵包大師，什麼紅豆包、奶黃包、花生包，甚至菠蘿包都做得有模有樣！尤其是剛從烤箱出來時那份麵包香，就讓人抵擋不住。老婆在台灣時就喜歡麵包，到卡城後是完全沒有機會吃到，一聽説有位麵包大師立刻就拜師學藝，也確實學會了作她最喜愛的麵包，尤其讓我意外的是，菠蘿麵包真的學得有模有樣的，剛剛烤出來的時候真是色香味俱全，好吃！而這麵包絕藝，也就這麼的老學生教新學生，新學生變老學生的一代一代的傳了下來。

　　除了麵包之外，我們也學會了肉圓，而且風味不輸台灣有名的彰化肉圓，吃起來還比一些台灣普通賣的家常肉圓還要好吃。不過也因此知道為什麼知名的肉圓，例如南機場夜市的彰化肉圓，一點半開賣兩小時賣完就算了，為什麼不多作一些？自己做過之後才知道肉圓真的很費工，拿個小碟子先鋪好底層加上內餡後，再把上層鋪上去。一個、一個的手工做真的很花時間，也發覺肉圓真的靠手工，賣肉圓的錢還真的不好賺啊！

Part II

Chapter 1

 **零食解饞**

1 主題對話

Michael is in a supermarket shopping with Judy.
Michael 跟 Judy 在超市買東西。

Michael	What do we need to buy today?	今天要買什麼？
Judy	Let me see. Besides the usual vegetables, fruits, pork, beef and chicken, we need to restock on some **snacks**. We are mostly out of snacks. You know I cannot live without it.	我看看，除了一般需要的蔬菜、水果和豬肉、牛肉、雞肉外，我們還要買些點心零食，零食都快沒了需要補貨。你知道沒零食我可活不了。
Michael	Okay, let's go to the produce section first for the vegetables.	好吧，先到生鮮蔬果區吧！

In the produce section, （在生鮮蔬果區）

Michael	Spinach, cabbage, lettuce and celery, anything else?	菠菜、甘藍菜、萵苣、芹菜。還有嗎？
Judy	We have all the vegetables. Let's go to the meat, seafood and **poultry** section.	都買齊了，該到海鮮肉禽類區了。

In the meat, seafood and poultry section, （在海鮮肉禽類區）

| Michael | Let me see. Pork chops, beefsteak, leg quarters, fish **fillet**, we are done here, right? | 看一下：豬排、牛排、大雞腿、魚排都買齊了對吧！ |

| Judy | Yes, let's go for the snacks. | 沒錯。該到點心區了。 |
| Michael | After you. | 你先請。 |

In the snack section,（在點心區）

Michael	My favorite, Oreo, let's have some.	我最喜歡的 Oreo 餅乾，買一些吧。
Judy	Pepperidge Farm, my favorite brand, let's have Milano and Chessmen.	我最喜歡的 Pepperidge Farm，我要買 Milano 和 Chessmen。
Michael	I love the Goldfish **crackers**.	我喜歡金魚餅乾！
Judy	Done with cookies and crackers, lct's go for the chips.	餅乾買好了該去去買些馬鈴薯片。
Michael	Lay's, grab some barbecue and sour cream & onion.	Lay's, 買些烤肉和酸奶油洋蔥口味。
Judy	I'll get Pringles, Original and Texas BBQ Sauce.	我買 Pringles, 原味和德州烤肉。
Michael	Let's buy some tortilla chips.	買些墨西哥玉米片吧！
Judy	Then, we need to buy salsa.	那就要買 salsa 醬了。
Michael	You like Tostitos or Pace?	你喜歡 Tostitos 還是 Pace？
Judy	Let's try Tostitos.	試試 Tostitos。
Michael	Anything else?	還有嗎？
Judy	Beef jerky, I know American jerky isn't as tasty as Taiwanese ones, but let's buy one.	牛肉乾。我知道美國牛肉乾不比台灣的好吃，不過還是買一個吧。

Part II

Chapter 1

| Michael | Okay. | OK。 |
| Judy | Got it. We are ready to check out. | 找到了。可以結帳了。 |

At the checkout counter, （在收銀台）

Clerk	The total is 60.75 with tax.	總共是 60.75 含稅。
Michael	Here's 61.	這是 61。
Clerk	(gives out the receipt) 60.75, (gives out one quarter), makes it 61. Thanks and please come again.	（給了收據） 60.75,（再給個兩毛五硬幣），這樣就是 61，謝謝歡迎再度光臨。
Both	We will.	會的。

❤ 2 心情小語

❤ Living in College Station, there aren't too many snack choices for Taiwanese. The cookies are mostly too sweet for us. My guess is that they are the desserts for coffee. cookies are delicious with coffee, but not as good when offered with other beverages. Besides cookies, Americans have crackers, which are crispy and a little salty. Personally, I prefer crackers. There are many snack brands, and I am only familiar with the followings: Oreo is well-known in Taiwan; Pepperidge Farm is a bit more expensive. Chips Ahoy is basically chocolate chips of different flavors and **textures**. Those three brands are also sold in Taiwan. For all other domestic brands, I'll just skip them here.

住在卡城實在沒有太多的零嘴選擇，多數的美國餅乾都太甜，我想可能是用來配咖啡吧！跟咖啡配在一起當點心味道就還不錯，但如果配上其他飲料就不很合適了。除了餅乾以外，美國人還有脆餅，基本上就是比較脆而且有點鹹的餅乾，我個人比較喜歡脆餅。美國餅乾廠牌很多，以下我就介紹幾種大家比較熟悉的品牌。除了在台灣大家都知道的 Oreo 以外，Pepperidge Farm 的價格上比較貴一點，而 Chips Ahoy 則是各種風味和口感的巧克力餅乾。這三種品牌在台灣都有得買，至於其他許多比較美國本土的品牌，我就在此省略了。

❤ Now, let's talk about other snacks. One of the most popular American snacks for Chinese people is potato chips. The common brands are Pringles, Ruffles and Lays. There is one **distinct** feature that I like about Pringles: Their long **cylindrical** can package. The chips are made into same size, and are stacked in the can. It prevents the chips from becoming crumbs, at the same time allowing more chips to be backed into the can. Other brands are mostly packed in bags, and the bags are filled with **nitrogen** as **cushion** to prevent any damage during shipping. The problem is, when buy a big bag of chips, there aren't that many chips laid in the bags.

　　現在該聊聊點心了。對我們而言最受歡迎的美式點心應該是洋芋片了。比較熟知的品牌應該是 Pringles, Ruffles 和 Lays。Pringles 有個我們喜歡的特色，就是它的圓柱型罐子包裝，所有的洋芋片都做成同樣大小，一片片堆疊在罐子裡。這樣洋芋片比較不會碎，同時也可以在罐子裡裝進更多的洋芋片。其他廠牌多數以袋子包裝，袋中充滿氮氣緩衝減少運送途中的傷害，以避免洋芋片碎裂，問題是一大袋的洋芋片，裡面卻裝不了多少片。

Chapter 1

♥ There is another kind of chips for Americans, and it is called tortilla, which usually served with salsa sauce. For Americans, they must have tortilla and potato chips for parties. **Beverages** are always served with the chips, because chips are salty. Besides sodas, beers are really popular among American college students.

> 在美國還有一種墨西哥玉米片，吃的時候還需要莎莎醬。對美國人而言，聚會時幾乎一定要有玉米片和洋芋片。這些零嘴基本上都比較鹹，所以也會提供飲料，除了汽水以外，啤酒對美國大學生來説是很平常的。

♥ Finally, I'd like to talk about beef jerky. For people from Taiwan, American beef jerky is very different from what we have in mind. American beef jerky, unlike "our" beef jerky, doesn't have any spicy taste at all. It's chewy, but not in a good way. To me, it is more like chewing a rubber band. I just don't like it at all. However, for some reason, my son enjoys it. I believe when he gets a chance to taste jerky in Taiwan, he would prefer the hot and spicy taste.

> 最後我想談談牛肉乾，美國的牛肉乾和台灣人吃的牛肉乾很不一樣，美國牛肉乾一點都不辣，很有嚼勁，但卻不是好嚼勁，對我來説，更像是在嚼橡皮筋！我是一點都不喜歡，但很奇怪，我兒子倒是蠻喜歡的。不過我相信等他吃過台灣牛肉乾以後，他就會喜歡上那個辣味了。

3 單字與例句

snack　*n.* 點心、零嘴

Being really busy today, I just grabbed a quick snack for lunch.
今天很忙我也就買了個點心當午餐。

poultry　*n.* 家禽

Poultry farms usually breed chickens, ducks and geese.
家禽農場通常飼養雞、鴨和鵝。

fillet　*n.* 肉片、魚片

You need a very sharp knife to trim away the skin on each fillet.
你需要一把很利的刀來切掉每片肉片的皮。

cracker　*n.* 脆餅、餅乾、爆竹

I am not hungry, just some crackers would be enough.
我不餓，幾片脆餅就夠了。

texture　*n.* 結構、質地

Silk possesses a distinctly smooth texture.
絲綢有種獨特的柔滑質地。

distinct　*adj.* 明顯的、清楚的、有區別的

The identical twins have distinct tastes.
完全一樣的雙胞胎有不同的品味。

cylindrical　*adj.* 圓柱形的

Beer cans are usually cylindrical.
啤酒罐通常都是圓柱形。

nitrogen　*n.* 氮氣

About 80% of the earth's atmosphere is nitrogen.
地球大氣層約有 80%是氮氣

cushion　*n.* 坐墊、靠墊、緩衝器

There is a layer of cushion under the carpet.
地毯下面有一層軟墊做緩衝。

beverage　*n.* 飲料

Beverages are not allowed on Taipei Mass Rapid Transit (MRT).
台北捷運不可以喝飲料。

知識備忘錄

　　上次談到在美國德州留學期間，老婆學會了做麵包、肉圓，其實她也學會了例如蛋糕、小籠包和巧果之類的點心。

　　在美國做蛋糕其實很簡單，超市裡就有賣現成的蛋糕粉，買回來以後照著它的說明書調製就可以了。更方便的是美國的公寓都會提供烤箱，這個烤箱可不是台灣一般賣的小烤箱，而是用來烤大火雞的烤箱，所以做蛋糕完全不是問題。

　　再來講到小籠包，其實做小籠包最大的困難就是揉麵團和發麵團，棒的是在美國也有現成的麵糰，就是原先老美買來做比斯吉的麵團，也就是老美所謂的 biscuit dough，通常都是買最普遍的 Pillsbury 廠牌的 biscuit dough。買回來以後直接就用來包小籠包，不用揉麵也不用發麵，包好以後用蒸籠蒸就可以了。不過問題就出在這裡了，美國哪來的蒸籠啊！還好在休士頓買就有了，為了品嘗可口美味的小籠包，買個蒸籠算什麼！就算是新生一開始覺得有點捨不得買蒸籠，找老學生問一下通常可以借到。說實話，這樣做出來的小籠包，還真有台灣的味道。

　　最後講到最麻煩的巧果了，先要把麵團加點芝麻，然後切成小條小條的用油炸，有時候為了好看，還要先兩條兩條的捲一下，美國基本上都是平底鍋，沒有油鍋，很不適合用來油炸，整個過程真的很麻煩！做了一次以後就再也沒做了。

　　後來搬到灣區矽谷，華人多，又有薪水，於是都買現成的，再也沒動手做過了。

 適合環境的服裝

1 主題對話

Michael is talking to Steve about the recent weather and what to wear.

Michael 跟 Steve 談到最近的天氣與穿著。

Michael	It sure feels cold and it seems like winter is coming.	天氣變冷了，感覺冬天真的到了。
Steve	From the weather report this morning, it is **predicted** that it will get colder and colder in the next few days.	今天早上的氣象預報預測說接下來的幾天會越來越冷。
Michael	Time to get the winter clothing out of the closet.	該把冬天衣物從衣櫥裡搬出來了。
Steve	I am prepared for it already. This is your first winter in US, right?	我早準備好了，這是你的第一個冬天對吧！
Michael	Yes, I brought some sweatshirts and sweatpants from Taiwan for the winter here.	是的，我從台灣帶了一些 sweaters 和 sweatpants 來應付冬天。
Steve	You are talking about the **thermal shirt** and **thermal pants** or just **thermal underwear**, right? Actually, you don't really need any thermal underwear here.	你說的是 thermal shirt 和 thermal pants 或是統稱 thermal underwear 對吧！事實上你不需要衛生衣褲。

Michael	How come? Thermal underwear really keeps me warm in Taiwan.	為什麼？我在台灣就是靠衛生衣褲保暖的。
Steve	We have heating systems for the winter here. The underwear would keep you warm outside, but once you get inside with the heater on, it would not be convenient for you to take off the thermal underwear underneath all the clothes and jean. Imagine you are inside an 80-degree room with all the thermal underwear on.	在這兒冬天都有暖氣，衛生衣褲讓你在室外保暖，但是一進到開暖氣的室內就不是那麼方便的能把它們脫掉。想想看在二十八、九度的室內穿著衛生衣的樣子。
Michael	Then, what do we need?	那該怎麼辦？
Steve	Just prepare a puffer coat or winter jacket would be enough. It would keep you warm outside, and you can easily take it off once you are inside.	準備個羽絨衣或厚夾克就可以了，在室外穿上保暖進到室內就直接脫掉。
Michael	But I don't really have anything like it.	可是我沒準備耶！
Steve	Don't worry. Just go to Walmart, Target, or any department store in the mall, and you can find something that fit your need and budget.	不用擔心到 Walmart, Target, 或是百貨店，就可以買到一些適合你預算的冬季衣物了。
Michael	Thanks. I'll go on shopping for winter clothing this weekend.	謝謝，這個周末需要去買衣服了。

Part II

2 心情小語

● When I was choosing a graduate school, one of the main **criteria** is not too far north. I cannot imagine myself being in a place that is extremely cold with occasional **blizzards**. In this regard, College Station, Texas is the perfect place for me, but the **scorching** hot summer in Texas is not a pleasant memory. Luckily for us, air conditioning is always on in school all year around.

> 　　當初在選研究所時，其中一個條件就是不能太北邊，我無法想像我呆在一個超冷又會有暴風雪的地方。以這點而言，卡城倒是很完美，但是德州熱到爆的夏天還真不是很舒服。運氣不錯的是學校內全年都有空調。

● As a student without any income, we cannot afford to turn on the air conditioner all the time during summer. We usually spent the whole afternoon in the library, or just went to the school video room watching movies to kill the summer heat. Summer dressing is never a problem for us, and T-shirts and short pants can get us through the hot season. During winter time, it could get really cold sometimes. Watching TV and wrapped around with **comforters** was the coziest way for us. The occasional cold winter days did come with the best gifts, especially for Taiwanese. On the average, every two to three years, it would snow at College Station. I could still remember seeing the **sleet** for the first time. We all went crazy, running outside in circles, screaming and yelling. The neighbors were looking at us, wondering what was happening. There was one time, it snowed on Christmas Eve and the snow didn't stop until the next day. The temperature was below freezing for the next few days. The snow piled up on the road side, and did not melt until after the New Year Day. It literally gave the town a special white Christmas. One local resident told me it was the first time in more than ten years.

身為沒有收入的學生，我們沒本錢在夏天時整天開冷氣，通常下午我們就待在圖書館，或是學校的影音室看電影殺時間。夏天的穿著一直都不是問題，T-shirts 和短褲就可以了。冬天有時候還真冷，不過包棉被看電視就很舒服了。對台灣人而言，寒冷的冬天偶而會帶來最棒的禮物：平均每兩、三年卡城就會下雪。我還記得第一次看到雪雨時，我們像瘋了一般地衝到外面繞圈圈，鄰居看著我們還搞不懂發生了什麼事！有次正好在平安夜下雪，一直下到第二天的聖誕節，接下來幾天溫度都在冰點以下，路旁的雪一直到新年後才融化，整個城鎮真的度過了個白色聖誕節。一位當地居民跟我說這可是十幾年來的第一次！

Part II

❤ Six years of dull life in College Station did give us some fabulous and exciting winter fun time.

　　六年在卡城的無聊生活，確實也給了我們一些很讚又興奮的冬天歡樂時光。

3 單字與例句

predict　*v.* 預測

With such a close race, it is hard to predict the outcome.
比賽這麼接近，很難預測結果。

thermal shirt, thermal pants, and thermal underwear　衛生內衣褲

criterion（複數：criteria）　*n.* 標準、準則

What are the criteria you are using to choose the winner?
你用來選優勝者的標準是什麼？

blizzard　*n.* 暴風雪

The snow will hit us soon and we are expecting a blizzard later tonight.
馬上就要下雪而且今晚稍晚預期會有暴風雪。

scorch　*v.* 燒焦、烤焦

The grass is being scorched by the hot summer sun.
草地正被夏天的大太陽燒烤著。

comforter　*n.* 被子

We need to buy some comforters for approaching cold front.
為了即將到來的冷鋒，我們需要買些被子。

sleet　*n.* 雪雨

With the slowly rising temperature, the snow is turning into sleet.
溫度緩慢上升，下雪慢慢變成雪雨。

知識備忘錄

　　或許是卡城不算特別冷吧！那幾年下雪的次數其實不多，不過也因為如此，每次碰到下雪時我們都還蠻興奮的，尤其是第一次看到雪時，還真的差點瘋掉，跑出去又叫又跳的。妻子還特地拿熱水瓶出去接了一點雪，想多保留一陣子。還記的當天其實是美國人所謂的 sleet，也就是混著一點雨的雪，而且雪花一掉到地上就融掉，雖然只是一點小雪，卻也讓人難忘。

　　後來慢慢知道其實冷鋒剛到的第一天會比較溼，但真正冷的是接下來的幾天，所以多數情況會下一點 sleet，但接下來的幾天就會冷到爆。唯一一次的積雪就是前面提的聖誕夜，當晚就很冷，雪也幾乎下了一整天，接下來的幾天更是冷到不行，也首次經歷了路邊有積雪。

　　後來慢慢知道在卡城其實下雪問題不大，怕的是冷鋒剛來的第一天天氣還在冰點以上，因為天氣濕就先下雨，白天下雨後晚上氣溫慢慢降低到冰點以下原先積在路面上的雨水就慢慢的就結冰，接下來的一兩天溫度繼續降低到冰點以下，開車最怕的路面結冰就發生了！

　　有次發生一件讓華人學生興奮的事情。在美國念書自然就會有個問題，農曆過年都是在學期中，基本上就不會放假。有次正好除夕白天下雨，經過一晚後，路面就結冰了，第二天學校怕開車危險，宣布全面停課，大家都賺到難得的年假。記得跟些北方學校的同學提起這事時，還曾被笑你們這些南方佬哪有結冰就不能開車的，不過也因為如此我們才能過年放假啊！

Chapter 2

 要洗衣服怎麼才好

1 主題對話

Michael is talking to Nancy about dry cleaning services.
Michael 跟 Nancy 談到了乾洗服務。

Nancy	Welcome to Discount Cleaners. How can I help you?	歡迎到 Discount Cleaners，有什麼需要服務的嗎？
Michael	I'd like to have this shirt and business suit cleaned. How long will it take?	我想要乾洗，這件襯衫和西裝需要多久？
Nancy	For the shirt and suit, it will take one day.	乾洗襯衫和西裝需要一天。
Michael	How much is the price?	價錢呢？
Nancy	The price is $5.99 for both the shirt and suit, and you can pick it up tomorrow.	襯衫和西裝總共 $5.99，明天就可以拿。
Michael	I am in a hurry. Do you have same day service?	我很急，能不能當天拿？
Nancy	If you can get it in by 10 AM, you can get it by 4 PM today. But if it's after 10 AM and before noon, same day service will cost you 4 dollars more.	如果早上十點以前給我，下午四點就能拿了。但若是在十點到中午之間給我，又要當天拿，就要多給四塊錢。
Michael	How about this evening gown?	那這件晚禮服呢？

Nancy	$6.49 to dry clean it.	乾洗要 $6.49。
Michael	It's 10:15, so I should be able to have them all cleaned and ready for pickup this afternoon, right? It's only 15 minutes late, please.	現在是 10:15，我應該可以在下午四點拿吧！只不過晚了十五分鐘，拜託啦！
Nancy	OK, but for this time only and the total price is $13.38 with tax.	好的，但就這一次。總共是 $13.38 美元，含稅。
Michael	Do you take Visa?	收 Visa 卡嗎？
Nancy	Yes, we do.	收。
Michael	Here it is. By the way, do you own the **Laundromat** next door?	信用卡在這裡，順便問一下，隔壁的洗衣房是你們的嗎？
Nancy	Yes, we do. Any problem?	是的，有什麼問題嗎？
Michael	The number 3 washer is not working, and I spent 4 quarters on it.	3 號洗衣機壞了，我丟了四個兩毛五硬幣。
Nancy	I am sorry about that. Here is one dollar for the refund. I will have it checked and fixed. Thanks for letting me know.	抱歉。我先退給你一塊錢，我會找人修理，謝謝你。

2 心情小語

♥ When working on my **Bachelor** degree in Taiwan, I usually hand-washed my dirty clothes. However, this is not the case in US. From what I learned, American generally don't hand wash clothes. Instead, they either install washer/dryer unit inside their **residency** or let coin operated washer/dryer do the work for them.

當我在台灣念大學時，通常都手洗髒衣服，但在美國就不一樣了，就我所知，美國人基本上不會手洗衣服，要不就是用家裡裝的洗衣、烘乾機，或是到外面的洗衣房用硬幣解決。

♥ For the first few years living off campus, we went to Laundromat. It cost us less than two dollars. Unlike the ones in Taiwan, Laundromat in US is usually self-service, which means you do all the work and nobody is there to help you. All it has is a phone number posted on the wall in case you have problems. Relatively few of them provide wash and fold (per pound) services. I guess the labor cost is just too high to have the business model working. The larger ones come with different sizes of washers, each with different prices for you to choose from. One wash, one price. As for the dryers, you get to make the payment based on the time it takes to dry the clothes. You probably need two to six quarters depends on the amount of clothes you have. It is obvious that you need to prepare some quarters to wash and dry your clothes. Of course, there is usually a coin exchanger in the room.

前幾年住校外時，我們也是在洗衣房解決，花不到兩塊錢。跟台灣不同的是，美國的洗衣房都是自己來，也就是說，一切自己動手，沒有他人服務。要有的話就是一張貼在牆上的電話號碼，有問題時可以和他們聯絡。沒幾家洗衣房會提供洗衣、折衣（按重量計算）的服務，我猜是美國的勞力成本太貴，無法提供這類的服務。大一點的洗衣房會提供各種大小的洗衣機和價格讓你選擇。洗一次收一次錢，而烘乾機則是由你自己決定衣服有多少，要烘多久來付多少錢。通常兩個到六個兩毛五硬幣就夠了，主要還是看你衣服量的多少。很明顯的，你會需要一些兩毛五的硬幣來洗衣服、烘衣服，當然洗衣房裡通常都會有換幣機。

❤ Later on, we moved into graduate student housing **equipped** with washer and dryer. Our Laundromat day finally ended since then. One thing I noticed in US is that American don't really hang dry their clothes; they use dryers all the time, and you just don't see any clothes hung around outside.

> 後來我們搬到有洗衣機和烘乾機的研究生宿舍，從此就不需要造訪洗衣房了。在美國我倒是注意到一件事，美國人幾乎都不晾衣服，都是用烘乾機，在美國你很難有機會看到晾在外面的衣服。

❤ During my graduate student days, we don't really need dry cleaning service. We only needed dry cleaning services for the graduation ceremony and for job interviews. Besides cleaning, we get the shirts ironed neatly, which is a must for the job interview. I wouldn't say the neatly ironed clothing got me the job, but it surely helped.

> 學生時代還真不需要乾洗服務，直到畢業典禮和工作面試時時，才去找了乾洗服務。除了乾洗外，當然也會把襯衫燙好，面試時還真需要筆直的襯衫。我倒不是說筆直襯衫幫我找到了工作，但不可否認的，的確有幫助。

Part II

Laundromat *n.* 洗衣房

There is a Laundromat in the corner of College Ave. and University Drive. You can have your clothes washed and dried there.

在 College Ave. 和 University Drive 的轉角處有個洗衣房。你可以在那裏洗衣及烘乾。

bachelor *n.* 單身漢、學士（通常 B 大寫）

After five years of hard working, he finally got his Bachelor degree.

在五年的辛勤努力之後，他終於拿到學士學位。

residency *n.* 住所

To prove your residency, please provide a copy of a bank statement, utility bill or mortgage bill.

請附上銀行月結單，水電或瓦斯帳單或是貸款帳單影本作為居住地址證明。

equip *v.* 裝備，配備

We equip our children with a good education.

我們讓孩子們受良好的教育。

知識備忘錄

　　剛到卡城時我曾一度異想天開的要手洗衣服,不過後來知道連洗帶烘不到兩塊錢,就都交給洗衣房了。說實話,在美國還真沒看到有人把衣服掛在外面晾乾,大家都是硬幣解決。也因此常常需要累積硬幣,尤其是兩毛五的 quarter。住在外面比較麻煩的是洗衣房往往不在附近,除非你住的是密集的學生公寓。在卡城這類的大型公寓並不多,這時就需要開車載著衣服去洗了。

　　在搬到學校宿舍後這個問題就小多了,有部分的研究生宿舍直接附了洗衣機和烘乾機,就算你的宿舍沒有,因為宿舍密集,通常在走路可到的距離內,就會有洗衣房,也就省了開車洗衣的煩惱。說到洗衣、烘衣我倒想起當時的一個問題:一些衣服,尤其是台灣帶來的衣服,在高溫烘乾之下會越縮越小,到後來甚至沒法穿。

　　至於乾洗,因為學生時期衣著基本上都很簡單,也就不需要乾洗服務。這一直到畢業前開始找工作才有所改變,在德州找工作時,開個幾個小時車去面試可說是是常態,如果到外州,那搭飛機更是少不了。回來後為了準備下一場面試,也就需要找乾洗服務,除了洗的比較乾淨以外,襯衫也燙的很專業。另外為了確保搭飛機時西裝襯衫能保持整潔,還買了西裝專用的行李箱。這也是沒辦法的,為了找個理想的工作,只好花錢送乾洗,買專用行李箱,畢竟比起日後的收入,這些真的是小錢。

Part II

Chapter 2

Unit 13　服裝禮儀

1 主題對話

Michael is talking to Tony about the Chinese New Year banquet.
Michael 跟 Tony 談到了過年晚宴。

Tony	Are you going to the Chinese New Year banquet?	你會參加過年晚宴嗎？
Michael	Sure I am. How can I miss my first Chinese New Year celebration here?	當然，我怎麼可能會不去參加第一個過年晚會。
Tony	Aren't you good at singing and playing guitar? Are you going to **participate** the talent show after the dinner?	你不是會唱歌、彈吉他嗎？你會參加之後的才藝表演嗎？
Michael	I have not played guitar for quite some time. I am afraid I am not good enough.	我好久沒彈吉他了。我擔心表演的不夠好啦！
Tony	Don't worry about it. The **talent** show is mostly just for everybody to have a good time. Everyone there knows the performers are amateurs, and the **audience** is not expecting too much.	不用擔心，才藝表演只是讓大家開心一下，大家都知道上台的都是業餘的，觀眾不會要求太多。
Michael	Okay then, who should I contact for joining the talent show?	好吧，那我該找誰報名參加呢？

Tony	Just call the talent show organizer, Jack Hu.	就找才藝表演主辦人 Jack Hu。
Michael	Okay, I will, but is there any dress code for the banquet and the show?	我會的。但是當天的晚宴和表演需要什麼正式服裝嗎？
Tony	For male students, a suit would be good enough, and for females, formal dresses should be fine. Fancy dresses aren't necessary.	男士只要穿西裝，女士穿著稍微正式的服裝就可以了，不需要太華麗。
Michael	I brought a suit and tie, and I haven't really had a chance to wear it.	我有西裝和領帶，但一直都沒機會穿。
Tony	This would be the best time for it.	這可是最合適的場合。
Michael	Thanks, and I'll probably need to **iron** the shirt first.	謝謝，我可先要燙一下襯衫。
Tony	Don't forget to call Jack and show us how good a singer you are.	不要忘了跟 Jack 聯絡，讓我們知道你多會唱歌。
Michael	Trust me, I am not that good, but I would call him for sure.	相信我，我沒那麼棒。不過我會打電話給他。

Part II

② 心情小語

♥ There really isn't much chance for formal **attire** while studying in US college. Regular student clothes would be more than enough to get you through most of the school activities.

> 在美國大學念書通常不會有太多機會穿著正式服飾，一般的學生衣著足夠應付大多數的學校活動。

♥ As mentioned previously, Chinese New Year almost always falls in the middle of a school semester. There isn't really a sense of Chinese New Year around College Station, except for the Chinese students. Still, Chinese New Year was a big deal for us, and Chinese New Year banquet and the talent show sure was a great way to remind all of us that the New Year is upon us, and this annual Chinese New Year banquet is the only regular circumstance for us to be formal dressed.

> 如同前面所提的，農曆年往往都在學期中，除了華人同學外，卡城實在沒什麼過年氣氛。但過年對我們還是很重要，過年餐會和表演節目是個告訴自己農曆年到來的最好機會，而這個晚會也是唯一需要正式著裝的場合。

♥ Through International Student Association, there was one time that we were invited to a Thanksgiving Dinner in a local resident's home. At first, we were worried about what to wear for the occasion. After contacting the host, we were told it's just a family party, semi-formal would be more than appropriate. Besides a few similar events, the formal dresses usually stay in the closet.

> 　　經由國際學生組織介紹，我們有一次參加一個當地家庭的感恩節大餐，一開始還擔心不知道要怎麼穿著才合適，問了主辦人後，他告訴我們這只是個家庭聚會，不需要很正式，一般的半正式的穿著就足夠了。除了這類的聚會之外，晚宴正服往往都留在衣櫃裡。

❤ My wife did not purchase any gown until we moved to Silicon Valley and I started working. Working in a US company is way different than being a student. There are more formal social events and official banquets. It was then that my wife bought some formal suitable gowns.

> 　　我太太一直到我們搬到矽谷、我開始工作後，才買了禮服。在美國公司工作和學生生活有很大的不同，正式的社交場合和晚宴比較多，我的妻子也才為此買了些晚禮服。

❤ I would say there isn't much to worry about in terms of dressing and wearing for a student.

> 　　對於學生而言，真的不用太擔心正式服裝的問題。

Part II

3 單字與例句

banquet *n.* 宴會、盛宴

A banquet is going to be held in honor of the retiring president.
這個晚宴是用來表彰退休的總經理。

participate *v.* 參加、參與

Professional singers are not allowed in the contest.
職業歌手不可以參加這個比賽。

talent *n.* 才能、天資

Her artistic talent is clearly shown in this drawing.
她的藝術天分在這張畫裡明顯的展現出來。

audience *n.* 觀眾

The audience was immersed in the fabulous performance.
觀眾沉醉在完美的表演裡。

iron *v.* 熨衣、燙平

You need to iron the wrinkled shirt.
你需要去燙平那件皺了的襯衫。

attire *n.* 衣著、盛裝

Formal attire is required to join the banquet.
需要正式衣著才能參加晚宴。

知識備忘錄

　　說實話，在卡城六年，還真沒什麼機會穿正式服裝！真要有固定機會的，就是每年的過年晚會了。所有台灣學生聚在一起，有時也邀請美國朋友來參加，讓他們感受一下華人的過年氣息。一頓比較正式的晚宴是少不了的，當然隨後的晚會表演也不能少。對多數女士而言，這很可能是唯一展現身材的機會。我在的那幾年，也因此認識了幾位真的很會唱歌的學長。其中一對夫妻，當年在晚會上彈吉他合唱一首「神雕俠侶」，轟動全場。男主角現在已經在台灣最大的 UC 公司擔任非常高階的主管，我相信他公司的同事應該沒幾個知道他們夫妻的唱功。在第一次要參加過年晚會時，聽說只要上台就可以免費吃當天的大餐，我也就厚著臉皮報名參加，從此以後為了那頓免費晚餐，年年上台表演口琴，終於在第六年被台上主持人開玩笑的說，來卡城沒聽到 TC 吹口琴，不算是過年！說完後全場鼓掌哄堂大笑。

　　對於想要出國的學生，我會建議學一項國樂樂器或是扯鈴、踢毽子之類的技藝，會很有用處。對晚會還有其他以美國人為主的聚會，國樂表演和傳統技藝甚至中國功夫，絕對是最受歡迎的演出。更棒的是能讓美國人對我們的文化有更多的認識，學會了一定有機會用上。

Part II

Unit 14 選住宿舍或在外租房

1 主題對話

Michael is talking to Glory about graduate student housing application.

Michael 跟 Glory 談到了研究生校內租屋。

Michael	Hi, I am a new graduate student here and I'd like to apply for graduate student housing.	我是剛來的研究生，想申請學校宿舍。
Glory	We have different sizes and floor plans for you to choose from. Please take this **brochure** for more detail information.	我們有各種不同大小和平面配置讓你選擇，請拿這本小冊子，看看裡面的詳細說明。
Michael	How about the price?	那價錢呢？
Glory	The price information is also shown in the brochure. It is listed right beside the apartment information.	價錢在小冊子裡，就列在各種公寓訊息的旁邊。
Michael	The monthly rent looks really attractive. How about utility, is it included?	每月租金看來很划算，那水電費呢？是不是算在房租裡了？
Glory	All except the electricity are paid for in the rent.	除了電費以外都包含在房租裡了。
Michael	How about furniture?	傢俱呢？

| Glory | All of them are fully furnished apartment, and some include washer/dryer unit. There is just one problem though. | 所有的公寓都含傢俱有些還包括洗衣機和烘乾機，不過有個問題。 |

| Michael | What is it? | 什麼問題？ |

| Glory | There are a lot of students applying for it, and it has a long waiting list. The wait time is usually longer than two years. Are you a master student? If yes, are you going to **pursue** a Ph. D degree? | 已經有很多學生申請，候補名單很長，通常要等兩年以上，你是碩士生嗎？如果是的話，你有考慮要修博士嗎？ |

| Michael | Does it matter? | 這有關係嗎？ |

| Glory | As I said, the waiting time is more than two years, and the master degree would usually takes two years. You will probably be graduating before moving in, but you can still apply for it though. | 如同我說的，申請通常要等兩年以上，而碩士一般需要兩年，在輪到之前可能已經畢業了，不過你還是可以申請。 |

| Michael | I am thinking about further study after getting the master degree. | 碩士後我是考慮繼續求學。 |

| Glory | In this case, just go ahead and apply for it. If you need more time to look at the different options, just take the **booklet** and carefully read at it. You can come back when you make a decision. We are open Mon. through Fri. from 9am to 5pm. | 那就直接申請吧！如果你需要些時間看看各種大小的公寓，把那小冊子帶回家仔細研究看看，決定後再回來申請。我們的開放時間是週一到週五，早上九點到下午五點。 |

| Michael | Thanks, and I'll be back for the application. | 謝謝，我會回來申請。 |

Part II

2 心情小語

❤ Depends on the college and the local **community**, you have different options for apartment renting. Most of the schools will provide student housing for both undergraduate and graduate students.

> 依你的學校和當地社區的不同,租公寓會有各種不同的選擇,多數學校都會提供住宿給大學生和研究生。

❤ Some schools require undergraduate student to live in campus for at least one year. Some others, however, do not even have enough space for incoming freshmen. University apartment is usually cheaper than renting off campus. However, there is one disadvantage living in campus, especially for international students. For long vacations like summer and winter breaks, or sometimes even spring breaks, the university housing, especially those for undergraduate students, would be closed since most of students would go home during the breaks. The international students would then have to find a place during those days, which is a short term rental, and it is usually tougher to find one. It is rather inconvenient. For graduate student housing, there is no such problem. Since most graduate students are from overseas, graduate student apartments would generally open all year round.

> 有些學校要求大學生至少要在宿舍留宿一年,但有些學校提供住宿房數不足,甚至給大一新生住宿都有困難。通常在學校住宿比在外面便宜,但是住學校裡會有個問題,這個問題對外國學生尤其嚴重:在暑假、寒假甚至春假等長假期間,因為多數學生都會回家,宿舍也在休假期間關閉,外國學生就需要找短期住宿的地方,這通常不好找,也十分的不便。研究生宿舍就沒這個問題,因為多數研究生來自國外,宿舍也就幾乎全年開放。

● Although the rent is probably higher, living off campus does have its own advantages. You get to choose the **neighborhood**, be closer to grocery stores, convenient for shopping, , and be closer to a playground or a park for the kids. There are always **trade-offs** between quality and price. Get the best one based on your requirement. Go on the internet, check the local newspaper classified ads, and ask around. Visit not only the apartment, but also the surrounding area. Walk a couple of blocks and feel the community. It is the place you probably need to spend for the next six months to a year or even longer. Don't rush into a decision for which you might regret later.

> 　　住在校外雖然比較貴，但也是有好處。你可以自由的選擇地點，找到比較靠近食品雜貨店、方便購物、或是附近有供小孩活動的運動區或公園。在價錢和品質上你也需要有所取捨，可以在網路上找，或看看當地報紙的分類廣告。找房子時不只要參觀公寓，你還需要看看鄰近區域，到附近走走看看，感受一下整個社區。這可是你接下來要住半年、一年甚至更久的地方，不要急著做一個日後可能會後悔的決定。

Part II

3 單字與例句

brochure　n. 小冊子

Please take the brochure which lists all of our vacation packages.
請拿本手冊裡面列出了我們所有的旅遊套裝行程。

pursue　v. 追求、追尋

The criminal is being pursued by police.
罪犯正被警方追趕中。

booklet　*n.* 小冊子

This booklet describes the procedures of setting up all the functions.
這本小冊子描述了設定所有功能的步驟。

community　*n.* 社區

The festival was a great way for the local community to celebrate the holiday.
這個慶祝活動是個很棒的方式來讓本地社區慶祝節日。

neighborhood　*n.* 鄰里、街坊

The whole neighborhood participates in the protest.
整個社區都參加了示威抗議。

trade-off　利弊、得失

This is an inevitable trade-off between quality and price.
這是個在品質與價格間無可避免的利弊權衡。

regret　*v.* 後悔

If you don't do it now, you'll only regret it.
如果你現在不做的話,將來一定會後悔的。

知識備忘錄

　　我在卡城六年，差不多有兩年多的時間租校外的公寓。剛到卡城時，承蒙一對馬來西亞僑生提供暫時的住所，為了避免增添他們的麻煩，在一位老學生的介紹下，很快地找到一間雖不滿意，卻也可以接受的公寓。日後對環境比較熟悉、知道合約到期日後，也比較有時間多做比較，後來搬到一間比較便宜、華人鄰居也較多的公寓。

　　當初一到卡城時，我就在老學生的建議下，先申請學校的研究生宿舍，雖然當時並不確定是否會讀博士班，就還是先申請再説。在卡城的校外公寓多半是小單位，畢竟是個大學城，公寓都是租給學生，八間、十間就算大的了。後來搬到學校的研究生宿舍就不同了，一整片幾十間、上百間，走路距離之內就有好幾位華人同學、朋友，不只是價錢便宜了，暖氣也從校外用電改成校內瓦斯，省了一大筆暖氣錢。，也不必抱著棉被看電視了。其他就算電價另計，也因為用的是學校發電，電價五折，也就比較捨得在夏天開冷氣。其實錢還是小事，四處都有華人鄰居、朋友，也讓生活更加舒適一些，閒來沒事大家一起來個 potluck，看球賽、聊台灣的最新八卦，可真是愜意。

Part II

 租屋有撇步

Chapter 3

1 主題對話

Telephone conversation（電話對話）

Michael Chen	May I speaking to Mr. Watson?	請找 Mr. Watson。
Eric Watson	Speaking.	我就是。
Michael	I am looking to rent an apartment. Do you have anything available?	我想租個公寓。請問有公寓出租嗎？
Eric	We do have some one-bedroom and two-bedroom ones. Would you like to take a look?	我們有一房和兩房的，要不要過來看看？
Michael	I'd like to. How about this afternoon at 3?	好啊，下午三點如何？
Eric	Sure, we are at 458 Santana Row San Jose, CA 95130. Just follow the direction shown in the front gate, and you can easily find the manager's office. By the way, you can visit www.santanaapartment.com for information regarding to our apartment.	沒問題，我們的地址是 458 Santana Row San Jose, CA 95130。隨著大門口的指標走，你就可以找到經理辦公室，你也可以到以下網址：www.santanaapartment.com 看看我們公寓的相關訊息。
Michael	Thanks for the info, looking forward to seeing you.	感謝，下午見。

At the manager's office（當天下午，經理辦公室）

Michael	Is Mr. Watson here?	請問 Watson 先生在嗎？
The receptionist	Yes, please take a seat. He'll be right with you.	他在，請稍坐，他馬上來。
Eric	Hi, You are Michael, right?	Hi, 你是 Michael 對吧！
Michael	You must be Mr. Watson.	你一定是 Watson 先生嘍！
Eric	Just call me Eric. What kind of apartment are you looking for?	叫我 Eric 就可以了，你想找的是哪種型態的公寓？
Michael	I want one with two bedrooms and one and a half bath.	我想要兩房、一套半的衛浴。
Eric	We have one like that. Would you like to take a look?	我們正好有一間，要不要去看看？
Michael	OK.	OK。

In the apartment（在公寓裡）

Michael	It looks like an unfurnished apartment.	這間公寓不附傢俱嗎？
Eric	We only have unfurnished ones.	我們不提供傢俱。
Michael	But I need a furnished apartment.	但我需要一間有傢俱的公寓。
Eric	It's easy. Right across the street, there is a **furniture** renting store. You can go there and pick whatever you need. It's more flexible and affordable to you.	這簡單，對街就有間傢俱出租店，你可以去看看，並選出你需要的傢俱，這麼彈性比較大，也更便宜。

Part II

Eric	As you can see, here is the living room, and the kitchen is right over there.	如你所見，這裡是客廳，廚房就在那裏。
Eric	At the end there is the full bath, and one bedroom on each sides. The half bath is inside the master bedroom in the left.	全套衛浴就在盡頭，左右兩邊各有一間臥室。另一個半套衛浴就在左邊的主臥室裡。
Michael	Looks fine. How much is the rent, and does it include the utilities.	看來還不錯，租金是多少？含不含水、電、瓦斯？
Eric	Monthly rent is $1,200, including water and gas, but not the electricity. The deposit is one full month rent.	每月 $1,200，包水和瓦斯，但是不含電費，押金是一個月的租金。
Michael	How about **garbage** disposal fee?	垃圾處理費呢？
Eric	It is included.	也包含在內！
Michael	Good, when can we move in?	好，什麼時候可以搬進來？
Eric	As you can see, it's in move-in condition. However, we need to check your credit, which would take two days. If there is no other questions, would you like to go back to the office and fill out the apartment forms to start the whole process?	如你所見，這間公寓隨時可以入住，但是我們要先查一下你的信用狀況，這會需要兩天。如果沒有其他問題的話，要不要回辦公室填一下相關表格？
Michael	No problem, you first.	沒問題，你先請。

2 心情小語

💜 Six years of studying in Texas and nine years working in Silicon Valley, I sure had a fair amount of experience looking for apartments, moving from one place to another, and living with neighbors from different cultures.

> 六年在德州求學與九年在矽谷工作的經歷，讓我累積了許多找公寓、搬家，及與跟各種文化背景的鄰居相處的經驗。

💜 Living with my wife in Texas as a poor graduate student, you could probably guess that monthly rent was my primary consideration while choosing an apartment. Still, I looked for an above average community.

> 當時我是一個和妻子住在一起的窮學生，你可以想見租金是我們找公寓時的首要條件，不過我們同時也很在意居家環境。

💜 At that time, we got the apartment-for-rent information mostly from Chinese Student Association. To save money, sometimes we picked up abandoned furniture, such as desks and chairs. There was one time we found a **mattress** in pretty good condition. Actually, it was better than the one we were sleeping on. Without any hesitation, we called our friends and tried to move it into our apartment. To our disappointment, however, it was picked up by another person before we could get a suitable car for it. It may sound funny or even ridiculous, but that was the life for poor graduate students.

Part II

> 當時相關的租屋訊息，多數是由中國同學會的朋友裡得知。當時為了省錢，我們也會從路邊撿回別人丟棄的桌椅等傢俱。有一次我在路邊看到一套被丟棄的床墊，走近一瞧，發現比家裡用的還來的好！我立刻四處打電話，希望能找朋友幫我搬回家。可惜的是，還沒來的及搬，床墊卻已被別人搬走！這看來或許有點好笑，甚至是有些荒謬，但那可是窮學生的生活！

♥ Before graduation, I got two job offers, and we moved to Silicon Valley when I made my decision. The company provided one month free apartment renting as part of the offer. Suddenly, I was not a poor graduate student anymore. Our only reaction after seeing the arranged apartment was like "WOW"! It was like moving from hell to heaven. Thinking maybe we can just live there after that one month, we immediately asked for the monthly rental, and there was another bigger "WOW" from us. Again, we were looking for an apartment in that one month, but at least, as a well-**compensated** engineer this time. I naively believed that it would be a piece of cake to find an apartment, since money isn't much of a concern now. I could not be more wrong. The economy of Silicon Valley was **booming**, almost all the electrical and computer engineers were moving in. There was once we took a couple hours considering one particular apartment, but to our **astonishment**, it was rent out to another guy in an hour. I suddenly realized that it's a lot easier to get a job than to get an apartment. I could still remember calling my poor student friends in Texas A&M and told them to come here quickly, and I said "if you can find an apartment here, you can get a job." Near the end of that one month free rental, we found an apartment that was OK according to our standard, but the rental was much higher than our expectation. At least we got a place to live, and it gave us more time to find another apartment. After that, we moved two more times, and eventually settled down in an apartment near a Chinese supermarket, with all seven neighbors coming from Taiwan. Three years later, we bought a house and finally stopped living in an apartment, and started a new chapter of our life.

Chapter 3

畢業前我被二家公司錄取，在我做出決定後，就搬去矽谷。當時公司提供頭一個月的免費住宿，從此我不再是個窮學生了！當時第一眼看到公司所安排的公寓，心中只有一個字：哇！這好像從地獄搬到天堂！當然我立刻詢問那間公寓的租金，沒想到聽到結果後，也是一個更大聲的哇！我也就立即開始另尋租屋，不過這次總算是以一個薪水還不錯的工程師身分來找了。當時很天真的以為，既然預算不再是最大的問題，找公寓應該非常容易才是。我可真是錯得離譜啊！那時的矽谷經濟大好，感覺上幾乎所有的電機、電腦工程師全到矽谷來了！有次花了兩小時考慮一下，打電話回去時卻發現，屋子在一小時前便租出去了！這時我才發現，公寓比工作難找！還記得我曾打電話給 Texas A&M 的朋友，叫他們快點來，我還說 "只要你在這找到房子，你就可以找到工作！" 而在公司提供的一個月到期前，找到一間還算 OK 的公寓，它的租金比我們預期的還高了許多，但至少這間公寓讓我們有個緩衝期去找下一間公寓。那次之後我們又搬了兩次家，最後住到一個中國超市附近的公寓，七個鄰居都是台灣來的。三年後我們正式買了房子，也結束了租屋生活，同時開啟了另一頁的生活！

單字與例句

furniture　　*n.* 傢俱

We need to buy some brand new furniture for our new house.
有了新家，我們需要買些全新的傢俱。

garbage　　*n.* 垃圾

The garbage disposal fee is included in the monthly rent.
垃圾處理費已經包含在房租裡了。

mattress *n.* 床墊

box spring *n.* 床座

foundation *n.* 原為基礎在此也當床座

bed frame *n.* 床架

A complete bed should include a mattress, a box spring or foundation, and a bed frame.
一個完整的床應該包含床墊、床座和床架。

compensate *v.* 補償、報酬

a well-compensated engineer 薪水還不錯的工程師

The price of the item has been reduced to compensate for a defect.
這物品的價格已經降低來補償它的缺陷。

boom *v.* 繁榮、激增

With the economy booming, it's time to invest in stocks.
經濟繁榮可是投資股票的時機。

astonishment *n.* 驚訝

To our astonishment, he really completed the job on time.
讓我們訝異的是，他竟然真的準時完成工作。

Chapter 3

知識備忘錄

　　我在德州六年以及加州的前五年都是租公寓碰到各式各樣的鄰居，也發生了一些糗事與趣事。求學時鄰居基本上都很單純，多半是學生。只是有些學生會開 party，有時大半夜還吵吵鬧鬧，幸好只要打電話給警察，十幾分鐘後警察就會出現勸導，也就沒事了。在搬進學校的研究生宿舍以後，就跟那些華人學生做了鄰居，大家多了照應。當時還有個不成文的傳統，要是有哪個留學生的老婆回台灣，他基本上就可以到處打牙祭。有老婆的同學也會偶而找找幾位單身的好朋友到家裡，加菜聚餐。尤其是當有重要的球賽時，不管是棒球、籃球或是美式橄欖球，大家都多少會聚在一起看電視。

　　搬到加州以後，前幾年都是住在大型的公寓建築裡，也是有各種鄰居，有和各種文化交流的機會。還記得我們的對門鄰居，丈夫是伊朗人、老婆是日本人，兩人都很客氣。每到週六或週日，就會有兩個小男孩來找他們，而且多半是老公帶他們出門，或者是跟他們在公寓或公園裡玩。有次聊起來，這日本老婆抱怨她老公不想生小孩。我老婆就好奇問了，不是還有兩個小男孩嗎？這才知道，原來這兩個小孩是她老公上一段婚姻的孩子，需要付贍養費，也有探視權。她老公不願意生，怕的就是萬一再次離婚，再多一筆贍養費會要了他的命！這日本老婆當然也抱怨老公薪水付了贍養費後所剩不多，養家還真難！另外還有一對日本夫妻，我兒子常跟她小孩玩。還記得常看兩個小孩，一個中文一個日文的雞同鴨講，兩人還講得津津有味！好玩的是我兒子就這麼學了點我們也不懂的日文！只是後來搬家，我兒子的日文也就耽擱了。而買房子之後，就少了這些與各種文化交流的機會了。

Part II

Unit 16 考駕照經驗談

1 主題對話

Michael is talking to Eric about obtaining a driver's license.
Michael 和 Eric 聊到考駕照。

Michael	I have an international driver's license. Does it work here?	我有張國際駕照有用嗎？
Eric	Unfortunately, it doesn't, and you'd better try and get one here. Since you already have a driver's license from Taiwan, it should not be a problem for you.	很不幸的，沒用。你最好考一張駕照。既然你已經有了台灣駕照，考一張應該不是問題。
Michael	How do I get it?	怎麼考？
Eric	First, you need to go to California Department of Motor Vehicles, fill out a form, pass the vision exam and written test. Then, pay the application fee, and you can get a driving permit.	首先要先去 DMV 填表，通過視力測驗和筆試後，繳清申請費用，可以拿到學習駕照。
Michael	What is the driving permit and what does it do?	學習駕照是什麼，又有什麼用？

Eric	With the permit, you can legally drive a car while accompanied by an adult with a driver's license, which means you can practice your driving skills. By the way, it would save you a lot of time if you call DMV and make an appointment first.	有了學習駕照，只要身邊有個有駕照的人，你就可以合法地開車，也可以練習開車。另外我也建議你打電話和 DMV 先約好，可以省下不少時間。
Michael	How about written test? How do I prepare for it?	筆試呢？又該怎麼準備？
Eric	Go to the DMV web site, and you can get some sample tests that you can try. Just work on those and you should be fine.	到 DMV 網站你就可以看到一些考古題，你可以用來試試看，寫個幾張以後就夠了。
Michael	Do I need to pass any driving test?	有路試嗎？
Eric	Yes, you need to pass the driving test.	有，你要過了路試才能拿正式駕照。
Michael	How does it work?	路試是怎麼進行？
Eric	Again, you need to make an appointment with DMV for the test. On the test day, an officer would sit on the passage seat and conduct the test. He is the one to say if you pass or fail.	你要先跟 DMV 事先約好，測試當天有位考官會坐你旁邊，由他來判定你過還是沒過。
Michael	Is parallel parking a part of the test? Is there anything else I need to know?	有測試路邊停車嗎？還有什麼我該知道的事嗎？

Part II

Eric	No, but during the driving test, you would probably be asked to pull up alongside of a curb. The officer would ask you to drive around residential area and business area. You did drive in Taiwan, right?	沒有，不過路試中他會讓你停在路邊，他也會請你在住宅區和商業區開開看，你在台灣開過車吧？
Michael	Yes, around one year.	差不多一年。
Eric	Then, it would not be a problem. Just listen carefully and follow the officer's instruction, and good luck.	那問題不大，只要仔細聽並且遵循他的指示就可以了。
Michael	Thanks a lot.	謝謝你。

2 心情小語

♥ Parallel parking is officially a part of the Texas driving test but it is not included in the California test. In Texas, you need to pass the parallel parking first. If you fail on that, you fail the exam. Believe it or not, parallel parking is not that easy for **rookie** drivers. The written tests are basically the test for traffic laws and signs. You may choose to take the Chinese test if available. Trust me, the Chinese version is way easier than the English one.

> 在德州的考試包含路邊停車，加州的考試則沒有。在德州，如果路邊停車沒過，那就不用再考了。信不信由你，對新手上路而言，路邊停車可不是那麼容易！筆試也就是所謂的交通條例和標誌的考試，如果可以考中文版的，就考中文版的吧！

♥ The good things about taking the driving test in US are that you don't need to do a reverse garage parking, and you don't have to do a reverse

Chapter4

S turn in middle of the street. However, in the driving test, you have to show the instructor that you are experienced and careful. You have to know that there is a fine line between being an experienced driver and a **reckless** driver.

> 講到美國路考，最棒的事情是，你不用倒車入庫，也不用在路上做 S 形前進和後退。但在路考中，你必須證明你是個有經驗且小心的駕駛。有經驗的駕駛和魯莽的駕駛之間可只有一線之隔。

❤ During the test, the officer would probably ask you to drive around residential and business areas. Just based on common sense, you know you would need to drive a bit slower in a residential area. In a business area, obviously, you need to step on the gas **pedal** a bit more. Just be aware of the speed limit and follow it carefully.

> 路考官很可能會要你在住宅區和商業區繞繞，根據常識你也該知道， 住宅區要開慢一點，而在商業區可以多踩一下油門。當然要注意速限，不要超速。

❤ There are four skills that you need to show to the officer.
- Control: You must show him that you can steer and have full control of the car.
- Observation: You must show him that you are constantly aware of drivers around you and any **hazardous** conditions.
- Positioning: You must be able to keep the car in your lane and smoothly and safely change it to another lane when instructed.
- Signaling: You must appropriately use the turn signals.

路考時你需要展現以下四個技能：

- 控制：你要能轉向並能完全的控制車子。
- 觀察：你要能展現，你隨時注意四周的駕駛人並且注意任何危險狀況。
- 位置：你要能夠把車保持在你的車道上，並在接到指示時平順、安全的換另一個車道。
- 燈號：你要能適時地打方向燈號。

❤ Following the advice stated above, you should be able to get the license in no time.

遵照以上的忠告你應該能很容易的考到駕照。

3  單字與例句

rookie   *n.* 菜鳥

The rookie needs to be partnered with an experience worker.
那位菜鳥需要跟個有經驗的工人在一組。

reckless   *adj.* 魯莽的、不在乎的

The construction worker was fired because of his reckless behavior.
那位建築工人因為魯莽的行為被開除

pedal   *n.* 踏板

He stepped on the brake pedal really hard to try to avoid a collision.
他狠狠的踩在煞車板上試著避免碰撞。

hazardous   *adj.* 危險的、危害的

Smoking is really hazardous to your health.
抽菸對你的健康有很大的危害。

知識備忘錄

　　留學前，我和妻子先在台灣的駕訓班學開車，當時就知道國際駕照在美國不適用，學過開車後，我們沒考駕照就直接出國了。到了美國的前幾個月，當時住在一間靠近超市的公寓，有需要時就找朋友搭便車，也就暫時不需要駕照。

　　後來去考筆試，拿到了所謂的學習駕照，買車之後，找了那位接機的馬來西亞僑生複習了一下，每個周末就到學校裡的超大停車場練習。練了幾個星期，並且在社區附近車比較少的街道開過幾次後，就決定要去路考了。

　　美國路考是由一位考官坐在你旁邊，首先要看你的證件，還有確認車子的保險，接下來在德州要先來個路邊停車。由於美國車大小差很多，從 2000 cc 到 5000 cc 都有，所以路邊停車的位置還蠻大的。當時就有老學生說，如果自己是個大車，就先借個小車來路試，不要跟自己過不去。如果開的是小車，路邊停車就容易了。接下來要倒車，看你倒車會不會微調，保持車子的直線後退。過了之後就正式上路，然後告訴你下個路口右轉，接下來要你先換車道，接著來個左轉，最重要的就是看你有沒有經驗，開的穩不穩。

　　前面說過，一位路考官可以決定你的生死，當時在卡城共有三位路考官，其中一位最胖，也最嚴格，只要你有些許遲疑，或讓他感覺你經驗還不夠，你就過不了。另兩位就容易多了，尤其一位女性考官，很容易過。路考不需要預約，當場報名當場考，我運氣好，碰上女考官，一次就過了。不過在加州人多的城市，路考往往需要預約，就很難照辦了。

 **想買一輛車**

① 主題對話

Michael is talking to Jack about buying a used car.
Michael 和 Jack 談到買舊車。

Michael	Now that I got my driver license, I'd like to buy a car. Any suggestion?	既然考到駕照，我想買部車，有什麼建議嗎？
Jack	Are you looking at a new one or used one?	想買新車還是舊車？
Michael	New ones are too expensive for me, so I am considering a used one.	新車太貴了，我想買舊車。
Jack	You got to be careful while buying an used car. Buying a new car is more expensive, but it comes with services and warranty. You would have less worry about the car.	買舊車要小心一點，新車是比較貴，但是會有維修保證，麻煩比較少。
Michael	I don't have enough money for a new car. Besides, being a student without a job, it would be tough for me to get a car **loan**.	我的錢不夠買新車，而且我是個學生，又沒工作，申請不到車貸。
Jack	How many years have you been driving?	你有幾年的開車經驗？
Michael	I have been driving in Taiwan for a year, but I don't think I know much about cars.	在台灣開了一年，但我不是很懂車。

Jack	You need to first check Kelley Blue Book, which lists the prices of used cars for almost all models and all years. It's a pretty good starting point for price **negotiation**. Also, get an exprcrienced driver to test drive for you. With his help, you'd be able to tell the condition of the car, and see if it is worth buying. By the way, is there any particular brand that you are looking for?	你要先去查一下凱利藍皮書，它有幾乎所有年份舊車的價格，可以拿來參考。還有找個有經驗的人幫你試車，會比較能知道車的狀況值不值得買。對了，有哪些廠牌是你有興趣的？
Michael	I like the Japanese cars better, like Toyota or Honda. How and where can I find the information about used cars?	我比較喜歡日本車，例如豐田或本田。我要怎麼去找相關的資訊呢？
Jack	You can take a look at the local newspaper classified ads or just go to a car dealer. You can usually find some used car for sale there.	你可以看看報紙的分類廣告，或是到車商那裏去看，車商往往都有些舊車在賣。
Michael	Thanks for the information. I'll check the Blue Book first.	謝謝。我會先看看藍皮書。
Jack	Let me know if you need any help.	有問題再找我。
Michael	Thanks, I will.	謝謝，我會的。

❷ 心情小語

♥ As I mentioned previously, the first apartment we chose was close to a supermarket to reduce the **dependency** on a car. In the first few months, we were able to get around without much trouble.

如前所述，我們挑的第一棟公寓靠近超市，以降低對車子的依賴，前幾個月也沒什麼大麻煩，就這樣過去了。

♥ However, after a while, we were seriously thinking about getting a car, since it would be much more convenient and flexibility. After talking to several friends about different car makers, we decided to buy a Japanese one. But the problem was, we didn't have much driving experience, and we didn't know much about cars. We needed someone to help us with the test driving.

但不久後我們開始認真考慮買車，因為有車還是比較方便。在和朋友討論後，我們決定買輛日本車。但問題是，我們不但沒什麼開車的經驗，也不太了解車子；我們需要有人協助我們進行試乘。

♥ First we looked at the classified ads on local newspaper. However, it's time consuming and troublesome. In local ads, fewer Japanese used cars are available, and even if it does, the cars would be sold quickly. Later, we went to a Toyota dealer and told the salesperson that we'd like to buy a car. He immediately led us to a 1988 Mazda 323. It was pretty new, about one year old, yet with over 60,000 miles on it. The good news was those were for sure mostly highway mileages, and it meant less damages to the car compared to local mileages.

我們當時先看分類廣告，不過這很麻煩，又浪費時間。廣告裡日本車原本就比較少，就算有，也賣得很快。後來我們就直接到豐田車商，告訴他我們要買車。業務當下就介紹了一台 1988 年的 Mazda 323，雖然車齡只有一年，但是卻開了 60,000 英哩，好消息是，這些里程多半是高速公路上開的，對車子的損傷比較小。

● We asked a friend to test drive for us, and after that we decided to purchase the car. Since it was almost five in the afternoon, we decided to come back the next day for price negotiation. The price was 4,500, and our budget was 4,000. I didn't speak English well at that time, but we finally got the salesperson to agree on 4,000. He gently led us to the manager of the finance department because he thought we would probably need a car loan. He was really surprised when we were going to pay by cash. It was the first time I realized that Americans usually don't have thousands of dollars on hand. They use loans for all the expensive appliances, furniture and cars.

> 找了朋友幫忙試車後，我們就決定要買了，不過當時已經下午五點，我們就決定隔天再去殺價。當時的開價是 4,500 美元，而我們的預算則是 4,000 美元。當時我的英文不好，但最後還是讓業務同意 4,000 元的價格。他以為我們要申請貸款，立刻帶我們去找財務部門的經理。等我說要付現時，他看起來非常驚訝。當時我才明白，美國人是不會特別準備幾千塊美金的。只要是買較貴的電器、傢俱和車子，他們就是用貸款。

Part II

● I still remember that Christmas Eve when we officially bought the car. It was the coldest Christmas in decades. Snow stayed on the road side until New Year. However it was a happy day for us. For the first time in my life, I had a car. One thing really amazed me was that the car lasted a lot longer than I expected. The car was shipped to Silicon Valley after I got a job, and I continued to drive the car until I decided to move back to Taiwan. The car, which was still in a good condition, was donated to charity. Even today, I still miss that reliable and **rugged** yet Mazda 323.

Chapter4

　　我還記得正式決定買車的那個聖誕夜，當時是數十年來最冷的一天，地上的積雪直到新年才退。天氣雖冷，但我卻很高興，因為這是我生平第一次買車。讓我意外的是，那輛車比我想像中的耐久，直到我回台灣前，我都還在開那輛車。後來我把車捐給慈善機關，但直到今日，我仍想念那輛可靠又堅固的馬自達 323。

3 單字與例句

loan　*n.* 貸款

We need to apply for a car loan because we can only afford to pay the down payment.

錢只夠付頭期款，我們需要申請車貸。

negotiation　*n.* 協商

With both sides putting down their weapons, the peace negotiation finally starts.

在雙方放下武器後，和平協商終於開始。

dependency　*n.* 依靠、信賴

To have a better economic future, we need to reduce our dependency on foreign oil.

為了更好的經濟未來，我們必須降低對國外原油的依賴。

rugged　*adj.* 粗糙的、高低不平的、粗壯的、耐用的

You need a fairly rugged vehicle to cross the rough terrain.

你需要一部耐操的車子來橫越這艱困的地形。

● **知識備忘錄**

　　抵美四個月後我買了一台馬自達 323，也去考了學習駕照上路，沒多久後就考到駕照，正式成為有車一族。

　　買車過程也遭遇到一些小問題，首先，我們不懂車。每次看車，都得請有經驗的學長幫忙試開，為了一輛車勞師動眾真的很麻煩，後來就決定到車商那兒去看。美國人買車時多半會把舊車一併賣給車商，因此賣新車的車商，手上都會有許多舊車要賣，每次去都有較多的選擇。當時決定要買日本車也造成了一些麻煩，二手美國車比二手日本車多多了，而且日本車也比較好賣，真的不容易找；有幾次差點想放棄了，但都在一些買了美國車的學長勸告下堅持下來。

　　我還記得那次到豐田的 dealer，原本要看一台日本車，卻已經賣掉了，在銷售員的介紹下看了上述的馬自達，車齡只有一年，卻有超過六萬英里的里程數。我在 Bluebook 找不到建議價格，畢竟這麼新的車有這麼高的里程數真的不常見，當時我猜多半是租車公司的車子。另外那輛車其實有個小問題：擋風玻璃上有個被小石頭砸到的圓圈，因此那輛車並不好賣。不過我和妻子的個子小，不會擋到我們的視線，對一般美國人就會是個問題。我想是這些原因讓價格低了下來，也造就了我和這輛車的緣分。

　　那輛車隨著我們從德州搬到加州，除了時間到就該更換的配件，例如輪胎、煞車、消音器等之外，都沒出過什麼大問題，那輛車跟了我們超過十四年，一直到搬回台灣前才很捨不得的捐了出去，到現在我都還會想念它，真的是耐操又好用。

Unit 18　國內轉機

1 主題對話

Michael is talking to Tony about summer vacation.
Michael 和 Tony 談到了暑假旅遊。

Michael	Summer vacation is coming. Do you have any plans?	暑假就快到了，你有什麼計畫嗎？
Tony	Yes, I am going to visit my aunts in New York. How about you?	我要去紐約找我嬸嬸，你呢？
Michael	I am planning to go to Utah, where it has lots of National Parks worth visiting. I'd like to drive there and stay for 3 weeks.	我計畫去猶他州，那有很多值得拜訪的國家公園。我計畫開車去玩三個星期。
Tony	Wow that is a lot of driving. I'll take a plane to New York.	哇！那要開很久的車。我會搭飛機到紐約。
Michael	In this hot summer touring season, it would be really expensive to fly there.	在暑假旺季搭飛機很貴！
Tony	I know, and that is why I am not taking a direct flight.	我知道，所以我不打算直飛。
Michael	How do you get the information? Do you check with any travel **agent**?	那你在哪找的相關訊息？你找過旅行社嗎？
Tony	No, I just go online and search for the best possible price and schedule. I spent some time on it and got myself a bargain.	我就上網去找，考慮價格和時間後，選了最適合我的行程。我在網上花了些時間，找到了好價錢。

Chapter4

Michael	Could you tell me how to do it? I'd like to learn it and get some good deals.	能告訴我怎麼做嗎？我想學著去找到物超所值的行程。
Tony	It's easy. Just go to some of the most well-known online travel websites and spend some time there.	很簡單，只要上幾個最知名的旅遊網站，花點時間就對了。
Michael	Any recommended websites?	有推薦的網站嗎？
Tony	I usually check expedia and priceline. There are some other ones. You can just search for "online travel websites" on Google, and you will do fine from there.	我通常到 expedia 和 priceline，其實還有其他網站，你可以用 Google 直接搜尋旅遊網站就可以了。
Michael	Thanks, I will.	謝謝，我會的。

2 心情小語

💜 During my fifteen years of studying in Texas and working in California, I had a fair amount of **leisure** traveling experience by car or by airplane.

> 在我十五年的德州求學與加州工作的生涯中，我有許多開車旅行或搭飛機旅行的經驗。

💜 Being a student in Texas, I would not dare to think about taking airplanes for recreational activities except of course, for the first trip from Taiwan to US. We first took Delta Airline from Taiwan to Portland while stopping at Japan. We don't have to wait for too long since it's the same plane. However, the second part of the journey, from Portland to Dallas was a different story. Because it's an international flight connecting to

domestic flight while changing airlines, and the **layover** time needed to be arranged longer. Together with the unpredictable **Customs** clearance, the layover time was close to four hours in total. We had to sit in an unfamiliar airport and wait for the **connecting flight** after fifteen hours of travel.

> 在德州當窮學生時，我根本不敢搭飛機旅遊，當然首次搭飛機赴美是例外。我們搭機前往美國途中首先過境日本，由於是同一架飛機，也就不用等太久。後來從波特蘭到達拉斯就不同了，由於是從國際航班接國內航班，轉機時間較長，加上難以預測的海關檢查，轉機時間長達近四個小時；於是在長達十五小時的旅程後，我們仍必須留在機場等下一班飛機。

♥ Finally we got on the flight from Portland to Dallas, which was a four-hour journey. We were tired, but we couldn't get much sleep on the plane. The next part of the journey was better, because it's a domestic flight, and the layover time was only an hour. We didn't sleep for almost a full day, and we were exhausted on the plane to College Station. We are totally exhausted when we arrived at College Station.

> 終於搭上了要飛行四小時到達拉斯的班機，在飛機上很累卻睡不好，下一班也是國內航班又是同一家公司，等機時間就好多了，一小時，但是幾乎一整天沒能好好睡覺，在達拉斯到卡城的班機上，可真是累翻了，抵達卡城時是可真的累垮了。

♥ However, being a student does have its own advantage while traveling by airplanes. Students usually have more time, and you can choose to take connecting flights in order to save money. It's the most effective way to save money. With all the traveling websites, you get to compare the total amount of flight hours, the layover time, and the price you pay for the journey. Unlike ten years ago when you had no choice but to purchase plans from a travel agent, you can actually come up with your own travel plans. The difference is like Heaven and Hell. There is one suggestion to you: enjoy your hard earned summer and winter vacations and travel to other places in America. **Immerse** yourself in a different culture. That's the reason you choose to study aboard, right?

> 　　不過學生搭飛機也有個好處：你可以選擇用轉機來省機票錢，因為是學生有的是時間。現在有那麼多的旅行網站，你可以自行選擇合適的航程轉機時間和價錢。和十年前不同當時你只能到旅行社接受他們訂好的旅遊計畫，現在卻可以自己規劃出旅行計畫，這根本就像天堂與地獄的差別！給你個建議，好好享受你的寒暑假，去不同的地方，感受不同的文化，這才是你出國念書的目的！

Part II

3 單字與例句

agent *n.* 仲介人、代理人

travel agent 旅行社

To apply for a mortgage, we need a bank agent's help.
申請房貸我們需要銀行仲介的幫忙。

leisure *n.* 閒暇、空暇時間

What do you usually do in your leisure time?
空暇時間你多數是做什麼？

recreational *adj.* 消遣的、娛樂的

Camping is our favorite recreational activity.
露營是我們最喜歡的休閒活動。

domestic　*adj.* 家庭的、國內的

The startup company hopes to attract both foreign and domestic funding.
這家新創公司希望能吸引外國和國內資金。

layover　*n.* 臨時滯留

Our flight from New York to San Francisco made a layover in Chicago.
我們從紐約到聖地牙哥的班機臨時滯留在芝加哥。

connecting flight　銜接航班

The first flight would take you to Los Angles, and the connecting flight would bring you to the final destination, Phoenix.
第一個航班讓你搭到洛杉磯，然後銜接航班會讓你抵達最終目的地鳳凰城。

immerse　*v.* 使浸沒、使深陷

He is immersed in Chinese culture.
他浸潤在中華文化裡。

Chapter4

知識備忘錄

　　窮學生時沒什麼機會搭飛機，除了首次搭飛機到美國以外，印象中我只搭了另外三次飛機：一次回台灣，另一次則是因為一位長輩親戚到拉斯維加斯參加消費電子展，請我去當翻譯。那時候我的長子才兩歲，我在展場當翻譯，老婆則帶著小孩在 Circus Circus 玩遊戲，沒想到兒子完全不知道規則，隨便玩也贏了好些填充玩偶。我會談到這次的經驗，其實是要跟大家聊一件和跟搭飛機有關的事情，這樣的事情也很難在台灣發生。

　　當時因為消費電子展的關係，來往拉斯維加斯的班機幾乎天天客滿。當時又是一月，美國幾個比較北邊的機場很容易受到天候影響，時常會有誤點的情況。情況嚴重時甚至可能會如同滾雪球般的影響到其他機場，當時我們展覽結束搭飛機回卡城時，就發生了這樣的狀況。

　　飛機原先就客滿，又因為其他機場的問題，有些乘客被迫要擠進我們這班飛機。我記得當時飛機上多了五名乘客，那時才知道美國航空公司的處理方式就是喊價。為了讓五位乘客自願放棄這班航班，空服員對機上所有乘客開始出價，從兩百塊航空公司禮券開始，一路加碼到三百、四百，最後提出一張免費機票外加機場免費飲食。喊價開始時我就先和老婆説，反正窮學生什麼沒有，就是時間多，就決定價碼合適時加入。一聽到有免費機票外加餐飲，我就立刻舉手自願，我的第三次搭飛機經驗就是這麼得來的！當出價逐漸提高時，就會開始有人自願改乘航班，價碼越高，越會有人心動，在最後關頭如果你猶豫了，可能就會有人先一步搶走。至於前面舉手的人反而不用擔心，航空公司一律以最後的價碼給所有自願的人，這真的是好玩又刺激。

Unit 19 大眾運輸系統

1 主題對話

Michael is talking to Judy about a coming trip to San Francisco.
Michael 和 Judy 談到了即將來臨的舊金山旅遊。

Michael	Where do you want to go for the winter vacation?	寒假你準備去哪裡？
Judy	I'd like to go to San Francisco.	我想去舊金山。
Michael	I never went there before. Are there any places worth visiting?	我沒去過耶，有什麼值得參觀的地點嗎？
Judy	There are a lot of places for us to explore. The world famous Golden Gate Bridge is a must see.	舊金山有很多值得我們探索的地方，世界知名的金門大橋是一定要去。
Michael	I have heard of that, and I saw some pictures of it.	我聽說過，也看過一些照片。
Judy	Also, there is Pier 39 and Fisherman's Wharf, where you can take a ferry to Alcatraz Island.	還有 39 號碼頭和漁人碼頭，從那裏可以搭渡輪到惡魔島。
Michael	Alcatraz Island? That's a prison where the most **notorious** criminals like Al Capone were held.	惡魔島！那裡關了美國最有名的黑幫老大疤面卡彭。

Chapter4

Judy	There is also the Lombard Street, which has eight sharp turns that make it the **crookedest** street in the world. The coolest thing is that the street is surrounded by the residences' bright flower gardens. It's a must see especially when the flowers are in full bloom.	還有九曲花街，八個急轉彎讓它成為全世界最彎曲的街，最酷的是它被兩旁居民所栽植的亮麗花園所環繞，百花盛開時是一定要去的景點。
Michael	Wow, it sounds like a place we have to go.	哇！聽來像個一定要去的地方。
Judy	We should take the world renowned San Francisco cable car, which is also a tourist attraction in its own right.	我們該搭乘世界知名的舊金山纜車，它本身也是個觀光景點。
Michael	That's a lot of attractions. Is there anything else?	這麼多景點。還有其他的嗎？
Judy	Sure there are more. We could go to Chinatown, which is densely packcd with shops, markets and restaurants. We can also have a traditional Cantonese meal there.	當然我們可以去商店、市場和餐廳林立的中國城，吃頓道地的廣東菜。
Michael	Wow, I'd like to go there now.	哇！我現在就想去。
Judy	Sorry, you have to wait until the winter vacation.	抱歉，你得等到寒假才行。

Part II

2 心情小語

♥ When I first glanced at the topic of public transportation, I was thinking there is basically no such system almost anywhere in US except for a few metropolitan areas. One day a flash of light gave me the greatest idea: San Francisco. San Francisco doesn't have the most convenient public transportation in US, nor does it have the most complete network. It does, however, have one of the most **diversified** traffic systems.

> 　　頭一次看到這個大眾運輸系統的標題時，我就想除了寥寥幾個大都會城市之外，美國哪來的大眾運輸系統？有天靈光一閃想到了舊金山，其實舊金山並沒有最方便或也沒有最完整的大眾運輸系統，不過它卻有最多樣化的交通系統。

♥ First and the foremost, it's the highly **acclaimed** cable cars, which survived the great 1906 San Francisco earthquake and fires. Beginning public service on September 1, 1873, it is one of two National Historic Landmarks that move, with the other one being New Orleans' St. Charles streetcar. There are also the streetcars, which operates with restored historic streetcars from Milan, San Francisco, and other cities.

> 　　首先也是最重要的，是眾所周知的叮噹車，它熬過 1906 年的舊金山大地震與火災，1873 年 9 月 1 號開始服務群眾，它現在可是美國唯二會動的國家歷史地標，另一個是紐奧良的聖查爾斯街車。還有舊金山的街車，是以米蘭、舊金山，還有其他市區所重建的街車來運作。

♥ Operating with overhead electrified lines, the trolleybuses look like adult's cute toys. Caltrains provide regular train service between San Francisco and San Jose. The two-leveled trains look like regular trains in Taiwan, except it is much taller. My kids love it, and sometimes we just took the Caltrain to Hillsdale Shopping Center located right across Hillsdale Caltrain Station to enjoy a leisure afternoon.

> 　　運用車頂上的電線操作的電公車，看起來就像是可愛的大人玩具。加州火車提供了舊金山和聖荷西之間的火車服務，兩層車廂看起來就像台灣火車，當然比起來是高多了。我小孩很愛搭火車，有時候我們就坐火車到西爾斯戴爾購物中心逛，就在車站對面，享受一個悠閒的下午。

💜 The ferries can take you to Alcatraz Island and Angel Island. Often refereed as "The Rock", Alcatraz Island was built with facilities for a lighthouse, a military fortification and a prison. Starring Sean Connery and Nicolas Cage, the movie "The Rock" was filmed there. Angel Island is the largest island in San Francisco Bay area, and it is a historical place where you can go hiking, biking or even **kayaking**.

> 　　渡輪可以載你到惡魔島和天使島，惡魔島有時又被稱為「巨岩」，島上的設施包括燈塔、軍事要塞和監獄。史恩康納萊和尼可拉斯凱吉主演的絕地任務就是在那兒拍的。天使島則是舊金山灣區最大的島嶼，歷史悠久，人們可以在那兒健行、騎腳踏車甚至划獨木舟。

💜 There is also a modern transit system in San Francisco. Bay Area Rapid Transit (BART) Connecting San Francisco with East Bay cities and Oakland airports. BART provides fast, convenient service to local area residents.

> 　　舊金山也有現代化的捷運系統，叫做灣區捷運，它連接舊金山和東灣的城市，以及奧克蘭機場。灣區捷運提供附近區域居民快速、方便的服務。

♥ San Francisco is a unique city in US with various public transportation services and it sure is a city worth visiting.

> 　　有這麼多種類的大眾運輸系統，舊金山確實是個很獨特並值得拜訪的城市。

3　單字與例句

notorious　*adj.* 惡名昭彰的

The coach is notorious for his strict and harsh disciplines.
那位教練因他的嚴厲嚴酷的紀律而著名。

crooked　*adj.* 歪的、彎曲的

A brace is needed to straighten the crooked teeth.
需要個牙齒矯正器來矯正彎曲的牙齒。

diversify　*v.* 使多樣化

The company is trying to diversify customer base for its product.
公司想為它的產品拓展更多樣化的顧客。

acclaimed　*adj.* 受到讚揚的

Harry Potter is a highly acclaimed series of fantasy novels.
哈利波特是個很受讚揚的系列奇幻小說。

kayak *n.* 獨木舟

The wind blew my kayak onto the shore.
風把我的獨木舟吹向岸邊。

知識備忘錄

　　你可能聽說過在美國，沒車就像沒腳一樣，還真沒錯！除了幾個最大的城市外，美國幾乎沒有任何大眾交通系統。這也是我第一次看到這個主題時當場傻眼的原因。後來靈光一閃，想到了舊金山，解決了我的難題。在這裡我也簡單的介紹一下舊金山這個城市。

　　舊金山市個歷史悠久的城市，西班牙在 1776 就進入此地，1821 年墨西哥由西班牙手中獨立後成為墨西哥領土，美墨戰爭後正式成為美國領土。1849 年的加州淘金熱潮讓人口在一年多內劇增，也因此在 1850 年加州正式成為美國的一州，這也是舊金山美式足球隊被命名為 49ers 四九人隊的原因。

　　1906 年 4 月 18 日早上 5:12，大地震及隨後因斷裂的瓦斯管線所造成的大火造成約三千人死亡，並摧毀了 80% 的舊金山，超過一半的居民無家可歸。由於沒水可以救火，就用炸藥炸掉一些建築物來防止火勢的蔓延。當時舊金山市是西岸的財政、貿易和文化中心，全美第九大城市，同時也是西岸最大的城市。這場災難使得貿易、工業和人口轉向南方，讓洛杉磯在二十世紀中發展成為最大也最重要的西岸城市。

　　觀光業是目前舊金山最重要的產業，有許多景點值得參訪，連它的交通工具都成為景點之一，如果你有機會應該要去看看。

 選課與學習

1 主題對話

Michael is talking to Daniel about registration and courses selection.

Michael 和 Daniel 談到了註冊與選課。

Michael	The vacation is ending and new semester is going to start soon. Did you register yet?	假期快結束了，新學期也快開始了，你註冊了沒？
Daniel	Yes, I just finished online registration. How about you?	我剛剛線上註冊了，你呢？
Michael	I am still trying to decide which courses to take for this semester.	我還在決定要修那些課。
Daniel	What field interests you the most?	你最有興趣的是哪個領域？
Michael	It's still my first year, and I don't have a clear picture yet. It looks like parallel and distributed computing for now.	這是我第一年，我還不是很清楚，目前看來是平行與分散式計算。
Daniel	Did you take Object-Oriented Programming yet? It's more like a basic course and a good starting point for you.	你修過物件導向程式設計嗎？那是個基礎課程，也是個很棒的起點。
Michael	Who is the instructor for the course?	是誰教的？

| Daniel | It's Dr. Richard Su, who is famous for his **articulate** teaching, and for giving large amount of tough homework. | 蘇教授。他教學清晰，作業很多，也很難。 |

| Michael | Wow, sounds like a challenging class. | 哇！聽來很有挑戰性。 |

| Daniel | It is, but after all the hard work, you will be able to understand the subject comprehensively and build a solid foundation for your future study and research. | 沒錯，但努力後會有成果，你會對整個課題有完整的了解，也會對你未來的學習與研究建立一個堅實的基礎。 |

| Michael | Any other suggestions? | 還有其他建議嗎？ |

| Daniel | Since you are interested in parallel and distributed computing, how about Applied Networks and Distributed Processing, Parallel Algorithm Design and Analysis, and Parallel/Distributcd Numerical Algorithms and Applications? Some of them have **prerequisite**, so check with the course catalogue for details. | 既然你對平行與分散式計算有興趣，你可以考慮應用網路與分散式處理、平行演算法的分析與設計還有平行與分散式數字分析演算法與應用，有些課有先修課程，詳細情況你可以去查一下課程目錄。 |

| Michael | I need to look into it and I'll register for this semester tomorrow. | 我需要好好研究一下，我明天會去註冊。 |

| Daniel | Let me know if you have any further question. | 還有問題的話再跟我聯絡。 |

Part II

2 心情小語

♥ Even though it's over twenty years ago, I still remember registering for the first semester, trying to decide which courses to take. That year, there were ten new Electrical Engineering Graduate students from Taiwan, with another tens of upper-class Taiwanese students already there. There was no shortage of information sources for class selection.

> 雖然已經超過二十年了，我還記得第一學期的註冊，試著要決定修那些課。那一年總共有十位來自台灣的電機研究所學生，加上幾十個原先的學長，很容易找到人問問題。

♥ In order to build a strong and sturdy foundation for my master research, I asked around for well organized, in depth courses in the department. I could still remember the first two courses I took, Advanced Analog Circuit Design Techniques and Microprogrammed Control of Digital Systems. After discussing with friends within the department, I knew those are the two of the toughest graduate courses. Some suggested me not to take these two courses in the same semester. I decided to take those two courses at the same time, because these two courses were only opened in fall semester, and I only had two years to finish my master degree. To ease the burden, I chose an easier course for that semester.

> 為了要對我未來的碩士研究建立個堅強、厚實的基礎，我到處問一些系上架構完整、有深度的課程，我還記得最先修的兩堂課：先進類比線路設計技術和數位系統的微程式控制。跟系上的朋友討論過後，我知道這是兩堂很重的研究所課程，有些人建議我不要同時修。但我覺得這兩堂只在秋季班開，而我只有兩年時間完成碩士課程，於是決定一起修。而為了減輕負荷，我另外選了一門比較簡單的課。

Chapter 5

♥ For the Analog Circuit Design, the professor stated in the first class that he wants us to study analog circuit and think about analog circuit every day. If we dream about it from time to time, it would be a great success for him and for us. When I heard it, I instantly knew that this would be tough and challenging for me. Little did I know there was another surprise waiting for me: the professor for Digital System came from Georgia, with a **burdensome** southern accent. It took me two months just to understand what he was saying. You can easily imagine the stress being put on my shoulder. Somehow I survived, getting two As and one B in that semester. After being forced to study and think about analog circuit every day, I realized that I am not interested in and not qualified for this field, and digital hardware is my future.

> 　　類比線路設計第一堂課，教授就說要我們每天念、每天想類比線路，如果還偶而夢到那就成功了。聽到這裡我立刻知道這堂課不好混，也會是個挑戰。想不到的還有另一個驚奇在等著我，數位系統的教授是由喬治亞州而來，一口讓人聽不懂的惱人南方腔，兩個月後我才能聽懂他在講什麼。你可以想像我肩膀上的壓力，但結果我也活了下來，三堂課拿了兩個 A 和一個 B。在被強迫每天念類比線路、每天想類比線路後，我發覺我對這個科目沒興趣也沒天分，數位硬體才是我的未來。

♥ Although it was the toughest semester that I had ever gone through, I was still able to overcome the **agony** and challenge. After that semester, I was sure that there were no obstacles I could not **conquer**, and there's no hurdles I could not jump over. I knew at that time I was prepared for any challenges ahead.

Part II

> 雖然那是我有史以來最艱難的學期，但我還是突破了艱困的挑戰。那個學期之後，我確定沒什麼難關我過不了，沒什麼障礙我跳不過去，我清楚的知道我可以面對未來任何的挑戰。

3 單字與例句

articulate　*v.* 清楚的講話

The baby is beginning to articulate words and phrases, and clearly expresses its feeling.
那小小孩開始清楚的講出些字和片語，並能明確的表達他的感受。

prerequisite　*n.* 預修的、不可缺的

If you plan on building a wall, a supply of bricks is a prerequisite.
如果你計畫蓋一道牆，就要先準備好磚塊。

burdensome　*adj.* 惱人的、繁重的

The newly proposed standards for record keeping are really burdensome.
最新提出的填寫紀錄標準真的很煩人。

agony　*n.* 極度痛苦、苦惱

She was in a terrible agony after breaking her leg.
在摔斷腿後她痛苦萬分。

conquer　*v.* 征服、戰勝

The singer conquered the hearts of the audience with her enchanting voice.
那位歌者用她醉人的聲音征服了觀眾的心。

講到選課，我的經驗已經在前一節分享過，在這裡我就聊聊一般的選課與學習。

　　選課前我會建議先去打聽看看、問問學長或是修過這些課程的人，看看他們修過後對課程和教授的感覺，還有要知道這課的學習量多大。如果在一個學期內修太多很花時間和精神的課，等於是找自己的麻煩。但如果一學期都是輕鬆的課，那也只是把困難往後推而已。美國一般的大學都會有一定的標準，可不像台灣的大學一般的好混，每個學期把困難和簡單的課平均的分布，才不會讓自己面對太大的壓力。不過有一點倒是確定的：嚴師出高徒，對學生而言更是如此，不經一番寒徹骨，哪得梅花撲鼻香？既然出國學習就要學點功夫才對得起自己，對得起所要付出的高額學費。

　　選課時還要注意一點，先確認自己未來的目標，是要去業界服務還是要走學術路線？我的碩、博士指導教授就特別提醒這點，她曾說如果學生要去業界，那就修一些實用的課，而且找一些實用的題目來做論文。如果要去學術界，那學理的課就要多，而且多出幾篇論文就重要多了。

　　如果畢業後要在業界找工作，那更應該打聽目前最熱門的課題和科目。找不到適當的人問，就上網搜尋或是到 LinkedIn 之類的網站看看，多蒐集資料絕對不會錯！選課之後當然就是認真學習，該交的作業一定要交、該準備的考試就不放過，得到好的成績，不管是要到業界或學界，都會有很大的幫助。

 申請獎學金

1 主題對話

Michael is talking to Daniel about scholarship.
Michael 和 Daniel 談到了獎學金。

Michael	New semester is starting. Are you ready for it?	新學期就要開始了，你準備好了嗎？
Daniel	I am more than ready. I couldn't wait.	早就準備好了，都等不及了！
Michael	Sounds like you are having a good time studying.	聽來你讀書讀的很高興。
Daniel	Learning what I am interested in and working with my advisors for my degree, I am having the time of my life. By the way, how is your GPA (grade point average) for the last semester?	學習我有興趣的東西，和我的指導教授一起工作，為學位而努力，可是我夢寐以求的事。對了，你上學期的成績如何？
Michael	I got straight As. Why do you ask?	我全部拿 A，為什麼問這個？
Daniel	Straight As, you may be able to get some scholarships.	全 A！你可能可以拿獎學金。
Michael	I am not a US citizen, and neither do I have a green card. I was told it would be really tough for me to get a scholarship.	我不是公民，也沒有綠卡，聽說這樣很難拿到獎學金。

Chapter 5

| Daniel | It is tough, but not impossible. With your perfect GPA, you have a pretty good chance of getting one. Actually, I got a 1,000-dollars from scholarship last year. | 是很難，不過不是不可能；你全部拿 A 就有機會拿到。事實上，去年我就拿到一千塊的獎學金。 |

| Michael | Really! What should I do? | 真的嗎？我該怎麼做？ |

| Daniel | Go to the university website as well as the department website, and look for scholarship pages. You will get a lot of related information. The **grants** are mostly from the US government, and thus are for legal residents, but some of the scholarships emphasize more on **academic** achievement. Just look through the pages and you may find some surprises. | 到學校還有系上的網站找獎學金的網頁，你會看到很多相關訊息。獎學基金多半來自美國政府，所以對象都是合法居民，但是有些獎學金更強調學術成就。仔細看看網頁或許會有驚喜。 |

| Michael | Thanks. I'll look into it carefully and meticulously. | 謝謝。我會小心、仔細的看。 |

| Daniel | Now you have one more reason to get a good grade. | 現在又多了個理由來拿好成績。 |

| Michael | Yes, that definitely is a **motivation** for me. | 沒錯，這確實是個激勵。 |

Part II

② 心情小語

♥ US scholarships are mostly for legal residents, namely, citizen or permanent resident. For students holding an F-1 visa, however, there are still some scholarships available. In most of these cases, good GPA is a must.

> 美國大學獎學金多數是給合法居民，也就是公民或永久居民。可是對拿 F-1 學生簽證的外國同學，還是有些獎學金可以拿，多數情況下好成績是必要的。

♥ When I was in Texas A&M University, we had to check the Department bulletin board for scholarship information. Often it was spotted too late. With the internet, you can get all the scholarship information right on the websites, be it the one with the University, the College of your major, or your department.

> 當我在德州農工大學時，只能從系上的公布欄看獎學金的訊息，有時看到時已經太遲。現在有了網路，你可以在網站上看到相關的資訊，不管是學校的、學院的或是系上的。

♥ There are all kinds of scholarships coming from different sources. For example, it may come from some wealthy alumni who after making **immense** amount of money and decided to help the poor but gifted students. Perhaps it's from a retired professor, who wanted to assist his beloved students after a **prolonged** teaching career,.

> 　　不同的獎學金有不同的來源，例如有些高收入的校友會決定幫助有天分卻沒財力的同學；又或許是一位退休教授，在漫長的教書生涯後決定幫助他親愛的學生們。

♥ In rare cases, the scholarship can come from a regular person like you and me. Oseola McCarty, a local washerwoman in Hattiesburg, Mississippi, left a portion (60%) of her life's savings to the University of Southern Mississippi to provide scholarships for deserving students. Quitting school at sixth grade to care for her aunt, she later washed clothes for a living. She never had a car, and she would push shopping cart for nearly a mile to get groceries. In July, 1995, when Oseola was at the age of 87, she donated an amount estimated at $150,000 to the university.

> 　　在少數情況下，獎學金可能來自如同你我的一般人。Oseola McCarty 是一位住在密西西比州哈蒂斯堡的婦人，以幫人洗衣維生；她捐出部份（60%）的積蓄給南密西西比大學，幫助那些值得獎勵的學生。Oseola 六年級時為了照顧她的姑姑而輟學，後來以洗衣維生；她從來都沒有車，甚至會推購物車去一英哩外買雜貨，在 1995 年七月，Oseola87 歲時，她捐出大約為十五萬美金的獎學金給學校。

♥ In order to get scholarships for international students, a good academic achievement is almost always a must. In this case, what can be more convincing than to have a perfect, or nearly perfect GPA? Hard working will pay off some day. It may not be in the form of a scholarship, but you know hard working always gets rewarded.

> 　　要拿到外國學生的獎學金，好的學術成就幾乎是必要的。那什麼東西能比完美、或幾近完美的成績，更有說服力呢？付出努力總是會有成果，或許不是獎學金，但你知道，認真努力永遠會有成果。

3 單字與例句

grant   *n.* 授予物、獎學金、補助金   *v.* 同意、授予

You need to be a citizen to be able to receive the government grant.
你需要是公民，才有資格收受那份政府的獎助金。

academic   *adj.* 廣泛地、無所不包地

You need to have good grades to get the academic scholarship.
你要有好成績，才能領那份學術獎學金。

meticulously   *adv.* 無微不至

He stuck to that decision resolve meticulously.
他一絲不苟的堅持執行那一個決定。

motivation   *n.* 動機、激勵

Many voters have questioned his motivation in running for the mayor.
很多選民對他選市長的動機有所懷疑。

immense   *adj.* 巨大的、廣大的

Coming from a wealthy family, he inherited an immense fortune.
來自個富裕的家庭，他繼承了份龐大的遺產。

prolonged   *adj.* 延長的、拖延的

Prolonged sun exposure could cause skin cancer.
長時間的陽光曝曬，可能導致皮膚癌。

知識備忘錄

　　念研究所跟念大學有一點不同，念大學獎學金比較少，尤其對外國學生而言，機會可說是渺茫，除非你功課真的很棒，成績很好。念研究所就不一樣了，機會多多了。其實還有一個很重要的原因：老美一般念完大學就就業，念研究所的真的不多。美國各大學研究所老外都是多數，如果有獎學金也就不會僅限給老美。

　　研究生的獎學金一般分兩種：Research Assistantship（RA）和 Teaching Assistantship（TA），也就是所謂的研究助理獎學金和助教獎學金。TA 簡單講就是當助教，不要小看 TA，表現好的話（當然成績好也會有幫助），有可能在暑假教一些教授沒時間開或不想開的課，收入可能就是兩、三倍起跳。但這比起 RA 還是差一點，所謂 RA 就是幫教授做研究，好處是這個研究一般就是你以後的畢業論文，而 TA 則是研究以外的額外工作，是會佔掉你讀書和做研究的時間。

　　美國教授基本上也是要盡力拿 funding，從政府機關或從私人企業拿到 funding 以後，一部分要給學校系上，一部份用來買機器設備，一部分獎勵自己，還有就是用來請 RA。所以有沒有 RA 就看教授拿 funding 的能力。找有錢的教授做老闆就有這個好處，funding 不是很夠的老闆就會經常要爭取 TA，美國教授還真不是很容易當。

　　博士生要比碩士生容易拿到 RA，畢竟碩士一般只需要兩年，剛學會一點東西就要畢業了。而博士修課年限長，對教授而言，當然優先給博士生。同樣的當 TA 有缺時，教授一般也是偏好給博士生。講到 TA 有件事一定要強調，英文一定要好！畢竟你面對的是大學生幾乎都是老美，英文不好絕對會被抱怨。

 開學的新生訓練

1 主題對話

Michael is talking to Steve about new student orientation.
Michael 和 Steve 談到了新生訓練。

Michael	I was told to participate in the new student orientation. Do I need to go?	我有被告知要去新生訓練，真的需要去嗎？
Steve	Is this your first time in US? If yes, I will suggest you to go.	這是你第一次來美國嗎？如果是的話，那我建議你去。
Michael	Someone told me it's going to be a waste of time.	有人說那是浪費時間。
Steve	Not really. 'Cause you have never been here before, I think it's better for you to go and learn something about the University and its surrounding area.	不見得。你從來沒來過這裡，我認為你去參加比較好，去看看大學和附近區域。
Michael	Couldn't I get the information just by asking around?	這些事我問其他人，難道不行嗎？
Steve	Yes, you can just ask around and get **scattered** information, but you can get more information there, especially when you need specific information.	你是可以四處問問取得零碎的資訊，但去那邊的資訊更多，尤其是一些較為細節的資訊。

Chapter 5

Michael	So what can I learn if I go to the orientation?	那我去的話會學到什麼？
Steve	Members of the school would talk about academic requirement and what you should expect. You will also get to know what kind of help is available get from the school. You could learn something from their presentation.	學校教員會講解學業上的要求、學校對學生的期望。你也可以得知學校對學生提供什麼樣的幫助。從他們的演說裡，你真的可以學到些東西。
Michael	Anything else?	還有呢？
Steve	Staff within the University would let you know what kind of service is available for students with different needs. There is a lot of information that you can get in the orientation. Best of all, all the presentation material would be put into one package for you to take home for future reference.	學校職員會說明對不同需求的學生能提供什麼樣的服務，你可以從新生訓練裡得知很多訊息，最棒的是所有訊息都會被歸整成一套資料，讓你帶回家做參考。
Michael	Thanks. I'll take part in the orientation for sure.	謝謝，我會去新生訓練。
Steve	Good for you.	去了準沒錯。

Part II

2 心情小語

♥ Some say that new student orientation is just a waste of time. To me, that is definitely not the case. Being the first one in the family to get an education from an US college, I didn't know what to expect the moment I stepped into the campus. Going to new student orientation really helped me.

> 有人說新生訓練只是浪費時間，對我而言絕不是事實。身為全家第一個到美國接受教育的人，我踏進校園時根本不知道要怎麼辦。參加新生訓練真的很有幫助。

Chapter 5

❤ I learned about Aggie traditions, various resources available for graduate student, and all kinds of facility that we could take advantage of in the school and at the local community. The first thing I learned is of course how to correctly pronounce "Howdy!" Saying howdy to anyone exemplifies that I am in the friendliest campus in the world.

> 我學到了 Aggie（德州農工大學學生的暱稱）的傳統、各種研究生可以取得的資源、學校和社區可以使用的設施。我學到的第一件事當然就是如何正確的講出 Howdy。對人就講 Howdy，也確認了我是在全世界最友善的校園裡。

❤ Had I not gone to the orientation, I would not have known that Memorial Student Center (MSC) gets the name Memorial for a reason. It's a student center which is dedicated to all those Aggies who had lost their lives during the World Wars. It is a living memorial that when stepping inside the building, everyone has to remove the hat to pay respects to all the fallen Aggies.

> 如果我沒去新生訓練，我也不會知道 MSC 名字裡面的 Memorial 是有意義的，它是個對在世界大戰中犧牲的 Aggies 表達敬意的活動中心。為了表達悼念之意，一進到 MSC 就要立刻脫帽，以表達對所有犧牲 Aggies 的敬意

❤ Aggie **Muster** is an annual event that celebrates the **camaraderie** of the school while remembering those Aggies who have died in the past year. The "Roll Call for the Absent" honor Aggies who died that year. Aggies light candles, and one by one, the fallen Aggies' name would be announced, and friends and families of that Aggie would answer "here" when the name of their beloved one is "called". Is there any better way to remember and recognize the lost Aggies?

> Aggie 聚會是另一個年度聚會，來慶祝學校的同窗情誼，並紀念過去一年去世的所有 Aggies。學生會點上蠟燭，然後將當年去世的 Aggies 的名字一個一個的叫出來。而那位已去世的學生親友，會在名字被叫到時喊一聲 here。你認為還有其他比這更好的方式來紀念、表彰死去的 Aggies 嗎？

♥ Let's not forget all those sport related traditions like the Twelfth Man, with the student body watching the entire game standing, to show that they are always ready to join the game if needed.The Bonfire symbolizes the burning desire of Aggies to beat t.u. (University of Texas) in the annual football game, and the midnight yell, which is held the night before a home game in Kyle Field, or on Thursday nights before the away game. Can you imagine tens of thousands of students gathering at midnight to pump up the Twelfth Man and the team for the big game tomorrow?

> 更不要忘記了運動相關的傳統，如 Twelfth Man，是站著看整場美式橄欖球比賽來展現他們隨時願意下場的決心。營火代表學生要在年度橄欖球賽裡擊敗德州大學的激情。另外還有每次主場球賽的前一天晚上，或是星期四客場晚上的午夜隊呼，你可以想像幾萬人在午夜裡聚集，來為 Twelfth Man 以及球隊為了第二天比賽加油的情形嗎？

Part II

♥ From the moment I took part in the orientation, I've learned and experienced what an honor and **privilege** are for me to be part of the Aggie Family, "Once an Aggie, always an Aggie".

> 從我參加了新生訓練的那個時刻起，我學到了能加入這個 Aggie 家庭是我多大的榮耀，『一刻 Aggie，永遠 Aggie』

3 單字與例句

scattered　*adj.* 四散的、散亂的

Toys are scattered around the room.
玩具四散在房間裡。

muster　*v./n.* 招集、集合

Mustering all the strength, they finally pushed the rock aside.
使盡全身力氣，他們終於把那塊岩石推到旁邊。

camaraderie　*n.* （法語）同志間的友愛和忠誠

This match exemplified the great camaraderie among the teammates.
這場比賽具體展現了隊友間的友愛與忠誠。

privilege　*adj.* 特權、殊榮

Affordable health care should be a right not a privilege.
負擔的起的健保應該是（大家的）權利而不是（少數人的）特權。

知識備忘錄

　　如果要問我對新生訓練的看法，其實只有一個：去參加就對了！尤其當你是第一次來到這個社區，或第一次踏入這個學校。美國大學跟台灣大學有些地方真的是非常不同，而最簡單、最容易學習的場合，就是新生訓練。

　　新生訓練當然會提到學校對學生所提供的服務設備，例如圖書館、餐廳、各項運動健身設施，如何借用應該注意哪些地方？有哪些程序規定要遵守？還有校園以外的鄰近社區簡介，那些地方值得一看，又有那些地方應該迴避。更重要的是學校有那些傳統，例如每個美國大學都會有暱稱、學校的代表顏色、學校的 mascot 吉祥物，當然不可避免的世仇學校，還有許多事物，只要去一次新生訓練就可以學習到，何樂而不為呢？而且就我所知，美國大學的新生訓練也辦得越來越活潑，確實值得一去。

　　在美國念了研究所以後，對美國大學部印象最深的就是：對自己母校的榮譽感！而美國大學的兩大運動：籃球和美式橄欖球，更讓學生激發了團結心與求勝心。台灣大學裡唯一可以比擬的我看只有梅竹賽了。但是美國大學籃球和橄欖球總共超過七個月的球季，是只有幾天的梅竹賽無法相比擬的。畢業後校友對母校的感情，這點真的是美國大學所特有的。

Part II

Unit 23 選擇合適的指導教授

1 主題對話

Michael is talking to Daniel about choosing an advisor.
Michael 和 Daniel 談到了選擇指導教授。

Michael	Time for me to choose an advisor for my graduate degree. Do you have any suggestion?	是該為我的研究生學位挑一個指導教授的時候了，你有什麼建議嗎？
Daniel	Which fields are you interested in?	你對哪些領域有興趣？
Michael	As I told you before, I am interested in parallel and distributed computing.	就像我先前說的，我喜歡平行與分散式計算。
Daniel	Dr. Richard Su has been doing research on that for quite some time. Did you talk to him yet?	蘇教授在這方面做了很多研究，你跟他聊過嗎？
Michael	Not yet, but I was told he is a pretty tough professor and always sets a high standard for his students. I am afraid that he could be an **obstruction** in obtaining my degree and may even prolong my time here.	還沒，但是我聽說他很嚴格而且往往為他的學生設立高標準，我怕這會成為我拿到學位的障礙，甚至可能延後我的時程。
Daniel	But he is also the director of the Parallel and Distributed Computing Laboratory, and a world **renowned** scholar. Sometimes his students would get a job just because they got a degree under his **supervision**. More importantly, he is an IEEE fellow.	但是他也是平行與分散式計算實驗室的主任，也是個世界知名的學者，有時候他的學生就因為是由他指導拿到學位，而得到工作。更重要的是，他是 IEEE 的傑出會員。

Michael	What does that mean?	傑出會員是什麼？
Daniel	It means his contribution in Parallel and Distributed Computing is highly recognized.	意思是他在平行與分散式計算上的貢獻受到高度肯定。
Michael	Any other professors?	還有其他教授嗎？
Daniel	How about Dr. Alex Livingston? He is good at helping students working on research tasks. He is young, energetic and fun to be with.	李文斯頓教授如何？他會幫助學生做研究，年輕、有活力、人也風趣。
Michael	He is an Assistant Professor, right?	他是個助理教授，對吧！
Daniel	Yes, he is. He is new to the school, and on tenure track. His tenure review is at least three years away, so you don't have to worry about that.	是的，他剛來，還在教授評鑑中，不過至少還有三年，所以你不用擔心這個問題。
Michael	Thanks for your suggestions. I'll think about it in the next couples of days.	謝謝你的建議，接下來的幾天我會好好考慮。

2 心情小語

♥ Choosing your advisor can be your first big step in obtaining your degree. As I mentioned in the class selection section, taking challenging courses could **drain** a lot of your time and energy, but at the end, hardworking always pay off, and you would be able to **reap** delicious fruit of hard work. A tough professor would make your life miserable for the next few years, but once you get your degree, it will really benefit your career.

選擇指導教授會是你拿到學位前的第一個重大步驟。如同我在選課與學習那一部分裡所提，修一些有挑戰性的課可能會耗掉你很多的時間與精力，但努力總會有回報之後就能收成你辛苦工作後的甜美果實。一位嚴格的教授會讓你接下來幾年的日子很難熬，但在你拿到學位後，將會對你的職場生涯有非常大的幫助。

💜 I would say the first criterion is to find out your interest. What area do you have the passion for? After all, this could be your profession and your career for the rest of your life.

我認為，第一個標準是找出你的興趣，搞清楚你的熱情在哪裡？畢竟日後這可能就是你的職業和你的生活。

💜 Some say you can choose a well-respected professor who has been with the school for quite some time. Having achieved almost everything achievable, he or she may ease up a bit and make your life less **tormenting**. The problem is there are only a few of them out there, and to be honest with you, they would uphold the standard to preserve their reputation. In most cases, however, I would suggest you to find his kind of professor as your advisor, if there is a chance.

有些人說你可以挑個在學校非常資深、廣受敬重的教授。這種教授通常已完成大部分的成就，可能會稍稍放鬆一點，讓你日子好過一些。問題是這樣的教授不多，而且事實上他們還是會維持一定標準，以求保持他們的名聲。但多數情形下，如果有機會，我還是會建議你選這樣的教授。

♥ Choosing an assistant professor does have its advantages and disadvantages. Being on tenure track, the professor would work hard and try to help his students as much as possible, because your research could be the stepping stone he needs in getting the tenure promotion. However, there is one thing you need to know before you choose a tenure track assistant professor. How much time does he or she have left? What is the status for his tenure review? Can he pass the review? If your advisor is rejected in the process, he or she would have a limited amout time in the school, and that could really put you in an awkward position. Changing your advisor in the middle of your research work is one of the worse things that can happen to a graduate student.

> 選助理教授有好有壞，這些正在評鑑中的教授，通常會努力工作，並盡力幫助他的學生，因為你的研究也可能成為讓他通過評鑑的助力。在選擇這樣的教授時要注意一點，就是他還有多少時間？評鑑的狀況如何？他能通過評鑑嗎？如果你的指導教授沒有通過教授評鑑，他在學校就只剩非常有限的時間，可能會讓情況變的非常棘手。對研究生而言，在研究途中更換指導教授是最糟糕的情況了。

♥ Just be careful and ask around for opinions and suggestions before you choose an advisor. Good luck!

> 找指導教授要很小心，多問問別人的意見和建議，祝你好運！

Part II

3 單字與例句

obstruction *n.* 阻塞物、障礙

We need to remove the obstructions to clear the road for drivers.
我們必須清理掉障礙物才能幫駕駛開路。

renowned *adj.* 有名的、有聲譽的

This restaurant is renowned for its sea food.
這家餐廳以海鮮著名。

supervision *n.* 監督、管理

Young children need constant supervision from their parents.
小孩需要父母時時的監管。

drain *v.* 排出、耗盡，名詞 *n.* 消耗、排水管

Prolonged civil war has drained the country's wealth and resources.
長期的內戰耗盡了這國家的財富與資源。

reap *v.* 收割、收穫、獲得

Our firm is reaping a big profit from the new product.
我們公司從新產品上獲得巨大的收益。

torment *v.* 使痛苦、折磨 名詞：痛苦、煩擾

Since that terrible accident, he has been tormented by nightmares.
自從那可怕的意外後他一直受到噩夢的折磨。

Chapter 5

知識備忘錄

選擇合適的指導教授真的是研究生生涯的第一個重要步驟，選的好就有了好的開始，自然為日後奠下一個紮實的基礎。運氣好的話有可能順利啟航，從此一帆風順；運氣不好的話，可能會變成受苦受難的開始。

在修碩、博士學位時，最開始也是最重要的是：確認自己感興趣的領域。其實這也是台灣學生最弱的一件事，畢竟多數台灣學生都遵循父母親的意見，對自己的未來想法自然比美國人少多了。我一直相信先找出自己的興趣最重要，因為這很可能就是你日後的一輩子的職場生涯，先確定這點再來找相關領域的教授。

再來就是選教授了，簡單的說可以分成找正教授或副教授，或是找助理教授。前兩者因為在系上地位穩固，比較不用擔心教授被迫離開的狀況，而找助理教授就要注意這點。什麼時候會有教授評鑑結果？會不會沒過而出現問題？當然有些表現很好的，過的機會很大，也就不用擔心。但副教授以上的往往會有很多學生，如果指導不多，你是否有能力自行完成研究，這也是考慮因素之一。而助理教授因為教授評鑑的關係，自然會比較積極，對一些比較需要督促的人，會是比較好的選擇。

Unit 24 使用學生服務的資源

1 主題對話

Michael is talking to Tony about the library.
Michael 和 Tony 談到了圖書館。

Michael	I was told the library provides a lot of services physically or online. How do I use it?	我聽説圖書館提供很多服務，不管是線上或是實體，我要怎麼使用？
Tony	Didn't you go to the New Student Orientation?	你不是去過新生訓練嗎？
Michael	I did, but without much of physical **demonstration**, I am not sure how to use their services.	我是去過，不過沒有實際示範，我還是不很清楚如何使用。
Tony	You shouldn't have much trouble **navigating** the website, right?	你在使用圖書館網站上應該沒問題，對吧？
Michael	I did walk through the library website, and I am starting to get a feeling for it. I think I'm fine with the online services.	我是看過幾次，感覺不錯，網路服務這方面應該沒什麼問題。
Tony	I have time this afternoon. Let's meet at the front door of the library at 2 PM?	今天下午我有時間，要不要下午兩點圖書館門口見？
Michael	Sure, see you there.	沒問題，到時候見。

Chapter 5

Later in the afternoon, inside the library, （當天下午，在圖書館）

Tony	As you noticed, each floor has different category of books. The first floor is the front desk and the reading areas, with newspaper and magazine being displaced here. If you are not really used to read on the computer screen, this is a great place for you. The front desk takes care of any library related requests, and you can ask questions there.	如你所見，每層樓都有不同種類的書。一樓是前台服務區和閱讀區，書報雜誌也在這裡，如果你不習慣在電腦螢幕上看書，就可以來這裡。前台負責提供所有圖書館相關的服務，你也可以跟他們提出你的問題。
Michael	With air-conditioning system, I think I'll spend some time here during scorching hot summer time and frigid winter time.	有這兒的空調，我看在炎熱的夏天和酷寒的冬天我會常來這裡看書。
Tony	There are more reading areas on the second floor.	二樓還有更多閱覽區。
Michael	More air-conditioned reading areas for me, this is good.	更多的空調閱讀區，這樣很好。
Tony	There are some study rooms for graduate students on the third floor.	三樓有一些研究生的研讀室。
Michael	Graduate student study rooms? What are they for?	研究生研讀室？用來做什麼？
Tony	As a graduate student, you can apply for one room here, so you can quietly study here without any interference.	每個研究生都可以申請一個房間，讓你可以不受干擾的讀書。
Michael	That's great. How and where do I apply for it?	這很棒，我要怎麼申請？在哪裡申請？

Part II

| Tony | Just go to the library front desk and ask for an application form. | 就到前台跟他們要申請表。 |
| Michael | Thanks. I'll do it right now. | 謝謝，我現在就去。 |

2 心情小語

❤ One benefit of going to a big public university in US is that it usually has relatively more international students. To **accommodate** these overseas students who need special assistance, it usually has an International Student Services Office. And this is the best place for you to get information and help.

> 去美國公立大學的好處就是，學校通常有較多的國際學生，也會設立國際學生服務處，為國際學生提供服務，解決各種問題。國際學生服務處是國際學生尋求協助的好地方。（選擇就讀美國大型公立大學的好處之一就是通常會有較多的國際學生。為了因應這些有特殊需求的學生們，校內會設有國際學生服務處。而這是你能獲得資訊及協助的最佳場所。

❤ Through ISS, we once found a special "Thanksgiving dinner with a local family" program. We applied and were later invited to a traditional Thanksgiving dinner with an American family. We had the chance to know the tradition and history of Thanksgiving and other holidays. Also, we had the opportunity to introduce our own culture to the family. You would be surprised by how little Americans know about Taiwan. This is the best way to enjoy great food, to learn each other's life style and culture, and to have a great time.

透過國際學生服務處，我們得知「與當地家庭享用感恩節晚餐」計畫。在申請後，得以到當地的一個美國家庭享受傳統的感恩節大餐，並了解感恩節和其他節日的傳統和歷史。我們和對方分享我們自己的傳統及文化。你會很訝異於一般美國人對台灣的認知真的很少！這是一個可以享受美食、互相學習生活方式和文化並享有快樂時光的最佳機會。

♥ From ISS, you can also get some information about the local community. There may be some special programs held in community center, some of which specifically designed for international students. Most local residents do not wander far away from home. Some of them might be spending their entire life within the city. The public university is the best resource for them to get to know the outside world. Thus, ISS is the place they get to know people from overseas. Discovery programs held by the First Baptist Church, College Station, really helped my wife in fitting into the local community.

從國際學生服務處你也可以得到一些當地社區的消息。社區中心有時還會有特殊的方案，其中有些是針對國際學生而設的。多數的美國人很少出遠門，有些人一輩子就待在同一個城市裡；對他們來說，大學就是讓他們了解外面世界的地方，國際學生服務處則是他們認識外國人的據點。卡城第一浸信會所辦的 Discovery 課程， 就讓我太太融入當地的社區。

♥ From ISS, we learned about another great program called Friendship International House, which invites international students to spend the Christmas and New Year holidays with an American family. I applied and was approved by the program, and we had the chance to live with a family in Orlando, Florida and got our best Christmas vacation in US ever. The details of the trip will be described in another section.

Part II

> 　　從國際學生服務處，我們也打聽到友誼國際家庭計畫，這個計畫提供國際學生和美國家庭共度聖誕節及新年假期的機會。在申請並獲得核准後，我們得到機會前往佛羅里達州的奧蘭多市，並在當地一個家庭過了一個最棒的聖誕假期。詳細的內容會在另一個章節裡描述。

❤ Get to know more about your school's International Student Services. There is a lot of treasure for you to find out.

> 　　多多了解學校的國際學生服務處，那可有很多的寶藏等你去挖掘。

3 單字與例句

demonstration   *n.* 證明、展現、示威遊行

Students participated in the nonviolent demonstration against the government.
學生參與了那個反政府的和平（非暴力）遊行。

navigate   *v.* 航行、駕駛、導航

Only the smaller boats can safely navigate the canal.
只有小船才可以安全地在運河裡航行。

accommodate   *v.* 能容納、提供膳宿、通融、適應

New programs are being added to accommodate the special needs of international students.
加入了些新計畫來因應國際學生的特殊需求。

知識備忘錄

　　美國大學所在地多數是那個城鎮的經濟與知識中心，尤其是大型的州立學校，往往都會有國際學生服務中心。對我們這些外國學生而言，這也是最重要的服務資訊來源，多去逛逛、看看、問問可能就會有些收穫。

　　除此之外，當地的社區中心和教會，多多少少也會針對海外學生提供些服務。尤其是研究生因為年紀比較大，往往有些已經結婚，甚至有小孩，有些還會針對配偶和小孩來舉辦各種活動。前面提到的 Discovery Program 就是這類針對配偶和小小孩所提供的活動，內容包括英文、烹飪、手工藝、化妝課程，甚至設計了一些父母親跟小孩互動的活動。當然還有一些讓各國人介紹他們的飲食、服裝、音樂文化的活動，藉這個機會，我們也有機會讓美國人和其他國家來的人民認識台灣。我的妻子就很喜歡這個每星期舉行一次的教會活動。

　　社區中心也很清楚，一般而言，這些人的英文不是很好，因此也會提供簡單的英文課程讓他們練習。美國四處都有教會，所以大學附近的教會也會針對國際學生提供一些服務，或舉辦一些相關的活動，讓當地的教友有機會認識各國的人。這也是個很好的機會，一方面學習美國文化，也可以讓他們接觸台灣的飲食和文化。

　　到國際學生服務處多問問，跟老學生聊聊，就可以知道這類的活動與服務真的很棒！

Part II

 論文答辯

1 主題對話

Michael is talking to his roommate Daniel about Daniel's thesis defense.
Michael 跟他的室友 Daniel 聊到 Daniel 的論文答辯。

Michael	I was told you just defended your thesis. How did it go?	我聽說你已經答辯了，結果呢？
Daniel	It went smoothly, and with the help of my advisor, I passed it.	還順利，在指導教授的幫忙下我通過了。
Michael	Congratulations. How did you prepare for it? Anything I need to take note of?	恭喜，你是怎麼準備的？有什麼我該注意的地方嗎？
Daniel	First, you would probably find out during the process, your advisor is the only professor in the committee who really reads your thesis **thoroughly**. The others just **scan** through it, and you are the only one who fully understands what is going on in the thesis.	首先，在整個過程中，你會發現你的指導教授是委員會裡唯一完整看過論文的人，其他教授多半只是瀏覽過去，而你是唯一一個完全清楚論文來龍去脈的人。
Michael	Really?	真的嗎？

Daniel	Sure, just think about it. Those professors have their own research to take care of, they have their own students to keep eyes on, and they have their own lectures they need to prepare for. How much time do you think they have left to read your thesis carefully?	當然，想想看那些教授，他們有自己的研究、有自己的學生、有自己的課程，你認為他們會有多少時間仔細的看你的論文？
Michael	That makes sense, but what is the point out of this?	有道理，但重點是？
Daniel	Since you are the one that did a **comprehensive** and **meticulous** research on the topic and the only one that fully understand the topic, you should show your confidence in defending any question.	既然你是唯一一個做了廣泛研究的人，又是唯一一個完全了解這個主題的人，你應該在回應問題時展現你的信心。
Michael	Good point, but what if I show any sign of uncertainty or **hesitation**?	有道理，但是如果我顯現了任何不確定或是遲疑的徵兆呢？
Daniel	Please don't do that. The committee members besides your professor would **pounce** on any sign of weakness, which would get you in trouble, sometimes big trouble.	拜託不要！除了你的指導教授以外的委員，都會針對弱點進行攻擊。這會讓你惹上麻煩，甚至是大麻煩！
Michael	I will remember that.	我會記得這點。
Daniel	Knowing that you are the only one that **scrutinizes** the subject, you should be able to keep your **poise** and confidently answer any question.	清楚知道你是唯一一個詳細研究這個專題的人，你應該能保持鎮定，有信心回答任何問題。

Part II

| Michael | Thank you, and now I have more confidence in my own work. | 謝謝，現在對我的研究更有信心了。 |
| Daniel | My pleasure. | 我的榮幸。 |

❷ 心情小語

♥ Thesis defense is probably the last **hurdle** for you to pass before getting your degree. Needless to say, you have to be well prepared for it. However, without the approval of your advisor, there would be no defense at all. During the whole process, the only thing you need to keep in mind is that in your advisor's opinion, your work is already worthy of a degree.

> 論文答辯可說是你在拿到學位前所要通過的最後一道關卡。不用說，你是該好好的準備一下。當然如果沒有指導教授的核可，根本就不會有答辯，因此在整個過程當中，你要記住，對你的指導教授而言，你的研究已經值得拿到這個學位了。

♥ Attend other defenses if possible. You will see how the defenses work. Go through a practice defense if possible. Be prepared for the following questions:
● Why did you decide to go into this direction and not others?
● Why didn't you try this?
● What could have been done better?
● What would be the next possible research topic?
● Any other possible solutions you explored on?

可能的話，去參加其他的答辯，看看別人的答辯是怎麼進行的。可能的話，來一次答辯演練，並準備好以下的問題：

- 你為什麼決定往這個方向研究？
- 你為什麼沒試過其他辦法？
- 有哪些可以做得更好？
- 下一個可能的研究專題？
- 探討過其他的解決方案嗎？

♥ If a question puzzles you, ask for **clarification** and that would buy you some precious time to **formulate** your answer. Don't be afraid to say "I have no idea (for now)." Don't assume you have every question covered. Professors would surprise you. Show your passion but don't be too aggressive. Professors like to see students who really care about their work, know how to conduct a scholarly debate, and take critique constructively. I know there is only a subtle line between being passion and being aggressive, so saying "have no idea (for now)" could be good. After the defense, It is common to be asked to add more data, or to do some more work on certain areas.

答辯中，如果有問題卡住了，可以先要求更詳盡的說明，這會讓你得到一些寶貴的時間來思考答案。不要害怕說：我（目前）不清楚。不要假設你已經準備好了所有的問題，有些教授會讓你驚訝。展現你的熱誠，但是不要顯得強辯。教授喜歡看到一個全心關注研究，同時也清楚如何主導辯論，並能接受建設性的批評的學生。我知道在熱誠與強辯之間的界線很微妙，所以說：我（目前）不知道，可能是個還不錯的選擇。答辯後被要求加些資料，或是加強一些工作，是很正常的。

❤ There is an unwritten rule for preparing thesis defense in US. The rule is to bring donuts and coffee to the defense, especially if it is in the morning. If it's in the afternoon, some cookies would be good, but donuts would still be fine. Also, ask for any dietary restriction for all the committee members. You don't want to have some food that somebody doesn't like. Sweet dessert is usually better than the salty snacks. Make sure you have the dishes properly set up beforehand.

> 在美國論文答辯有個潛規則，那就是準備甜甜圈和咖啡，尤其是在早上。如果答辯是在下午，一些餅乾也還不錯，但甜甜圈一樣可以。同時先問一下委員會教授，是否有些飲食上的禁忌，可不要準備了某些教授不喜歡的食物。甜點通常比鹹的點心好，並確定盤子在答辯前要擺好。

❤ Once again, remember that your advisor already believed your research is good enough to get a degree, and that is why he/she allows you to have this defense. Also, you are probably the only one that has done a thorough job in this topic, so nobody knows it more than you do. Be confident and go for it.

> 再次記得，你的指導教授已經認為你的研究足夠讓你拿學位，這也是他讓你答辯的原因。同時你很可能是唯一一個對題目做過完整研究的人，所以沒人比你更懂這個研究。以信心面對答辯吧！

3 單字與例句

thoroughly *adv.* 徹底地、仔細地

They studied the problem thoroughly and made sure that every possible solution was investigated.
他們徹底地研究了這個問題，並確認每個可能的解決方案都調查過。

scan   *v.* 粗略的看、瀏覽

He always scans the headlines of the newspaper in the morning.
他每天早上都把報紙頭條瀏覽過。

comprehensive   *adj.* 廣泛的、綜合的

A comprehensive search is needed to find the missing girl.
需要完整的搜尋才能找到那位走失的女孩。

meticulous   *adj.* 精細的、一絲不苟的

The teacher described the subject in meticulous detail to make sure all the students have a complete understanding.
老師仔細地描述了這個主題，以確認所有學生都完全的了解。

hesitation   *n.* 遲疑

He jumped into the lake without any hesitation to save the drowning boy.
他毫不遲疑地跳進湖裡，去救那位淹水的男孩。

pounce   *v.* 猛撲、襲擊

The lion did not hesitate and pounced on the zebra.
那隻獅子毫不遲疑地猛撲向那斑馬。

scrutinize   *v.* 詳細檢查、細看

The police scrutinized the suspect's house, looking for any evidence linking him to the crime.
警察仔細的檢查了嫌犯的家，尋找任何能證明他犯罪的證據。

poise   *n.* 鎮定、自信

The young gymnast showed her remarkable poise in preforming her routine.
那位年輕體操選手在表演他的體操程序時，展現無比的自信。

Part II

hurdle   *n.* 跳欄、障礙、困難

The company overcame severe financial hurdles this year and kept making profit.

這公司克服許多財務困難並持續地賺錢。

clarification   *n.* 澄清、說明

I need further clarification in order to answer the question.

在回答問題前，我需要更詳盡的說明。

formulate   *v.* 公式化、系統性的說明闡述

It is important to formulate a plan before tackling any problem.

在解決問題前，先設想好個計畫非常重要。

知識備忘錄

　　我的論文答辯是個少有的情況。當時研究做得差不多了，在指導教授的同意下開始專心寫論文。同時也開始準備履歷，開始找工作，正好又碰上網路爆炸性成長的那段時間，慢慢的，電話或是正式面試的機會也越來越多，當然也就影響到我寫論文的進度。還記得當時就跟老婆講，找到工作只是遲早的事，要專心寫論文了。結果幾天後，就拿到一些工作機會，只剩不到一個星期的時間要把論文寫完。還記得要搭飛機到加州的那天凌晨才完成我的論文，當時電子郵件附件檔案的大小受限，根本不可能電子郵件寄送，只好交給一位大陸朋友，請他轉交給我的指導教授。

　　抵達矽谷後便開始工作。每隔幾個星期問教授看論文的進度，一直都沒什麼確切的答案，不知何時可以看完。其實指導教授當時已轉往行政職，並成為工學院助理院長，根本沒時間看我的論文。等到半年後公司的計畫告一段落，我覺得拖下去只會更糟，就直接問她何時可以進行答辯？她要我挑一個日子，我查了一下學校的行事曆，找了個公司計畫不忙，又不至於耽誤到我畢業日期的日子。結果一提出來教授就答應了。

　　我當然就開始準備我的答辯，經過了半年多重新看我的論文，卻發覺我好像不認識它了！有些關鍵點甚至我都懷疑，是不是真的是我寫的？有些公式我又得重新思考、推導來確認。還好幾天後感覺就回來了，於是在有點信心卻也有些懷疑的情況下，搭機回德州答辯。

　　結果整個過程比我想像中的順利，只有幾個比較艱澀的問題，有些我回答的還不錯，有些指導教授稍稍幫忙，然後就被趕出房間。接下來的十幾、二十分鐘，可真讓我度日如年。要是沒過，我已經在矽谷工作了，根本不可能重回德州做研究。還好開門後只聽到恭喜之聲，在答應做一些補強工作後，我通過了拿到學位，正式展開我的職場生涯。

Unit 26　社交聚會

1　主題對話

Michael is talking to Janet, an International Student Services (ISS) staff, about the possible Thanksgiving activity.

Michael 和 Janet 一位 ISS 的職員談到了感恩節可能會有的活動。

Michael	Is there any special program for international students to attend in the coming Thanksgiving holidays?	有什麼國際學生能參加的感恩節活動嗎？
Janet	Yes, there are several of them. What kind of programs are you interested in joining?	是有幾個，你對什麼樣的活動感興趣？
Michael	I'd like to spend the holiday with an American family, and get to know more about history and traditions.	我想跟個美國家庭一起過節，也想知道節日的傳統與歷史。
Janet	The local church has a program like that. They ask local residents if they are interested in inviting international students to their Thanksgiving dinner. Would you like to sign up for that?	本地教會有舉辦類似的活動，他們向本地居民詢問是否有意邀請國際學生一起舉行感恩節晚餐，你要參加嗎？
Michael	Sure, I'd love to. Is there any dress code? Do I have to prepare any dish?	當然。有需要穿著正式服裝嗎？或準備餐點嗎？

Chapter 6

Janet	The only thing you have to bring is your **appetite**. You are more than welcome to bring some homemade dishes or dressed up with your traditional clothes from your home country.	唯一要帶的就是你的胃口，當然也歡迎你準備一些家鄉食物或是穿著你自己國家的傳統服飾。
Michael	Do I need to be a Christian, since it is a church related activity?	既然是教會所辦，一定要是基督徒才能參加嗎？
Janet	No. Actually, they welcome any religionist or **atheist**.	不用，任何宗教或是不信教都歡迎。
Michael	Great, how do I sign up for it?	很棒，我要如何申請？
Janet	Here is the application form, and please leave your name, address and phone number on it, so we can get in touch with you once it's approved.	這是申請表，請填上你的姓名、住址和電話，好讓我們在核可後跟你連絡。
Michael	Do you have a pen?	有筆嗎？
Janet	Here it is. You can sit over there to fill out the form.	這裡，你可以坐在那裏填表。
Michael	Thanks. I am looking forward to it already.	謝謝，我已經等不及了。

2 心情小語

❤ For college students, there aren't many formal social events to go to. Annual Chinese New Year celebration banquet is one, and being invited to a local family for Christmas or Thanksgiving dinner is another. Other occasions are **few and far between**. The **casual** ones, however, are more often.

> 以學生而言，正式的社交聚會場合真的不多，除了每年的過年慶祝晚宴，另外就是被邀請到當地家庭享用聖誕或感恩大餐，其他的則較少。不過非正式休閒的聚會就比較多了。

❤ Sometimes, the professor would invite all of his/her graduate students to lunch together or to have a dinner party at home. This is the chance for you to have a casual chat with your advisor and colleagues, to have fun, and to take a break from all the hard work. Of course, this is also an opportunity to learn about other country's custom, and the best moment to promote our own culture.

> 有時候教授會邀請他所有的研究生吃午餐，或到家裡吃晚飯。這可是讓你能輕鬆地跟同僚和老師愉快聊天，並在繁忙的工作後休息的機會。當然也可以藉此學習世界各國的風俗，並也是推銷我們自己的文化的最佳時機。

❤ Taiwanese students would occasionally have potlucks. Every family or individual brings in one or two dishes to share with all the other ones. Best of all, each person or family would prepare his/her own specialty, and thus, everyone has the chance to **devour** the most delicious food. **Bachelors** who are not good at cooking would attend the party with fruit, snacks, or drinks. Even with a scholarhip to cover for the living, life of a graduate student is not that much fun for most of the time. It is even worse for overseas students because they are far away from their families. Having a potluck or any kind of social gathering is a great way to let you forget those **dull** moments at least temporarily.

Chapter 6

台灣學生通常會辦分享餐會。每個家庭或個人帶一兩盤食物與眾人分享，最棒的是大家都會準備拿手菜，所以每個人都有機會可以張開大口吃到最美味、可口的餐點。那些比較不會烹飪的單身漢則準備水果、點心或飲料。研究生生活多數都不會很有趣，就算有獎學金，金額也不高，對於海外學生無法跟親人相處更是可憐，而這類的分享餐會或社交聚會就是個很棒的場合，讓你至少暫時的忘記無聊的研究生生活。

♥ In Taiwan, families usually have a reunion on the three major Chinese holidays, namely, Chinese New Year, Moon festival and Dragon Boat Festival. For students studying in US, it is hard to have gatherings on those occasions, since they usually don't fall on weekends. Sometimes, the holidays just passed by without anybody noticing it. However, we still try our best to have friends coming together to enjoy the holiday whenever there is a chance.

Part II

　　在台灣，家人通常會在三大節日時聚在一起，三大節日分別是過年、中秋和端午。在美國唸書的學生就很難在這些節日裡聚會，畢竟多數不是周末。甚至有時節日過了都沒有人注意到。但只要有機會，我們仍然試著找朋友來一起慶祝佳節。

3 單字與例句

apparel　*n.* 衣著、服裝

With spring coming, winter apparel is on sale.
春天即將來臨，冬裝開始打折。

appetite　*n.* 食慾、胃口

Some common flu symptoms are tiredness, fever, cough, running nose and loss of appetite.
流感的一般症狀是疲倦、發燒、咳嗽、流鼻涕和沒有食慾。

atheist　*n.* 無神論者

Not believing in any God, he is an atheist.
不信仰任何神，他是個無神論者。

few and far between　稀疏、很少

Wonderful and enjoyable family movies are few and far between.
拍得很棒又好看的家庭電影片真的很少。

casual　*adj.* 非正式的、休閒的、碰巧的

Casual dress is not appropriate for this ceremony.
非正式休閒的服裝對這個典禮並不恰當。

devour　*v.* 吃光、狼吞虎嚥

After two hours of intensive exercise, he devours everything on his plate.
在兩小時的密集操練後，他把盤子裡所有的東西吃光了。

bachelor　*n.* 單身漢、學士 (B 常大寫)

Never getting married, he was a bachelor all his life.
從未結婚他成了一輩子的單身漢。

dull　*adj.* 無聊的、昏暗的、隱約的

There is never a dull moment in that exciting adventure movie.
那部刺激的冒險電影沒有任何沉悶的時刻。

知識備忘錄

　　在台灣，有活動大多是以家庭聚會為主，回老家過節更不可免。但是在美國時，一般家人都不在身邊，生活社交圈真的很小。所以幾乎所有同學、朋友住的距離都不會很遠，因為出門在外確實有很多的不方便，這個時候，相互間的幫忙與照料自然不可免，或許也就因為這樣，大家一起社交聚會的機會也就多了，大家比較常聚在一起吃飯、聊天、唱卡拉 OK。在海外，朋友、同學間的關係確實比台灣更加緊密，畢竟大家都離鄉在外，多少就會聚在一起聊天，說說台灣最近發生的事，講一些八卦。

　　學生時代跟美國人的聚會不多，偶而邀請他們到餐廳或家裡吃個飯、聊聊天，定期的聚會更少。畢竟生活習慣與文化不同，共同的話題不多，偶而為之。美國人一般都對運動，尤其是美式橄欖球、籃球和棒球較有興趣，通常談論的都是鄰近的職業隊或是大學隊，除非在美國待過一陣子、看過一些球賽，才有辦法跟他們聊，所以吃飯聚會也僅於偶而為之。

　　在美國待的比較久一點的學生，自然而然的也就入境隨俗的看起了球賽，遇到重要的大學死敵比賽，或是當地職業球隊的季賽和季後賽，更是大家相聚一堂、呼喊加油的時候，這幾乎是不可免的運動球賽聚會。

Part II

Unit 27 旅遊樂趣多

1 主題對話

Michael is talking to Tony about a Colorado skiing trip for the coming winter break.

Michael 和 Tony 聊到了在寒假裡，要到科羅拉多滑雪旅遊。

Michael	I just got some information about a Colorado skiing trip from ISS.	我從 ISS 那裏聽說有個科羅拉多州的滑雪行程。
Tony	Wow, a skiing trip to colorful Colorado, one of the Rocky Mountain States. Do you have detailed information?	哇！去落磯山州之一的多彩科羅拉多州滑雪！你有詳細的資訊嗎？
Michael	One of the local churches is working with their sister church in Colorado to plan for a trip there. It would be a ten-day visit, including sightseeing and skiing.	本地的教會跟它位於科州的姊妹教會計畫要辦個十天的旅遊，包含觀光遊覽和滑雪。
Tony	How much is it?	多少錢？
Michael	It is 250 dollars per person, including lodging, meals, and transportation. Skiing costs is extra.	每人 250 塊，包含住宿、餐飲和交通，但是滑雪費用另計。
Tony	Is there any religious activities? Can non-Christian join the trip?	有任何教會活動嗎？非教友可以參加嗎？
Michael	Yes, there is some casual bible study, and non-Christian can still join it.	有些輕鬆的聖經研讀，非教友也可以參加。

Chapter 6

Tony	You mentioned about sightseeing, any place in particular?	你說了觀光導覽，有說要去哪些地方嗎？
Michael	They are going to Denver, the state capital, which is also known as the Mile-High city. They will visit the Colorado State Capitol Building, which is a **distinctive** gold **dome** building consists of real gold plate. They're also going to the Red Rocks Amphitheatre and some other places, but I can't remember all of them.	會去科州首府，號稱一哩高城市的丹佛。還會去看黃金蓋頂的州政府建築。行程裡還有紅岩劇場，和一些我不記得的地點。
Tony	Sounds fun. I am interested in skiing but I never tried it before. Is that a concern?	聽來不錯。我想試試滑雪，不過我從沒滑過。這會是問題嗎？
Michael	No, a lot of tourists are first time skier. There is also cross country skiing besides regular downhill skiing.	不會，很多旅客都是第一次滑雪，而且除了高降滑雪外，還有越野滑雪。
Tony	What's the difference between them?	有什麼不一樣嗎？
Michael	Come join us and you will know.	參加就知道了。

Part II

2 心情小語

♥ Speaking of leisure traveling, we sure have a lot of experience. As I said, graduate student life in US is boring. Living in the middle of Texas makes it even worse. Whenever there is a summer vacation or winter holiday, almost all Taiwanese students go out to have trips.

講到休閒旅遊我們確實有些經驗，如我所言，美國研究生的生活確實無聊，而住在德州只會更慘。只要有暑假或寒假，多數的台灣學生就會出去旅遊一番。

❤ Once, I went to ISS and got information regarding a special program called Friendship International House (FIH), which is organized by churches around US. They invite international students to join local American families for Christmas and New Year Holiday. They can stay with the host for more than a week to enjoy their hospitality.

有次我去 ISS 得知一個名為國際友誼家庭（FIH）的特殊計畫，基本上由美國各地的教會邀請一些外國學生，到當地的美國家庭過聖誕節和新年。參加者可以在美國家庭住宿超過一星期，並感受美國家庭的熱情招待。

❤ We decided to go to Florida, and we signed up for three cities: Orlando, Tampa, and Jacksonville. Luckily, we were chosen by a church in Orlando. My wife prepared a decoration Chinese paper-cutting figure for the host family as the Christmas gift. The church planned a sightseeing tour, and the **itinerary** includes Disney World, Busch Gardens in Tampa, and St. Augustine Old Town. We lived in a fabulous room, and the church arranged all transportation. It's the best trip in our life.

報名時我們決定去佛羅里達，並在申請單上填了佛州的奧蘭多、譚巴和傑克森維爾三個城市。幸運的是，我們被奧蘭多的教會選上。我太太還特別準備了剪紙，送給寄宿家庭的主人當聖誕禮物。教會準備了很棒的行程，包含迪士尼世界、譚巴的布希花園、聖奧古斯丁老城區等。寄宿家庭的房間很棒，交通也由教會安排，這實在是我們這一輩子最棒的旅遊。

❤ The three day spent in Walt Disney World **Resort** was without question the **pinnacle** of the **journey**. There are three **theme** parks: Magic Kingdom, Hollywood Studios, and Epcot Center. It was a life time experience. The Busch Gardens in Tampa really surprised us. I had never heard of it before the trip. There were various roller coasters, a mini zoo, and all different kinds of shows. We had a great time there. Our host, Frank, was a lawyer, and his wife, Gina, was a nurse. They even gave us two tickets to watch an Orlando Magic game. After all these years, we still miss the trip to Florida.

> 　　迪士尼三日遊是旅程中的亮點。當時迪士尼有三個主題樂園：魔術王國、好萊塢影城,和未來中心。這真是讓我畢生難忘的經驗。讓我驚訝的是讓我們感到驚訝的是譚巴的布希花園。我去之前從沒聽過這個地方,那裏有各式各樣的雲霄飛車、以及小型動物園和各種表演,我們很喜歡那裡。住宿家庭主人法蘭克是一位律師,他的妻子吉娜則是一位護士,他們甚至給我們兩張奧蘭多魔術隊比賽的門票。這麼多年後,這趟佛州之旅仍讓我回味無窮。

❤ If you see a similar program, remember to sign up for it. You won't regret it. Also remember to show how grateful you are to the host. After all, you represent the image of Taiwan.

> 　　如果看到類似的計畫,記得報名參加!你不會後悔的!記得向住處的主人表達感謝,畢竟你代表了台灣的形象。

3 單字與例句

distinctive　*adj.* 特殊的、有特色的

The singer has a distinctive voice that can be easily recognized.
那位歌手有種很容易認出來的特別嗓音。

dome　*n.* 圓頂建築、圓蓋

Tokyo Dome is one of the most famous architectures in Japan.
東京巨蛋是日本最著名的建物之一。

itinerary　*n.* 旅程、路線、旅行計畫

Before going to Japan, please leave your itinerary so we can reach you in case of an emergency.
去日本前請留下你的旅行計畫，也好在有急事時可以找到你。

resort　*n.* 名勝、渡假村

There are many tourist resorts in Kenting.
墾丁有很多旅遊渡假村。

pinnacle　*n.* 山峰、頂點

After releasing the most popular song ever, the singer reached the pinnacle of his career.
在推出有史以來最賣座的歌曲後，這位歌者達到他生涯的頂點。

journey　*n.* 旅程、行程

"Sometimes it's worth lingering on the journey for a while before getting to the destination."- Richelle Mead
「有時候在抵達目的地之前，是值得在行程中逗留一下。" - Richelle Mead

theme　*n.* 話題、主題

Disney Land is one of the most prominent theme parks in the world.
狄斯奈樂園是世界上最著名的主題樂園之一。

Chapter 6

知識備忘錄

　　多數的美國大學都在一些半大不小的城鎮，就算是在大城市，每到假期，台灣學生多多少少都會想到美國各處玩玩，但是花費都不會少。在此除了前面提到的 FIH，我再介紹一個不用花太多錢，卻能同樣享受旅遊的經驗。

　　待過美國的就知道，美國教會到處都有，一般而言，教友都非常友善，對外國學生更是親切。我在美國的幾次便宜旅遊，都是教會或教友所主辦的。除了前一節的佛羅里達之旅，還有一次科羅拉多滑雪之遊。這是一位在卡城的美國人教友舉辦的，我在 ISS 裡認識他，他本身是在南美洲長大的 aggie，所以會説西班牙文和英文，他對中國文化也很有興趣，中文講得很不錯。透過科州教會，他找了十幾個卡城的華人，其中多數是大陸來的，一起到科州十天。

　　科羅拉多位於落磯山上，而丹佛市號稱 mile high city，正因為它標高不多不少，正好一英里（1,609.3 公尺）。可以想見，冬天這地方常下雪，又因為處於山地，所以有許多滑雪勝地。那次的旅程讓我知道滑雪還分 downhill 和 cross-country。Downhill skiing 就是我們常見的高降滑雪，而 cross-country skiing 則是越野滑雪。當然還有機會體驗冰刀溜冰，我也就是在當時學會滑雪。我們住在教會安排的小木屋，以火爐燒柴取暖，一進到室內就不會冷了。當時有一天下了整晚的雪，第二天早上起來看到，就看到風景明信片裡才能看到的雪景，實在令人難忘。

　　在美國念書，有空記得到 ISS 網站逛逛，隨時打聽一下這類的旅遊機會，認識幾個教友。不管你信不信基督都沒問題，既然來到美國就四處走走看看，體驗一下異國風情。

Part II

 觀看體育賽事

1 主題對話

Michael is talking to Tony about the upcoming football season.
Michael 和 Tony 聊到了即將來臨的美式足球季節。

Tony	It's going to be the football season soon. I can't wait for the games to start.	足球球季快開始了。我等不及了。
Michael	Football? Are you talking about the Association football, which commonly known as soccer?	足球？你是說一般足球嗎？
Tony	No, I am talking about American football. It's the most popular sport in US, college or professional.	不，我講的是美式足球，美國最受歡迎的運動，不管是大學或是職業隊。
Michael	I don't know much about it. Actually, I don't know anything about American Football at all.	我懂的不多，事實上我完全不懂！
Tony	To study in US, you have to learn to watch football games. Didn't you notice that recently some students are talking about the coming football season, especially about the revenge of losing last year's game to our **arch-rival** in the last minute?	在美國念書，你要學著看美式足球。你沒注意到最近學生們在談足球季，尤其是要一雪去年在最後一分鐘輸給我們死敵的恥辱嗎？

Michael	Oh, so that is the game they talked about last Thanksgiving. I **vaguely** remembered that there was a **disputed** call from the referees that completely change the game outcome.	喔！就是大家一直談的去年感恩節的比賽。我依稀記得裁判的一個爭議判決完全改變了比賽結果。
Tony	Yes, and that is why the students are talking about revenge. Football is a fun game, and you should learn to watch it. I wasn't really interested in the game at first, but once I got the hang of it, I started enjoying it.	是的，這也是學生們講一雪前恥的原因。美式足球很有趣，你該學著看看。我一開始也看不懂，但是捉到些竅門後就愛上它了。
Michael	I prefer watching basketball and baseball.	我比較喜歡看籃球和棒球。
Tony	Give football a try and I know you are going to love it.	試一下美式足球，我確信你會喜歡。
Michael	I know nothing about it. How do I start?	要怎麼開始？尤其是我什麼都不懂。
Tony	There must be some more students like you. Maybe we can talk to TSA and see if it's possible for TSA to arrange a tutorial about football.	應該還有其他學生跟你一樣，或許可以跟同學會談談，看看是否可以安排一次足球講解。
Michael	Sure, let's contact the President of TSA.	跟會長聯絡一下吧！

Part II

② 心情小語

💗 There are three major sports in US, namely, baseball, basketball and football. Baseball, also known as American **pastime**, has the longest history. However, it is now less popular than the rest of the two. Little League Baseball, enjoyed by elementary school kids and their parents, is still one of the most beloved activities in US, as elementary school kids and parents really enjoy it. With players like Chien-Ming Wang, Wei-Yin Chen and other Taiwanese players participating, Major League Baseball is getting more and more popular to Taiwanese.

> 　　美國有三大球賽，也就是：棒球、籃球和美式足球。棒球又稱為美國娛樂，歷史最久，不過棒球跟其他兩項球賽比起來歡迎度差一點。不過小學生和家長都喜愛的少棒還是很受歡迎。因為有王建民、陳偉殷和其他台灣球員的加入，美國職棒大聯盟在台灣也越來越受歡迎。

💗 Basketball is popular in Taiwan too. With the least amount of **gears** and space required, basketball is accessible to most people. The emerging of Jeremy Lin makes NBA even more attractive to Taiwanese than ever before.

> 　　籃球在台灣一樣受歡迎。籃球需要的場地和設備不多，適合大部分的人參與。林書豪的出現讓台灣人更加喜愛美國職籃。

💗 Although most people from Taiwan aren't familiar to football, or more specifically American football, it is the most exciting sport to watch. It is becoming the favorite sport in US. Super Bowl, the championship game for National Football League, is the most widely watched TV game every year, and the price for Super Bowl commercials are the highest. In 2013, a thirty-second ad on Super Bowl costs 4 million US dollars.

Chapter 6

台灣人多半不熟悉足球，或說是美式足球，但這卻是個很精采的球賽。在美國它已成為最受歡迎的運動，職業美式足球冠軍賽：超級盃，也是每年收視率最高的節目。當然超級盃的廣告也是最貴的，2013 年一段 30 秒的廣告要價四百萬美元。

❤ Life of a graduate student is mostly busy and dull, and naturally watching sport broadcasts on TV is one of the ways to escape the pressure. Baseball is the only major sport played in the summer, and watching MLB games, especially when there are players from Taiwan, becomes a must during the long and hot summer days. Its playoff games usually start in October, and the best-of-seven World Series decides the final championship. Football starts in September and runs all the way to the next February. College football games on Saturday and NFL games on Sunday accompany us through the fall semester. Thanksgiving holiday is also the college football rivalry weekend, and most of the rivalry schools play their annual football games in that weekend. To Americans, Thanksgiving is synonymous to football.

研究生的生活很忙也很無趣，看運動轉播就成為紓壓的方式之一。暑假中唯一有球季的運動是棒球，看棒球比賽，尤其是有台灣球員上場的比賽，就成為漫長暑假中的必要娛樂。季後賽通常十月開打，最後以七戰四勝的四屆大賽來決定冠軍。美式足球的球季從九月開始，一直持續到明年二月結束。下半年的學期中，陪伴我們的通常是週六的大學足球賽和週日的職業足球賽。感恩節假期也是大學的死敵周，多數的死敵學校都在那個周末比賽。對美國人而言，感恩節與足球畫上等號。

❤ Basketball season starts in November. Featuring 68 teams now, March Madness, a single-elimination tournament, decides the Division I college

Part II

basketball Championship. It is one of the most famous sporting events in US. With regular season ending and playoffs starting in April, the NBA championship game is usually played in June. With baseball starting in April, Americans never run short on sports games.

> 　　籃球球季由十一月開始。大學籃球則由 68 支隊伍進行單淘汰賽，並在瘋狂三月決定冠軍，這也是全美最知名的運動賽事。美國職籃在四月結束季賽，並隨後開始季後賽。冠軍賽通常在六月，而棒球又從四月開始，因此美國人決不缺運動娛樂。

3 單字與例句

arch-rival *n.* 死仇、勁敵

University of Texas and Texas A&M University are arch-rival.
德州大學和德州農工大學是死敵。

vaguely *adv.* 不清晰地、模糊地

The elderly man could only vaguely remember his childhood.
那位老先生只能模糊的憶起他的童年。

dispute *v.* 爭執、爭論

The two countries disputed over a small strip of land on the border for decades.
這兩個國家為了邊界上的一小塊土地爭執了幾十年。

pastime *n.* 消遣、娛樂

Her favorite pastime is playing guitar.
他最喜歡的消遣是彈吉他。

Chapter 6

gear　*n.* 工具、設備

I managed to pack all my gear into one box.
我設法把所有工具塞進盒子裡。

知識備忘錄

　　觀看運動賽事已經是美國生活的一部分，棒球、籃球和美式足球各有大學和職業球賽。這其中只有大學棒球比較少人看，也比較不流行。其他所有賽事不只是電視轉播受歡迎，也經常成為聊天的話題，如果你想跟美國人閒聊練習英文，最容易開始的就是相關的大學和職業隊伍賽事。

　　棒球季節從四月初開始，一直到十月末世界大賽後結束，球季長達七個月。不過美國職棒的受歡迎度卻慢慢地被美式足球搶走。美式足球不管是大學還是職業都是九月開始，大學球季通常在感恩節後結束，隨後而來的則是季後的各種杯賽，到一月初的冠軍賽結束。最受歡迎的職業美式足球冠軍賽超級盃則在二月初。如要跟美國人聊天，最容易的就是美式足球。了解一下自己大學和鄰近的職業球隊，絕對只有好處。

　　最後要談的是在台灣很受歡迎的籃球，在林書豪的加持下，NBA 在台灣更受歡迎。因為一般台灣學生多少都懂一點籃球，也就比較容易融入觀賞美國的比賽，美國所有大學都會有籃球隊，去現場看看體會一下氣氛，自然而然地就會融入美國的運動文化裡了。

Part II

Unit 29 看電影享受生活

1 主題對話

Michael is talking to Tony about Avatar the movie.
Michael 和 Tony 聊到了電影阿凡達。

Tony	Avatar the movie is being shown in AMC theatre.	阿凡達正在 AMC 上映中。
Michael	I heard a lot of good reviews about that movie, but it also cost a lot of money.	我聽到很多不錯的反應，但拍這部電影也花了不少錢。
Tony	According to some reports it cost 280 millions. However, as Roger Ebert, one of the most recognizable movie critics said "There is still at least one man in Hollywood who knows how to spend $250 million, or was it $300 million, wisely. "	據報導共花了兩億八千萬美金，但是如同知名影評家 Roger Ebert 所說的，好萊塢至少還有人，懂得怎麼明智的花兩億五千萬或者是三億美元拍電影。
Michael	Who is that one man he is talking about?	他說的人是？
Tony	James Cameron, the director of Avatar, who also directed Titanic, which was also the most expensive movie made at that time. He sure knows how to spend a boat load of money in making a movie.	阿凡達的導演，詹姆斯卡麥隆，他也執導了鐵達尼號，那是當時花費最高的電影，他顯然很會花大錢拍電影。

Chapter 6

Michael	I was told Avatar was a beautifully filmed 3-D movie, and some even proclaim it would start the 3-D **era**. Too bad, we couldn't enjoy the 3-D effect on those trailers.	我聽說阿凡達是部拍得很美的 3-D 電影，甚至有些人宣稱它會開啟 3-D 時代。很可惜，預告片裡看不到 3-D 特效。
Tony	Still, the visual on the trailers is stunning. It makes me eager to see the movie.	不過視覺效果仍讓人驚豔，讓我更想看了。
Michael	With green-environment and anti-war message being implied in the movie, the story line is intriguing too.	劇情暗示了綠色環境和反戰訊息，這也很吸引人。
Tony	It's a touching story about peace, friendship, and love. It's distinctly different from recent regular wall-to-wall action movies.	這是一部有關和平、友誼和愛情的感人電影，和最近只有打鬥的動作電影截然不同。
Michael	I would like to see it. When do you have time? How about Friday?	我想去看這部電影。你有時間嗎？週五如何？
Tony	I'll have a test on Friday. Can we go on Saturday morning?	週五我有考試，可以週六上午嗎？
Michael	Sure, I'll check the movie schedule and let you know the exact time.	沒問題，我去看一下時刻表再通知你確切時間。
Tony	Good, see you on Saturday.	好的，週六見。

Part II

2 心情小語

♥ Screenwriter William Goldman once stated, "Nobody knows anything about what makes a movie work." Is the movie going to be a **blockbuster** hit or not? Nobody knows the answer to the million dollar question until the movie is released. The problem is no film maker knows exactly what the audience wants, and the even bigger problem is, even the audiences don't know what they like.

> 劇作家 William Goldman 曾經説過：『沒人知道是什麼因素讓電影賣作』。這部電影到底會不會賣座？這個價值千金的問題，一定要到電影上映後大家才會知道答案。問題在於：沒有製作人能知道觀眾到底要什麼，更難的是，就連觀眾也不知道自己喜歡什麼！

♥ To get the firsthand view on how the young audience would react to the movie and the plot, some films are previewed in selected college campuses in order to **gauge** the reaction and interest from the audience. Thus, one of the good things studying in US college is the free movie previews. The previews are not trailers, but full length movies. The other benefit to watch free preview movies is that you are free to express your feelings and let out all of your stress, just like you are watching the movies in your own place. This is because all audiences around you are students from your college. You are free to howl like a wolf, or scream like a little girl.

> 為了要了解年輕人對電影的第一手反應，有些電影會選在大學校園試映，藉此評估觀眾的反應。於是在美國念大學的好處之一，就是可以看免費的電影。這可不是預告，而是完整的片子。有趣的是，看這些電影時，你可以像在家一樣紓解壓力，因為周圍的人都是大學裡的同學。你大可以學狼一樣的嚎叫，或像個小女孩一樣大聲尖叫。

♥ The first movie we watched in Texas A&M campus is Tremors. A small town gets terrorized by a strange underground creature, picking off people one by one. Even though it was not a particularly entertaining movie, watching it with all those crazy young college students made it a lot more enjoyable.

> 我在德州農工所看的第一部免費電影是『從地心竄出』，一個小鎮被一個怪異的食人怪物襲擊給。雖然這不是一部特別好看的電影，但是跟一群瘋狂年輕大學生一起看，確實讓你更享受電影。

❤ One of the free movies I watched was "My Best Friend's Wedding". The scene when Julianne, played by Julia Roberts, says the following line "to follow you in this dumb job, where you travel 52 weeks a year to College Station, Texas, and such" is still **vividly implanted** in my head. Upon hearing the term "College Station, Texas", the whole audience just went nuts. Everyone was **whooping**, yelling, **howling** and screaming **hysterically**. It was fun for sure. It was an irreplaceable memory to watch preview movies with a bunch ofenergetic, American college kids.

> 我看的第一部免費電影是『新娘不是我』。至今這部電影還有一個畫面深深烙印在我腦裡，那就是當由茱莉亞羅勃茲所演的茱莉安說到：『跟著你這個笨工作，一年 52 個禮拜到處走，去德州卡城這類的地方』這句台詞時，全場觀眾全瘋了似的呼喊、狂叫、狼嚎、尖聲，真的很有趣。跟一群有活力的大學生一起看電影，這可是無可取代的經驗。

3 單字與例句

era *n.* 年代、時代

We are now in the internet era.
我們現在在網路時代裡。

gauge   *v.* 量、測、判斷   *n.* 程度、範圍、容量

Retail sales provide an effective way of gauging the overall state of economy.
零售業銷量提供了個有效評估整體經濟的方法。

blockbuster   *n.* 大轟動、大賣座

Avatar is a blockbuster hit movie.
阿凡達是部大賣座電影。

vividly   *adv.* 生動地、逼真地

The picture book is vividly illustrated.
那本繪本的插圖畫得很逼真。

implant   *v.* 埋置、灌輸

The teacher tries to implant within the students with the love of reading.
老師試著要讓學生們愛上閱讀。

hysterically   *adv.* 歇斯底里地

Upon hearing the funny joke, he laughed hysterically.
在聽到那個有趣的笑話後,他歇斯底里地大笑。

whoop   *v.* (激動)高呼、高叫

After winning the championship game, the whole team was whooping hysterically.
在贏得冠軍賽後,整個球隊歇斯底里地狂喊大叫。

howl   *v.* 嗥叫、嚎啕大哭、大笑

The pack of wolves was howling all night.
那群野狼整晚的嗥叫。

知識備忘錄

　　看電影是學生時代最常見的消遣娛樂，在美國看電影更可以增進你的英文能力。美國的電影和電視節目有一點和台灣很不一樣，那就是：不管是電影或電視，都沒有字幕！電視你還可以買個字幕機把字幕顯現出來，電影就沒辦法了。不過說實話，字幕機其實沒什麼幫助，因為你看字幕的速度絕對跟不上角色說話的速度。

　　在美國看電影另一個不同的地方就是票價差別，尖峰和離峰時間的票差比台灣還大，可能會到五、六折左右。所以看電影一般都挑週一到週五上、下午時間或是週六日上午，可以省下一點錢。如果不介意看二、三輪片的話，Dollar Movies 就是最有價值的選擇。看名字就知道，這些電影的票價一律是一美元。當年我和老婆在美國所看的第一部電影，就是在卡城 Dollar Movies 看 Pretty Woman 麻雀變鳳凰。

　　當然如果有機會看大學裡的免費試映會更棒！免費試映對電影廠商幫助很大，其實麻雀變鳳凰原先要描述的是個現實的風月女子，所以結局是李察基爾把茱莉亞羅勃茲趕出車子後揚長而去。但試映幾次觀眾的反應都不好，才把結局改得像灰姑娘。而原片中茱莉亞羅勃茲使用毒品的情節也被完全刪除，正因為有試映，片商才能修改這些情節，使它成為賣座電影。

　　想知道學校電影試映的相關訊息，就多注意學校校內報紙和網站，並多和同學打聽看看。去試映不但可以看免費電影，還有機會看到別人看不到的情節與結尾，有機會一定要去。

Part II

Unit 30　購物樂趣多

1 主題對話

Judy is going to the local mall to buy cosmetic products. She is trying to ask Michael to go with her.

Judy 準備要去百貨購物中心去買化妝品，她要 Michael 跟她一起去。

Michael	I am done with my homework. I have some free time now.	作業做完了，我現在有時間。
Judy	Good, I'd like to go to the Galleria Mall to buy some cosmetics. Would you like to go with me?	好，我想去 Galleria（拱廊）購物中心買化妝品，想一起去嗎？
Michael	I want to know what you are going to buy first.	我想先知道你要買什麼東西。
Judy	I need to buy some **foundation** cream and moisturizers, and to see if there is a good deal for concealer.	我要買粉底霜和護膚保濕用品，並看看有沒有在促銷的遮瑕膏。
Michael	Is that all? Are you sure you are not going to buy more?	就這些？你確定不會多買？
Judy	You know me. If I spot a good deal, I'll buy it. In a way, I am saving money. Also, Clinique has a special offer with any purchase over $30.	你知道的，如果我有看到划算的價格我就會買，某種程度上，我可是在省錢耶！還有倩碧只要買 $30 以上，就會送禮品。
Michael	Really? OK, I'll go with you.	真的？那我跟你去。

Chapter 6

In the Clinique counter（在倩碧專櫃）

| Sales Clerk | Welcome to Clinique. What do you need today? | 歡迎光臨倩碧需要什麼？ |

| Judy | I am interested in foundation cream and moisturizers. | 我想看看粉底霜和保濕護膚品。 |

| Sales Clerk | We have some really good products for you. If you have dry skins, you should try this BB cream, specially designed for dry skins. Combined with our new "Dramatically Different Moisturizing Lotion", your precious skin will be moisturized and protected all day. | 我們有些很棒的產品適合你。如果你是乾性皮膚，你可以試試這瓶 BB 霜，特別適合乾性皮膚。再加上我們最新的「三步驟還原潤膚乳」，就可以全天候保濕，並保護你的寶貴肌膚。 |

| Judy | I used the BB cream before, and it's great. I'll also buy the moisturizer too. How much is it? | 我以前用過 BB 霜，很棒。我也要買潤膚乳液，總共多少？ |

| Sales Clerk | The total is $62.90 plus tax, and you get this free pack of gift with your purchase today. How would you like to pay for it? | 總共是 62.90 加稅，還有這個免費的禮物組給你，要怎麼付帳？ |

| Judy | I'll pay by credit card. | 用信用卡。 |

| Sales Clerk | Here is the receipt, the bag with all the products, and the gift pack. Please come again. | 收據在這裡還有這個袋子裡面有你買的產品和禮物，下次再來。 |

Part II

② 心情小語

♥ Consumer spending is the back bone of US economy. Naturally, all kinds of sales, discounts are offered to **spur** consumer spending. The most important shopping season is of course the Christmas shopping season. It starts from Black Friday which is the Friday after Thanksgiving. The name Black Friday may sound strange to you, but it was originally used to describe the heavy and disruptive pedestrian and vehicle traffic occurred on the day after Thanksgiving by Philadelphia police and bus drivers. Some other people believe it is the beginning of the period when retailers would no longer have losses (the red) and instead take in the year's profits (the black). Thus, it is called Black Friday.

> 消費者支出是美國經濟的主幹，所有的拍賣、折扣都是用來刺激消費。而最重要的購物季節就是聖誕購物季。購物季由黑色星期五開始，也就是感恩節後的第一個星期五。這個黑色星期五的名稱或許聽起來有點怪，這個詞起源於費城的警察和公車司機用來描述感恩節後民眾外出購物所造成的交通堵塞情形。有些人則認為，從這天開始，零售商不再會有虧損（紅色），而是開始賺錢（黑色），所以稱為黑色星期五。

♥ Almost all the department stores, warehouse clubs, discount stores and specialty stores would have some kind of sales to **lure** customers in. The Black Friday and the last Saturday before Christmas are two of the busiest shopping days in US. You can really get some good deals during the shopping season. Also, you don't want to miss the after Christmas sales from which you can get the best deal of the year. The best example would be the cheap **ornaments** for Christmas trees.

幾乎所有的百貨商店、大型會員式量販店、平價商店和專門店，都會以各種折扣來吸引消費者。黑色星期五和聖誕節前的最後一個禮拜六，是美國最忙碌的兩個購物日。在這個購物季節裡，你可以得到較好的折扣。另外你可千萬不要錯失聖誕節後的大拍賣，你可以找到一年內最好的折扣，最好的例了就是便宜到離譜的聖誕樹裝飾品。

❤ For those who are interested in cosmetics, I would recommend checking Ads from Clinique, Estee Lauder, Lancôme and Christian Dior regularly because those four brands have special offers from time to time. You can get free gift packs with purchase over a fixed amount of money, sometimes as low as $25 or $30. The gifts could be lipsticks, cream, lotion, **fragrance** and other kinds of cosmetics. Sometimes the prices on the free gifts are more than 25 or 30 dollars, especially if you compare the price in Taiwan. Thus, those free gifts are the best presents for you to bring back to Taiwan for friends and relatives.

對化妝品有興趣的人，我會建議經常看看倩碧、雅詩蘭黛、蘭蔻和迪奧的廣告，因為這四個廠牌時常會有特殊優惠，例如是在購買價值滿 $25 或 $30 的商品後，例如，就會送你一個禮物包，裡面可能有口紅、乳液、化妝水、香水或是其他化妝品。這些東西的價錢有時會比你付的 $25 或 $30 還要高，尤其是和台灣的價格相比。所以這些免費贈品，就是你帶回台灣送給親友最棒的禮物。

❤ Besides the great deals on cosmetics, there is one other thing worth your attention. That's the coupons on your local Sunday newspaper. Sunday newspapers is much more expensive than the weekday ones, but with the inserted coupon, you are going to get more than what you paid for. You can get coupons for cleaning products, food, medication, and other categories. Some grocery stores may even double or triple the coupons. It is a great way to save your hard-earned money.

> 除了化妝品的特殊優惠以外，還有一件事值得你注意，就是週日報紙裡的折價券。週日的報紙通常比平日的貴，但是裡面的折價券會讓你值回票價。你可以拿到清潔用品、食物、藥物和其他各種類的折價券，有些雜貨超市，甚至會給兩倍或是三倍的折價券優惠。這是個很棒的機會，可以省下你辛苦賺來的錢。

3 單字與例句

fragrance *n.* 香水、芬芳、香氣

The fragrance coming from lavender is rather lovely.
這薰衣草的香味很迷人。

spur *v.* 鞭策、鼓勵 *n.* 馬刺

The threat of losing its only professional sports team spurred the city council to approve the building of the stadium.
可能會失去唯一的職業球隊，正是市政府核可建造體育場，所需要的刺激。

lure *v.* 誘惑、吸引

An attractive window display can help to lure customers into the store.
一個引人的櫥窗展示可以用來吸引顧客上門。

ornament *n.* 裝飾品

I got punished after smashing my mom's favorite hair ornament by accident.
在不小心毀損了我媽最喜歡的髮飾之後，我被懲罰了。

Chapter 6

知識備忘錄

　　美國是個消費的國家，基本上美國人不儲蓄，幾乎都是賺多少花多少，而整個美國經濟，就是消費的經濟。所以消費者平均花多少錢購物，就成了美國最重要的經濟指標。當然消費者信心更是最重要的因素。只要消費者有信心，自然敢花錢買東西，如果消費者認為前景不看好，就不敢花錢。這也是為什麼美國新聞經常報導消費者信心指數。

　　因為市場大又重視消費，美國商店為了爭取顧客，多數商店都有買後一定期限內（多數是一兩周）的「no question asked refund」，也就是無論任何問題都無條件退貨。我們曾經買過一個打折的吸塵器，一禮拜後覺得聲音太大不喜歡，就退了，也沒有買其他的吸塵器，完全沒問題的拿到退款。一開始我岳母根本不信，哪有這麼好的事？一直到跟著我們拿到退款後，才問說這家公司怎麼不會倒？

　　其實不只是退貨，美國的購物比價退款，也比台灣來的更好、更大方。許多商店在賣出東西一兩周後，若你發現同一商店對同樣商品有折扣時，就可以比價退款。還有些商店，只要你能拿出別家商店同一時間價格較為便宜的廣告，就可以憑廣告退差價的服務。對於精打細算的台灣人來說，當然要注意這家店，以及對手商店的廣告了。這真的是看廣告還可以省錢。

　　最後我想跟大家說一聲，美國的退貨、退差價真的很棒！但是請不要濫用，畢竟賠錢的生意沒人做，更重要的是，不要破壞了我們的名聲。

Part II

Unit 31 如何辦理醫療保險

1 主題對話

Michael is talking to Janet, who is an ISS clerk, about insurance for international students.

Michael 和國際學生中心的職員 Janet 談到了外國學生的保險。

Janet	Welcome to ISS. What can I do for you?	歡迎來 ISS，有什麼可以幫忙的嗎？
Michael	I'd like to know more about the international student insurance plan.	我想知道一些關於國際學生保險的事宜。
Janet	Sure, what questions do you have?	你的問題是？
Michael	What kind of coverage do I have in this plan?	在這計畫下我有什麼樣的保障？
Janet	If you go to the Student Health Center, 100% of the cost is covered. If you receive treatment from a Network provider, 80% of the cost will be **reimbursed**. If you are treated by an out-of-Network provider, the coverage is only 60%.	如果你到學校的學生健康中心，一切費用都免費。如果是醫療網內的服務，能報銷 80% 的費用。如果是醫療網外服務，則只補償 60%。
Michael	What do you mean by Network providers and out-of-Network ones?	你所謂的醫療網內和醫療網外的意思是？

Janet	Here is a brochure which contains all the doctors and hospitals that are in our Network. Those who are not listed in the brochure are considered as out-of-Network providers. You can also go to the university insurance web site to check the list.	這裡有本小冊子，裡面包含所有醫療網內的醫院和醫生，沒被列在裡面的就是網外。你也可以到學校的健保網站去查相關的名單。
Michael	Any other things that I need to take note of?	有什麼其他我需要注意的事嗎？
Janet	The **deductible** is 300 dollars for each plan year.	每個保險年度的自付額是美金 300 元。
Michael	What do you mean by deductible?	自付額的意思是？
Janet	It is the amount you have to pay first before any insurance benefit kicks in. The maximum deductible you pay for one plan year is $300. If you go to a Network doctor and get a bill of $500, you need to pay the first $300 and the insurance would pay 80% of the rest of 200. If you have any other bill after that in the same plan year, you don't have to pay the deductible again. All you need to pay is 20% of the total amount. You can refer to the brochure for more detail information.	自付額就是在保險公司補償醫療費用前，你所要付出的金額。每個保險年度所要付出的自付額是 300 元，如果你到醫療網內的醫生看病，收到 500 元的帳單，你要先付 300 元，然後保險公司會補給你剩下 200 元中的 80%。如在同一年度又收到其他醫療帳單，就不需要付自付額，只要付帳單金額的 20%。你可以參考冊子裡的訊息。
Michael	Thanks, I'll check it thoroughly.	謝謝，我會仔細看看。
Janet	Let me know if you have any questions.	如果還有問題再問我吧！

Part II

② 心情小語

♥ As most of you probably know, Taiwan's National Health Insurance is the best insurance plan in the world, especially from patients' point of view. You would be shocked to hear the **premium** you need to pay in US and what kind of coverage you get with that **colossal** amount of premium.

> 相信多數人應該已經知道，台灣的全民健保可是全世界最好的保險，尤其從患者的觀點來看。當你得知在美國你所需要付出的保費，以及在那鉅額保費下所包含的範圍時，你可是會大吃一驚！

♥ One thing is certain. If there is a student health center in your university, go there first whenever a doctor's visit is needed. You will be paying a lot less money with or without insurance.

> 有件事是確定的，如果學校有個學生健康中心，需要看醫生時就去那裏，不管有沒有保險，費用都會低很多。

♥ There are certain things you need to know when we talk about insurance. The first is the premium, which is the amount of money you need to pay to get you registered into the insurance plan. You need to pay at least a few hundred dollars of premium in order to be enrolled in any kind of insurance plan for six months. Then, there is the deductible, which is the amount of money you need to pay for the medical bill before the insurance company shell out their cash. That is usually another couple hundred dollars for any plan year. If you think that is too much, the solution is to pay more for the premium.

> 在講到保險時，有些事一定要知道。首先是保費，也就是為了加入保險你所需要付出的金額，要加入任何一種保險，半年內最少也要付幾百美元，然後還有自付額，也就是在保險公司付出任何費用之前，你需要付出的金額。通常每年也要幾百美元，如果你認為自付額太高，多付一點保費就可以了。

❤ If you think that is the total amount of money you need to pay, I have a surprise for you. There is more. The co-payment, or co-pay, is the amount of money you need to pay every time you visit a doctor. Also, there is co-pay for pharmacy bills. The co-pays are usually fifteen to forty dollars, which means you need to pay at least thirty dollars every time you visit a doctor and get the meditation you need. The worst part is that the co-pay generally doesn't count as part of deductible. Deductible and co-pay are separate **obligations**.

> 如果你以為這就是你要付的錢，我還有個驚奇給你，其實還有所謂的掛號費，也就是每次看醫生你所需要負擔的金額。同時拿藥也有掛號費，金額通常在 15 到 40 塊之間。也就是說，每次看醫生、拿藥，你至少要付 30 塊美金。更慘的是，掛號費並不算在自付額裡面！掛號費和自付額，是兩個不同的義務。

❤ Are you confused? Look at the following example. If you had a $400 yearly deductible, a $15 co-pay and an 80% coverage, for a $300 doctor's visit, you would pay the $300 bill, which includes your $15 co-pay and $285 of your $400 deductible. At a **subsequent** $300 visit you would pay another $15 co-pay and the remaining $115 of your deductible, while your insurance would pay 80% of the remaining $170. You are also responsible for the remaining 20%. If there is another $300 visit in the same year, you only need to pay the $15 co-pay and 20% of the remaining bill. Now you know how great our National Health Insurance is.

Part II

搞糊塗了嗎？看看以下這個例子。如果你每年的自付額是 400 美元，15 元的掛號費，還有 80% 的保障。若看醫生花費 300 元，你要先付 15 元的掛號費，剩下的 285 算在自付額裡面。下次若又花了 300 美元，你還是要付 15 元掛號費，然後再付剩下的 115 元的自付額，接下來的 170 元中，保險公司會付 80%，而你要付 20%。如果同一年度你又花了 300 元看醫生，那你只需要付 15 元掛號費，以及剩下的 285 元中的 20%，現在你了解我們的全民健保有多棒了吧！

3 單字與例句

reimburse   *v.* 償還、歸還

Please keep all the receipts so company can reimburse you for your expenses.
請確定收好所有的發票，好讓公司可以歸還你的費用。

deductible   *adj.* 可減免的

The cost is deductible as business expense.
這項費用可以視為業務支出來抵稅。

premium   *n.* 獎金、高價、保險費

Most customers would be willing to pay a premium for organic vegetables.
多數顧客願意付高價買有機蔬菜。

colossal   *adj.* 巨大的、龐大的

They built a colossal statue of the country's founder.
他們建造了一個創建這個國家者的巨大雕像。

Chapter 7

obligation　*n.* 義務、責任

He failed to fulfill his obligation as an employee, and thus got fired.
他無法盡到一個員工的義務，也因此被解雇了。

subsequent　*adj.* 後來的、隨後的

These phenomena will be discussed in more details in subsequent chapters.
這些現象會在隨後的章節裡，有更詳盡的說明。

知識備忘錄

　　關於美國醫療費用的新聞，大家應該多多少少都聽過。既然醫療費用高，可以想見是，保險一定也會水漲船高。心情小語所揭示的數字，就是現在一般保險的情況，而類似這樣的保險，保費大概一年一千美金左右。可以確定的是，美國保險不是用來保小病痛用的。只要研究一下就會發現，一般小病痛無論保險與否，所付出的費用相差無幾，唯一的差別是保費！這些保費，其實是用來以防萬一，在你出意外時使用的。

　　目前許多美國大學都會強制要求外國學生一定要保險，有些直接在你註冊時，就把保費加到你的學雜費裡，不保也不行！如果你的學校規定如此，就乖乖的繳費吧！如果你的學校並不強制你保險，我勸你還是保一下吧，畢竟出門在外，沒人能保證天災人禍不會發生。如果幾年後你發覺，一直以來都只有些小病痛，幾千元甚至上萬元的保費都白繳了，你該覺得很慶幸，因為這證明你平平安安的，完全沒有嚴重的健康問題。如果人生中有什麼事不希望有賺到的感覺，就是保險！相信我，沒人希望自己出個意外，把保費給賺回來！最後就是，你該慶幸自己生在台灣，還有不要濫用這麼好的全民健保，不要想去賺回全民健保保費的錢！

Part II

 看牙醫

1 主題對話

Michael is talking about dental cleaning with a dental hygienist.
Michael 和一位牙醫助理談到了洗牙。

Denise	Welcome to Aspen Dental. What can I do for you?	歡迎到亞斯班牙醫,有麼可以幫忙的嗎?
Michael	I'd like to know more about dental cleaning.	我想知道關於洗牙的訊息。
Denise	Sure, did your have dental cleaning before? If yes, when was the last time you had your teeth cleaned?	好的,你曾經洗過牙嗎?如果有,是多久以前?
Michael	I haven't had my teeth cleaned in more than five years.	我已經有超過五年沒洗牙了。
Denise	In that case, I would recommend you to do a dental cleaning now.	這樣的話,我會建議你立刻洗牙。
Michael	What would happen if I don't?	如果不洗的話呢?
Denise	Without any dental cleaning in more than five years, you would already have **tartar**, or dental **plaque**, built up in your teeth. It is likely that you are having **periodontal** diseases. You might lose some of your teeth if it is not properly treated.	超過五年沒洗牙,你的牙齒應該已經有牙結石或是牙菌斑,而且很有可能已患牙周病。如果不治療的話可能會失去幾顆牙。

Chapter 7

Michael	I brush my teeth three times daily. Isn't that enough?	我每天刷牙三次，難道還不夠嗎？
Denise	No matter how thorough your brushing is, there would be still tartar on your teeth. Besides, there may already be some cavities, and it's better to have them treated before it is too late.	不管你刷得多完全，你的牙齒還是會有牙結石，而且可能有蛀牙；在狀況變糟之前治療會比較好。
Michael	I don't think I have any cavity. I would have toothaches already, if I have one.	我覺得我應該沒有蛀牙，如果有的話早就痛了。
Denise	Having toothaches usually means it is already too late. You want to treat it early. It is always better to treat it before symptom occurs. Getting dental treatment when your tooth is aching will not be a pleasant experience.	你需要早點治療，等到牙痛就已經太遲了，在症狀發生前就應該先治療。邊牙痛邊接受治療並不會是個令人感到愉快的經驗。
Michael	I'd like to have my teeth cleaned after talking to you. Can i make an appointment now?	和你聊過後，我想先洗牙了。可以預約嗎？
Denise	Let me check. How about next Monday at 10 AM? Since you have not had one in five years, I would recommend an X-ray check for your tccth thoroughly.	讓我看看，下禮拜一早上十點如何？既然已經五年了，我會建議用X光仔細檢查你的牙齒。
Michael	Sure, see you then.	沒問題，到時候見。

Part II

2 心情小語

💜 If you think health insurance in US is expensive, wait until you hear the dental insurance. The dental insurance is so expensive that some smaller companies won't even provide it to their employees. During my 15 years in US, we only have dental insurance when my company is providing it. To be honest, I would not recommend dental insurance to most of the foreign students, because again, it is expensive, and in most cases dental problems are not lethal.

> 　如果你認為美國健保很貴，等你聽到牙醫保險再說。牙醫保險貴到有些小公司根本不提供。在我美國十五年的生涯裡，只有公司有提供時，才有牙齒保險。老實說對外國學生我不會建議牙齒保險，因為很貴，而且多數情形下，牙齒問題不至於致命。

💜 However, having your teeth regularly cleaned and checked when you are in US is a must for all of you. First, you want to make sure that your teeth are professionally cleaned, and any minor cavity would be found early. Knowing that you have a minor cavity, you would have more time to decide whether if you want it treated during your next trip back to Taiwan. Besides, treating a minor cavity would be easier, as it costs less time and money. Forced to take an expensive dental visit because of toothache does not worth it. Spending a small amount of money to have a dental cleaning and have your teeth checked is the best way to find out problems early. Don't forget that periodontal disease is more pervasive in Taiwan.

Chapter 7

Part II

> 然而在美國時定時的洗牙和檢查牙齒，卻是必要的。首先你可以確認你的牙齒被專業的清洗過，而且任何的蛀牙都可以早期發現。知道你有個輕微的蛀牙，讓你有更多的時間去決定，是否要趁下次回台灣時治療？而且治療輕微的蛀牙比較簡單，時間也短，錢花得更少。因為牙痛而被迫看昂貴的牙醫真的不值那個錢，那個時間，更不用説那份痛！花點小錢來洗牙，檢查牙齒是最好的方式，早期發現問題，有更多的時間來找最好的解決方案。不要忘了，牙周病在台灣可是更普遍！

❤ From my experience, all the dental cleaning in US is performed by a dental hygienist, not the dentist. The dental hygienist would take X-ray of you teeth and clean them. Then the dentist would come in and check the X-ray and talk to you about the condition of your teeth, and any possible problems or treatments.

> 從我的經驗來看，美國洗牙一律是由牙醫助理，而不是牙醫來執行。首先會由助手來照 X 光、洗牙，然後才由牙醫來看片了，檢查牙齒，並告訴你情況，以及可能的問題或治療方式。

❤ I did not have my teeth cleaned before going to US, and I didn't realize I had a serious periodontal disease until I had my teeth cleaned in College Station. The cost was humongous, and I did not have any dental insurance. I waited until after graduation, and got a dental insurance from my company. In the meantime, all I can do is regularly have my teeth cleaned. It was still too late, and I lost two teeth because of it.

> 在去美國前我並沒有先洗牙，一直到我在卡城洗牙後，才發現我有嚴重的牙周病！由於沒有牙醫，保險價格又貴，只好等到畢業後，靠工作提供的保險，才接受治療。在這段時間，我只能定期洗牙，等接受治療時已經太遲，我也因此失去了兩顆牙齒。

❤ Take my advice, have your teeth cleaned and checked before going to US. Regularly have dental cleaning while you are in US, before any problem **arise**.

> 聽我的忠告，去美國前先洗牙，並檢查牙齒。抵達美國後定期洗牙以避免出問題。

3 單字與例句

hygienist *n.* 衛生學者、保健專家

General dental cleaning in US would be done by a hygienist.
在美國，洗牙一般由牙醫助理執行。

tartar *n.* 牙結石

You need a deep cleaning to have the tartar completely removed.
深層洗牙才能完全清除你的牙結石。

plaque *n.* 匾額、牙菌斑

The company gives him a plaque in honor of his contribution.
公司送給他一個匾額以獎勵他的貢獻。

Chapter 7

periodontal　*adj.* 牙周的

Regularly having your teeth cleaned is the most effective way of preventing periodontal disease.

定期洗牙是最有效避免牙周病的方法。

arise　*v.* 上升、升起

The problem arises because people try to avoid their responsibility.

因為眾人試著要規避責任，問題自然就產生了。

知識備忘錄

　　在美國有次陪著老婆看牙醫時，隨手翻著牙醫小冊子，才發覺洗牙的重要性！結果當天我立即預約洗牙。我還記得洗一次牙 37 美元，而且因為太久沒洗，還花了兩次療程才洗乾淨，並發現我有嚴重的牙周病！

　　以洗牙或看牙醫而言，現在只會更貴。不過這個錢我還是建議要花，畢竟美國的牙醫更貴，保險更不用說了，只有大公司才會有，一些小公司根本不提供。定期洗牙兼檢查牙齒，才能提早發現問題，讓你有更多時間來決定是否返回台灣看牙齒。不然等到牙痛痛到受不了時才去看醫生，到時候被迫要花昂貴的醫藥費，絕對划不來！牙齒不痛也不代表沒問題，像是我的牙周病就從來沒痛過。越早發現問題越好，最好能在出國前請牙醫把你所有的牙齒仔細的看過，該清的清、該洗的洗、該拔的拔，有任何問題就在台灣解決。

　　牙痛不是病，痛起來要人命，等你痛到受不了去看美國牙醫時，荷包更痛、心更痛，所以切記在出國前一定要看牙醫！

Unit 33 視力檢查配眼鏡

1 主題對話

Michael is talking to Gloria, an **optometrist**, about an eyeglasses prescription checking result.
Michael 和 Gloria 談到了眼鏡檢查結果。

Gloria	Here is the result. Please take a look.	這是檢驗結果,請看看。
Michael	I have no idea about all those medical terms. Could you explain the result?	裡面的術語我都看不懂,能不能解釋一下檢驗結果?
Gloria	Sure, in the first column, the D.V. and N.V. are the abbreviations for distance vision and near vision, respectively. The O.D. and O.S. next to them are the Latin terms for right eye and left eye, respectively, from the patient's point of view.	沒問題,在第一欄裡的 D.V. 和 N.V. 是遠距離視力和近距離視力,而旁邊的 O.D. 和 O.S. 則是拉丁文的右眼和左眼,從你的方向所看來的左和右。
Michael	This is really confusing. Why not use right eye and left eye instead of O.D. and O.S.?	這真的讓人很疑惑,為什麼不直接用右眼和左眼而是 O.D. 和 O.S. ?
Gloria	I know, and there are more and more optometrists and ophthalmologists using RE and LE instead. BE is used sometimes for both eyes.	我知道。現在有越來越多的驗光師和眼科醫師,開始用右眼和左眼,有時候會以 BE 來表示兩個眼睛。
Michael	What does **spherical** mean, and what are those corresponding numbers?	那 spherical(球面的)意思又是?相關的數字的意義呢?

Gloria	Correcting for nearsightedness or farsightedness is called a spherical correction, because it is correcting in all the directions equally. As for the numbers, let's start with the most simple and basic one for D.V., the number -1.0 means the person can see objects at one meter clearly, but anything farther is blurred. The number -2.0 means the person can see objects up to a 1/2 meter away clearly, and the number -5.0 corresponds to the person can see objects only up to 1/5 meter away. Similarly the number +1.00 for N.V. indicates the person can see objects at one meter clearly, but anything closer than that is blurred. The number +2.00 implies someone can see things at 1/2 meter and beyond clearly, but nothing closer.	近視和遠視的矯正被稱為球面矯正，因為它所調整的視力是全方面，不分角度。至於數字，我先給個最簡單最基本的數字也就是 -1.0，它的意思是患者可以看清楚一公尺距離的物品，但是再遠就看不清了。而 -2.0 則代表患者可以看清楚距離 1/2 公尺的物品，而 -5.0 則意味著只能看清楚距離 1/5 公尺的物品。同樣的 +1.0 表示可以看清處一公尺遠再近就模糊了， +2.0 則是看清楚 1/2 公尺，但是再近就不行了。
Michael	How about **cylindrical**?	那圓筒形的呢？
Gloria	Simply speaking, when a cylindrical lens acts as a magnifier, it magnifies only in one direction. The cylindrical correction is used for **astigmatism**.	簡單說以圓筒形鏡片作為放大鏡時，它只會放大一個方向。圓筒形矯正，是用來調整散光的。
Michael	Thanks for your explanation. I understand more about those terms.	謝謝你的解釋，我對這些術語了解比較多了。
Gloria	Let me know if you have other questions.	如果還有問題再問我吧！

Part II

❷ 心情小語

❤ Similar to dental insurance, vision insurance isn't as common as the regular health insurance. However, this is not because of the cost, but rather, in my opinion, because many American simply don't need vision insurance. For the company that covers dental, it would usually include vision.

> 跟牙齒保險類似,視力保險不如健康保險般的普遍,但原因不是因為費用,在我看來,是因為多數美國人用不到。有提供牙齒保險的公司,通常也會附加視力保險。

❤ In US, a vision check is considered as a form of medical practices, so an optometrist or ophthalmologist is required to perform the task. This is way different from what we have in Taiwan, where a trained technician can carry out the job. Generally, vision centers inside the US supermarket chains, like Costco or Wal-Mart, would have on-site optometrists to check your vision.

> 在美國視力檢查被視為一種醫療行為,所以一定要是驗光師或眼科醫師才可以進行,這和一般技術人員就可以驗光的台灣,有很大的不同。一般而言,美國連鎖超市,例如好事多或是沃爾瑪,都會有視力中心和駐點的驗光師,為你檢查視力。

❤ We had our eyes examined in US for a couple of times. To be honest with you, I don't see any difference in vision checkups done by an optometrist or a technician. Maybe I am too naïve or too **ignorant** to figure out the distinction, but then again, any vision center would have a licensed optometrists for sure. Also, the checking result is only valid for only one or two years. Maybe that is one of the reasons prescription glasses and contact lens are more expensive in US.

> 我們曾在美國由驗光師做過幾次視力檢查，老實説我不覺得驗光師和技術人員的檢查有什麼不同。或許是我天真或沒什麼見識，實在看不出有什麼不一樣。不過視力中心都一定會有擁有執照的驗光師。檢驗結果的有效期限只有一兩年，或許這也是眼鏡和隱形眼鏡在美國比較貴的原因之一。

♥ Generally speaking, Americans have much less near sight problem than Chinese, and for the second generation American Chinese, they may have the near sight issue, but it is not as server as the Taiwan counterparts.

> 一般而言，美國人近視的比率比華人低多了，而且第二代華裔美國人或許有近視，但是不像相對的台灣人般的那麼嚴重。

♥ Prescription eyeglasses or contact lens are big businesses in Taiwan simply because there are so many students needing it. However, it is not the case in US. Even for those Americans who need prescription eyeglasses, from what I know, the problem is a lot milder, with the numbers usually less than -5.0, which corresponds to 500-degree in Taiwan. For those who need a pair of glasses or contact lens for more than 500-degree, I would suggest getting an extra pair of glasses or bringing more than enough contacts before going to US. It would not be as convenient to get them in US, simply because of the fact that general US vision centers would not have those kinds of lenses on-site. It would take at least a couple of days to get the suitable one for you.

一般眼鏡和隱形眼鏡在台灣可是大生意，因為多數台灣學生都有近視。在美國就不是如此了，就算美國人有近視，問題也不大，一般都在 -5.0 以下，也就是台灣所謂的五百度以下。對於那些度數超過五百度的人，在來美國前，我會建議多買一副眼鏡或多準備一些隱形眼鏡，因為在美國不是那麼方便，一般的視力中心，很少有超過五百度的鏡片存貨，通常要等個幾天才能拿到適合你的鏡片。

❤ Similar to the advice I gave in the dental section, have your vision checked in Taiwan, and prepare an extra pair of glasses and/or more than enough contact lenses before you board the plane to US.

跟牙醫部分我所提供的忠告一樣，去搭飛機美國以前，在台灣先做視力檢查，然後多準備一副眼鏡，以及足夠的隱形眼鏡。

3 單字與例句

optometrist *n.* 驗光師

ophthalmologist *n.* 眼科醫師

An optometrist or ophthalmologist is needed to carry out vision checks.
需要一位驗光師或眼科醫師來檢查視力。

associated *adj.* 組合的、相關的

I would no longer want to be associated with him
我再也不想跟他有任何關聯。

spherical *adj.* 球的、球面的

The planet Earth is, in fact, not perfectly spherical.
地球事實上並不是完美的球形。

astigmatism　*n.* 散光

Astigmatism would get you blurry vision.
散光會導致視線模糊。

ignorant　*adj.* 無知的、沒受教育的

They may be ignorant, but not stupid.　They would learn quickly.
他們或許無知，但並不笨。他們會進步得很快。

知識備忘錄

　　台灣人戴眼鏡的比率真的比美國高多了，我覺得這跟環境有關，台灣到處是高樓大廈，而美國四處都是平地和公園，近視的機會就小多了。

　　美國的眼鏡市場比起台灣要小多了！而且因為度數都不高，通常超市附設的眼鏡行裡，也沒有高度數鏡片的存貨。像我將近八百的近視度數，每次都要請眼鏡行特別訂貨，總要等個幾天，而且一般沒有台灣所謂的超薄鏡片，價格也非常貴，因為都是客製品。

　　隱形眼鏡也是類似的情況，但跟普通眼鏡有一點不同的是，隱形眼鏡的附屬配備比較多；也因為市場小，所以這些配備也都比台灣貴。不管是 contact lotion（隱形眼鏡保養液）、saline water/solution（生理食鹽水）還是隱形眼鏡本身都比較貴。

　　跟牙齒一樣，我會建議先在台灣把視力檢查過後，買下兩副眼鏡；如果戴隱形眼鏡的話，更要把相關的保養配備買齊，會讓你省下不少錢。我小孩每次回台灣一定買相關的視力用品，就是這個原因。

Unit 34　過敏和花粉熱

1　主題對話

Michael is talking to Daniel about the cold symptoms that he is having.

Michael 和 Daniel 談到他目前的感冒症狀。

Daniel	Spring is coming, flowers are **blooming**, and weather is getting warmer. Things couldn't be better.	春天來了，花朵盛開，天氣也漸漸溫暖起來，真是太棒了。
Michael	I love spring too, but I got this terrible cold for more than a week.	我也喜歡春天，不過最近一個禮拜我感冒的很厲害。
Daniel	What happened?	怎麼了？
Michael	I've been having all kinds of cold symptoms, running nose, stuffy nose. Also, my eyes are itchy.	各種的感冒症狀我都有，流鼻涕、鼻塞，還有眼睛癢。
Daniel	Are you sure you are having a cold?	你確定是感冒嗎？
Michael	With all those symptoms, what else can it be?	有這些症狀，還會是什麼？
Daniel	You are probably not getting a cold. It could be a hay fever.	可能不是感冒，是花粉熱。
Michael	What is that? I've never heard of it.	那是什麼？從沒聽說過。

Chapter 7

| Daniel | Simply speaking, it's an allergic reaction triggered by pollen or dust. Common symptoms include sneezing, watery and itchy eyes, **nasal congestion**, running nose, and itchy throat. The funny thing is that fever isn't one of them even though it is named hay fever. | 簡單的説，就是對花粉或粉塵敏感的反應，一般症狀是打噴嚏、眼睛癢、流淚、鼻塞、流鼻水、喉嚨癢。好笑的是不會發燒，卻被稱為花粉熱。 |

| Michael | Is there any treatment? How do I deal with it? | 有方法治療嗎？我又該怎麼處埋？ |

| Daniel | The best solution would be avoiding any contact with the **allergen**, and in your case, probably some kind of **pollen**. Close your doors and windows, roll up your car windows while driving, put your washed clothes into the dryer instead of hanging them outside, and wear sunglasses to prevent pollen from your eyes.Also, check pollen counts before joining any outdoor activities. | 最好的方法就是避免跟過敏原接觸，以你而言可能就是花粉。關閉門窗，開車時關起窗戶，用乾衣機烘乾衣物，不要掛在外面曬，戴眼鏡以避免眼睛接觸到花粉，還有在做任何戶外活動時，先查看一下花粉數量。 |

| Michael | Pollen counts? How and where do I get the information? | 花粉數量？我要怎麼查？又該哪裡查？ |

| Daniel | Actually the numbers are reported as part of the weather forecast. You can also access the National Allergy Bureau's pollen count information at their web site (http://www.aaaai.org/nab/index.cfm). | 氣象預報時都會報導，你也可以到國家過敏局的網站 http://www.aaaai.org/nab/index.cfm 去看花粉數量。 |

| Michael | Thanks for the information. | 謝謝你的資訊。 |

Part II

2 心情小語

♥ Because of the **perennial** wet condition in Taiwan, people seldom suffer from hay fever or pollen allergy. They are **prevalent** in US as the weather is dryer. How to avoid hay fever or pollen allergy has become a big issue there.

> 因為台灣空氣潮濕，台灣人很少得到花粉熱。而美國則因為天氣普遍乾燥，花粉熱就多了！如何避免和治療花粉熱在美國是個大問題。

♥ I still remember what happened on that horrible day. One day when I was studying my graduate course materials, suddenly, I felt some kind of warm fluid running down from my nose. My nose was bleeding. Before that day, I had been having all kinds of cold symptoms. Thinking it should be a simple cold, I did not pay much attention to it. However, the bleeding nose really scared me. I was surprised when later on I was told I got hay fever, and nose bleeding is one of the more severe symptoms.

> 我還記得那可怕的一天發生的事，我在唸書的時候，突然覺得鼻子有些溫暖的液體流下來，我在流鼻血！在此之前我一直有些感冒症狀，但自認為是小感冒，也就沒什麼特別注意。但是流鼻血卻嚇到我了，後來被告知是花粉熱，而且流鼻血是較為嚴重的症狀時，還真有點訝異。

♥ Ever since that day, I had been suffering hay fever, or pollen allergy in spring and fall. Yes, you are reading it correctly, both spring and fall seasons. It really bothered me, and the worst thing is there's no absolute cure for it. Medication can only **alleviate** the symptoms, no matter it is over the counter or **prescription**. Also, medication could **induce** some unwanted side effects like **dizziness**, **drowsiness**, **upset stomach**, blurry vision, and a dry mouth/nose and throat. For example, from our experience, Benadryl can make us really sleepy.

> 在此之後只要是春天或秋天，我就會感染花粉熱。你沒看錯，春、秋兩季，真的很難受，最慘的是無論是藥房買的藥或醫生處方，都沒有有效的藥物能治療這個症狀。藥物只能緩解症狀，同時藥物也會產生不必要的副作用，例如：暈眩、嗜睡、胃痛、視力模糊、乾燥的嘴巴、鼻子或喉嚨。例如以我們經驗，Benadryl（減緩花粉熱症狀的藥品）真的會讓人想睡覺。

According to some research publications, many of the allergy suffers are allergic to **ragweed**, and about half of the patients are allergic to grasses. Avoid contacts with allergens is often proposed as one of the effective solutions to combat allergy, but it is easier said than done. Sometimes, you still need to go outside even when the pollen count is high. Over the counter medication is the usual way of me dealing with hay fever. If the symptoms persist, or the condition doesn't improve much aftcrovcr the counter medication, It is probably the time to see a doctor.

> 根據一些出版的研究，許多過敏患者是對豕草過敏，大概有一半是對青草過敏。常被提起來降低過敏的方法是：避免接觸過敏原，但是説的比做的容易！有時候就算花粉數高，你還是得外出。感染花粉熱通常就是買藥房架上的藥品，如果症狀持續，或是吃了藥狀況還是沒改善，可能就需要去看醫生了。

Part II

💗 For more information and treatment regarding hay fever, you can check the following websites, the Allergies Health Center of WebMD at http://www.webmd.com/allergies/default.htm and Hay Fever of MedicineNet.com at http://www.medicinenet.com/hay_fever/article.htm.

> 　　如果想獲知更多的花粉熱的資訊以及它的治療方法，你可以看看以下的網站：WebMD 的 過 敏 健 康 中 心，http://www.webmd.com/allergies/default.htm 以及 MedicineNet.com 的花粉熱專章，http://www.medicinenet.com/hay_fever/article.htm

3 單字與例句

bloom　*v.* 開花、生長茂盛

With all the flowers blooming, spring sure is coming.
百花盛開，春天確實到了。

nasal　*adj.* 鼻子的

We all breathe through the nasal passage.
我們都是透過鼻腔呼吸。

congestion　*n.* 阻塞、塞滿

There is always traffic congestion during rush hour.
上、下班時間交通一定會阻塞。

pollen　*n.* 花粉

The bee collects pollen from a blooming flower.
那蜜蜂從那盛開的花朵收集花粉。

Chapter 7

allergen *n.* 過敏原

You need to wear a pair of glasses to prevent your eyes from contacting the allergen.
你需要戴眼鏡以避免你的眼睛接觸到過敏原。

perennial *adj.* 終年的、常年的

Flooding is a perennial problem for people living by the river.
淹水是住在河邊人們常年的問題。

prevalent *adj.* 普遍的、流行的

Hay fever is prevalent in spring and fall.
花粉熱在春季和秋季很普遍。

prescription *n.* 命令、規定、處方、藥方

A doctor's prescription is needed for this medication.
這藥物需要醫師的處方。

induce *v.* 引誘、導致

The advertisement is meant to induce people to eat more fruit.
這個廣告是用來引導人們多吃水果。

dizziness *n.* 暈眩

After holding my breath for a while, I experience dizziness.
在屏住呼吸一陣子後，我感到暈眩。

drowsiness *n.* 困倦、睡意

Drowsiness hit her during the boring math class.
在無聊的數學課裡，她感受到些睡意。

upset stomach *n.* 腸胃不適、胃痛

Suffering an upset stomach, she was vomiting.
因為胃痛她嘔吐了。

ragweed *n.* 豕草

Ragweed is the most common allergen.
豕草是最普遍的過敏原。

知識備忘錄

　　美國普遍的乾燥氣候，使得花粉熱成為普遍的疾病，在台灣則因為潮濕，尤其常下雨，就較少有花粉熱的患者。我在台灣幾年來從來沒得過什麼花粉熱，但到美國第三年開始，有一天竟然毫無症狀，突然間開始流鼻血！幾天後跟老學生聊天時，才知道這竟然也是花粉熱的症狀之一，從此每年春、秋兩季就是我感染花粉熱的時候了。

　　如同我在保險那一章節裡所言，美國健保保的是大病，對小病其實毫無幫助。很不幸的，花粉熱正是如同這樣的小病。我唯一能做的也就是在症狀較為嚴重時，去買藥房架上不須處方簽的藥物來減緩症狀。多數時間就是忍過去就算了。

　　講到這裡，我也想說說一件搭飛機時遇到的美國人的事。這位小姐正好坐在我旁邊，在漫長的飛航途中就聊了起來。她在台灣已待了一陣子的時間，當我提到台灣的空氣污染時，沒想到她竟立刻反對，並說台灣的空氣比美國好太多了！我當時就愣住了，結果她說她有很嚴重的花粉熱，在美國春、秋兩季幾乎活不下去。這次到台灣一整年，花粉熱不藥而癒，她一輩子從沒呼吸過不會讓她過敏的空氣她甚至說，只要飛機靠近台灣，她立刻可以感覺到台灣的空氣。我還記就當飛機抵達台灣時，她立刻深呼吸一口然後說：What a fresh air. 真是清新的空氣！

Unit 35　銀行開戶與匯款

1　主題對話

Michael is talking to Steve about opening bank accounts.

Michael 和 Steve 談到了銀行開戶。

Michael	Do I really need to open a bank account?	我真的需要到銀行開戶嗎？
Steve	In US, you really need to have banking accounts. It is more convenient.	在美國你真的需要銀行帳戶，這也比較方便。
Michael	What kind of accounts should I have?	我要開哪種帳戶？
Steve	The most popular accounts are checking, saving and CD accounts.	最普遍的是支票、儲蓄和定存帳戶。
Michael	What are these, and what're their purposes?	那是什麼啊？目的又是？
Steve	A checking account allows you to write checks, but in most cases, you don't get any interest payment. You get a small amount of interest with a saving account, but the amount of checks you can write per month is limited.	支票帳戶讓你能開支票，但在多數情況下沒有任何利息。儲蓄帳戶裡會有一點點利息，但是每個月能從儲蓄帳戶裡開出的支票張數並不多。

Chapter8

Steve	CD stands for **Certificate** of **Deposit**, and you get the highest amount of interest in this account, but you cannot **withdraw** any money from the account for certain period of time.	CD 就是台灣所謂的定存，利息最高，但在指定期限內不能提款。
Michael	Why do I need checks? I was doing fine in Taiwan without checks.	為什麼我需要支票？以前在台灣沒支票也沒問題啊！
Steve	In US, people don't usually carry a lot of cash. People use credit cards or checks to pay large amount of money. Checks are safer and more convenient than cash.	在美國，人們不常隨身攜帶大量現金，要買比較貴的物品，不是用信用卡，就是用支票。支票也比現金來得安全、便利。
Michael	Sounds good. I'll probably go to a local bank and open an account.	聽來不錯，我該去附近開個戶。
Steve	If you need help, I can go with you.	如果需要幫忙的話，我可以跟你去。
Michael	That would be great. When do you have time?	那太棒了，你什麼時候有空？
Steve	How about tomorrow at 11?	明天十一點如何？
Michael	Sure, see you then.	沒問題，到時候見。
Steve	Bye.	再見。

Part II

2 心情小語

♥ For foreign students, banking accounts are essential. In US, people don't really carry any large amount of cash. When I was in US, I usually bring as much as 50 dollars with me.

> 對於外國學生而言，銀行帳戶是必須的。美國人通常不會隨身攜帶大量現金，我在美國時，身上頂多帶著五十元左右。

♥ You may wonder how American people buy some of the more expensive **merchandises**. They usually pay by credit cards or checks. Most foreign students can't **legally** work in US, and they usually have no taxable incomes. It would be really hard for these people to apply for credits. A checking account is thus necessary for them. Without an account, you would need to carry a huge amount of cash whenever you need to purchase expensive items, which is inconvenient and dangerous. Checks also provide extra security. In US, checks need to be **endorsed** first before it can be cashed or deposited. The bank can always trace the check to find out who gets the money.

> 你或許在想，那美國人怎麼買一些比較貴的東西呢？通常都是用信用卡或支票。外國學生剛到美國時，因為不能合法工作，也沒有所得收入，所以很難申請信用卡。這時候就需要支票帳戶。如果沒有支票，當要要買昂貴的東西時，就要攜帶大量現金。支票一般來說比較安全，因為在美國，支票要背書後才能兌現或轉存，銀行可以透過支票追蹤每一筆錢。

♥ Also, with a saving account, you get your money deposited in a safe place while earning some interest. If you have a good amount of money that you don't need, you can put it into a CD account for more interests.

> 儲蓄帳戶不但讓你存錢，也可以賺一點利息。如果你有一筆短期內用不到的錢，則可以開個定存帳戶，利息更高。

❤ Checking accounts are sometimes not enough for foreign students. Most retailers or dealers require valid identification cards before accepting checks. The most popular ID card in US is the driver's license, and that is why getting a driver's license means more than being able to drive a car. It also works as an official ID which enables you to write checks.

> 支票帳戶對海外學生而言不一定足夠。多數零售商和業者在收支票錢需要看證件。在美國，最普遍的證件就是駕照，所以拿到駕照不只意味著你可以開車，同時還是個身分證件，讓你可以開支票。

❤ Opening bank accounts sometimes gives you extra benefits. Some banks would offer you a credit card when you open a CD account, or when you deposit certain amount of money. When I was at College Station, a 1000 dollar CD account gave me a credit card with 1000 dollar credit. As I mentioned in previous chapter, getting your first credit card as a student may be hard. Check your local banks to see if they have any similar offers. If you see one, apply for it while it still lasts. Paying with a credit card is the easiest and the most convenient way to purchase stuffs in US.

> 開戶有時還有其他好處，有些銀行在你以一定金額開戶後，就會發給信用卡。當我在卡城時，開一個一千元的定存帳戶，銀行就給我一張一千元額度的信用卡。如同我在先前的章節所提到的，對學生來說，第一張信用卡永遠是最難申請到的。沒事可以多去附近的銀行看看有沒有類似的方案，就可以考慮申請一張信用卡。在美國用信用卡結帳，永遠是最簡單、也最方便的付款方式。

3 單字與例句

certificate　*n.* 執照、證明書

You need to submit your birth certificate and the application form to get a passport.

要拿到護照你需要遞交出生證明和申請表。

deposit　*v.* 放置、存放

Please deposit your baggage in your room and return to the hotel lobby.

請把行李放在房間然後回到旅館大廳。

withdraw　*v.* 拉開、取回、撤銷

She withdrew $600 from the ATM to buy the new computer.

她從提款機裡領了六百塊來買新電腦。

merchandise　*n.* 商品、貨物

The department store sells all kinds of merchandise.

那間百貨公司有賣各式各樣的貨品。

legally　*adv.* 合法地

Without a green card, foreign students cannot legally work in US.

沒有綠卡的外國學生不能在美國合法工作。

endorse　*v.* 背書、保證、認可

You must endorse the check before you deposit it in the bank.

在將支票轉存到銀行前你需要先背書。

Chapter8

知識備忘錄

　　在美國很少有小偷，在我看來，部分原因是因為美國人家中通常沒什麼現金，沒有儲蓄的概念，就算有儲蓄也都把錢存在銀行。而留學生也都是把現金存在銀行。在美國一般不習慣在身上放大把現金，有需要時就是用信用卡或支票付帳。我在美國時一般的帳單，像是水電瓦斯、電話等，也都是用支票付款。

　　在美國一般都至少會開兩種銀行帳號：支票帳戶和儲蓄帳戶。支票帳戶顧名思義就是用來開支票用的，所以沒有利息。而儲蓄帳號一般就是在有需要時，用來把錢轉到支票帳號裡，必要時還是可以儲蓄帳號來開支票。不過美國銀行通常都會限制每個月能從儲蓄帳戶裡開出的支票總數，還有它們也會限制每個月內，能從儲蓄帳號轉錢到支票帳號的次數，這兩點都要注意，以免被扣手續費。

　　如果你較常以支票方式付款，你還得時時注意帳號裡的現金數量，還有你所開出的支票與款項，避免有跳票的情況。當然有些銀行在支票帳戶餘額不足的時候，也提供由儲蓄帳戶自動轉帳的服務，不過這還是會有其他的限制。如果你注意一下，就會發現每張支票都有號碼，而且每本支票簿都有用來記帳的欄位。每開出一張支票，就要立刻把支票號碼、付款對象、票面金額記在支票簿裡，隔個幾天就細算一下，就不會出錯了。

　　現在網路風行，所有的美國銀行都會提供網路銀行的服務。你可以登入網路銀行，查看所有的交易狀況，比以前方便多了。

Part II

Unit 36 外幣現金兌換與旅行支票

1 主題對話

Michael is in a bank, trying to change NTD to USD.
Michael 在一家銀行要把新台幣換成美金。

Michael	I'd like to exchange my NT Dollars into US Dollars.	我想把新台幣換成美金。
Sophia	Sure, please fill out this form. By the way, why do you need US dollars?	沒問題，請先填好表格，順便問一下，你換美金是要用來做什麼？
Michael	I am going to US to pursue my master degree.	我要去美國念碩士。
Sophia	Good for you. What do you need, cash or traveler's check?	好棒！那你需要現金還是旅行支票？
Michael	It's my first time going there, so I have no idea. What is the difference?	我是第一次去，所以我不知道，有什麼不同嗎？
Sophia	Cash, as you probably know, is basically cash, which you can spend anywhere is US. As for traveler's check, you can see it as a special check. When you purchase it, you need to immediately sign on the upper half part of each check. When you need to buy something in US, you need to date and **countersign** the check on the lower half of the check.	現金基本上就是現金，美國任何地方都可以用。至於旅行支票，你可以把它看成一種特別的支票。你購買時要立刻在每張支票的上半部先簽名，等你到美國要買東西時，你要在支票後半部寫下日期並再簽一次名。

Chapter8

Michael	How about the exchange rate? Are they the same?	匯率呢？是不是一樣？
Sophia	You get a higher exchange rate for traveler's check. Usually, customers buy a little bit of cash with a larger amount of traveler's check. Cash is more convenient, while traveler's checks come with better exchange rates.	旅行支票的匯率比較高，所以通常客戶會買少量的現金和較多的旅行支票。現金方便，而旅行支票比較實惠。
Michael	I already have some cash in my pocket. I think I'll just buy traveler's checks.	我身上已經有些現金，那我就買旅行支票好了。
Sophia	What kinds of **denomination** do you like, 20, 50, or 100?	什麼樣的面額？二十、五十還是一百？
Michael	Please make it all in hundreds.	全部是一百的。
Sophia	Here you are, and please sign your name on the portion that says "sign here immediately upon receipt of this cheque" on each check.	旅行支票在這裡，請在每張支票裡標明『收到支票後立刻在此簽名』的地方，簽下你的名字。
Michael	Chinese or English?	中文還是英文？
Sophia	Up to you. You can sign both if you like. Actually, it would be better and more secure if you do both.	都可以，你可以兩種都簽，事實上這樣也比較安全。
Michael	Thanks.	謝謝。

Part II

② 心情小語

💗 To exchange local **currency** into US dollars, you have a few choices. The easiest way would be getting plain cash. Basically there is no restriction for cash. However, its advantages may also become its disadvantages. If you lose the money, whoever picks it up would be able to spend it. That's why I don't **advocate** carrying a large amount of cash. You can never be too careful with cash.

> 要把現金換成美元,你會有幾種選擇。最簡單的就是換成美元現金,在使用上幾乎沒有任何限制。但優點也有可能成為缺點,當你遺失現金時,任何人都可以把錢撿去用。所以我不建議身上帶太大量的現金,因為對錢,永遠是越小心越好!

💗 Traveler's checks provide better security. All you need to do is to sign you name on the proper space once you get them. Personally I'll recommend signing both your Chinese and English names, because it will be more difficult for others to counterfeit your signatures. If the checks are stolen, it is likely you will be able to get refunds. However, you also need an ID card and the receipt to apply for the refund. To be on the safe side, don't put your traveler's check and its receipt in the same place. It's OK to have one of them stolen, but not both.

> 比起現金,旅行支票安全多了。你只需在收到旅行支票後,立刻在適當的地方簽下你的名字。我個人建議中英文都簽,這樣一來,別人就很難模仿你的簽名。如果旅行支票遺失了,你還是可能可以退錢,只是通常會需要身分證明文件和收據。為了安全起見,不要把旅行支票和收據放在同一個地方,其中一種被偷還沒問題,但都丟了就沒了。

♥ Wire transfer or in traditional term, telegraphic transfer is another great way to transfer your money into US dollar. You need to know the **beneficiary** information and the related account information in order to do a wire transfer. Please go to your bank for further information. The **surcharge** and **commission** will be different from one bank to another, so check and compare before you get it. You can also try PayPal, but with a relatively high commission of 3.5%, in my opinion, other alternatives would be better.

> 另一個換美金的好方法則是電匯（telegraphic transfer 是較傳統的說法，意思為以電報通訊匯款）。你需要知道受款者的資料和他的帳號，想知道詳情，我建議你到銀行問問。每家銀行的手續費和佣金都可能不同，所以先確認比較看看。你也可以用 PayPal，但是相對之下，3.5% 的佣金有點高，我會建議用其他方法。

♥ You can also utilize credit cards or automated teller machines (ATMs). With the associated fee and charges, it would not be suitable for large transactions. It should be your last resort.

> 你也可以用信用卡或自動提款機，但考慮收費因素，這並不適合大金額的交易，應該把這當作是最後的方法。

♥ Finally, I would like to remind everyone to be careful with your own money. Make sure you know what to do when you lose it. Again, you cannot be too careful with your money.

> 最後我想提醒大家，對錢要小心，如果錢掉了，你要知道該做些什麼。再說一次，對於錢再怎麼小心都不為過。

Part II

3 單字與例句

countersign *v.* 副署、確認

The final report needs to be countersigned by your supervisor.
最後的報告要給你的長官副署。

denomination *n.* 名稱、面額

The gift certificates are available in $10 and $20 denominations.
禮品券的面額有十塊、二十塊。

currency *n.* 貨幣、流通、流傳

US dollar is one of the most popular currencies in the world.
美金是世界最普遍的貨幣之一。

advocate *v.* 擁護、主張

Martin Luther King, Jr. advocates civil rights all his life.
馬丁·路德·金恩終身倡導民權。

beneficiary *n.* 受益者

The beneficiary of my insurance policy is my son.
我保單的受益者是我兒子。

surcharge *n.* 額外費用、超載

The airlines add a $20 fuel surcharge on all international flights.
航空公司在所有的國際航線裡都加了 20 塊的燃料附加費。

commission *n.* 佣金

The sales person earns a 10% commission on every deal he gets.
業務員在每個他拿到的訂單裡都得到 10% 的佣金。

Chapter8

知識備忘錄

當年我出國時要換匯，基本上就是美金現金和旅行支票。我完全不懂，只好問銀行，我只知道旅行支票比較便宜，現金比較貴，而且旅行支票可以掛失，因此當時只換了幾百塊現金，其餘全是旅行支票就出國了。

還記得在飛機上，空姐就特別說明，只要攜帶超過一定數額的美金，就一定要申報。當年帶了兩萬多，也就老老實實的在飛機上填表，（請讀者注意，當年台幣兌美金是 25:1，加上股市上萬點，正是台灣錢淹腳目的時代。）結果一下飛機進海關時，就立刻見識到老美不隨身帶鉅額現金的事實。

還記得當時第一次到美國，拿著 I-20（美國大學入學許可）和簽證，戰戰兢兢地等候問話，在他看到我的學校 Texas A&M University 德州農工大學時，只說了 good school，好學校，就沒再問相關問題。但是在他看到幾萬美金時，立刻問為什麼帶這麼多現金？我沒好氣地說我是要去念 graduate school 研究所，所以就帶了這兩萬多，有問題嗎？我還記得僵了一陣子之後，他終於說出 OK，讓我入關。當時就覺得奇怪，怎麼會這樣？在美國待一陣子之後，真的發現沒幾個美國人會有這樣『鉅額』的存款。

談回外幣兌換，如果是一次要換大量的美元，我還是建議用旅行支票。等你一到美國，就立刻到銀行把它轉存到你的帳戶裡。這樣簡單、安全又方便。如果是小額消費，其實換現金、用當地的自動提款機，或是直接用台灣的信用卡也都可以。當然還是事先查一下提款卡和信用卡相關的手續費比較好。

 信用卡

1 主題對話

Michael is in a bank booth trying to apply for a credit card during a career & internship fair.

Michael 在參加職業與實習工作展裡，到一個銀行攤位申請信用卡。

Michael	I'd like to apply for a credit card.	我想申請一張信用卡。
Emily	Sure, please fill out this form. By the way, are you a foreign student?	OK，請填一下這張表格，順便問一下你是外國學生嗎？
Michael	Yes, I am working on my master degree in Computer Science.	是的，我正在攻讀資訊科學碩士學位。
Emily	Good for you. It should be easy to get a job when you graduate.	那很棒，畢業後應該很容易找到工作。
Michael	Thanks, I sure hope so. By the way, how do I fill out the Section 3 – Employment and income?	謝謝，我也希望如此。我要怎麼填寫第三項職業與收入？
Emily	Let me see. You are a student, right? Just put down student as your occupation. Do you have a work?	讓我看看，你是個學生對吧！請在職業欄填上學生。你有工作嗎？
Michael	Yes, I was a grader for the spring semester, and I am a teaching assistant now.	我在春季時曾經幫教授改過作業，而現在我是助教。

Emily	Good, then just write the university and its corresponding address for the Employer's name and address, respectively. Also, fill out the appropriate length of time at current employment.	很好，那就把學校和相關的地址，填到雇主名稱和地址，同時寫下擔任助教有多久時間。
Michael	How about the personal income? I just started working as a teaching assistant.	那收入呢？我才剛剛開始擔任助教。
Emily	Just estimate how much taxable income you are going to make this year, and fill the number there.	預估一下你的綜合所得，然後填上去就可以了。
Michael	There are several cards for me to choose from. Which one is the best for me?	有好幾種信用卡，你認為哪一個最適合我？
Emily	It depends on your need and financial situation. As shown in the form, there are basically three kinds of credit cards for you to choose from. The award card, the low fee card, and the low rate card. The award card gives you cash reward for your purchase; the low fee credit card has the least amount of annual fee, the low rates credit card has the lowest interest rate, of course. You can choose from these three cards and pick the one that's most suitable for you.	那要看你的需求與財務狀況，如同申請表上寫的，基本上有三種信用卡：回饋卡、低年費卡以及低利率卡。回饋卡會給你現金回饋，低年費卡就是年費低，低利率就是利率低。你可以互相比較一下，選張最適合你的。

Part II

Michael	I'll take the reward one. Here is the form.	我會選回饋卡，申請表填好了。
Emily	Thank you. We'll let you know the result in a week.	謝謝，一個禮拜後會通知你。
Michael	Thanks.	謝謝。

心情小語

♥ It's not safe to carry a huge amount of cash with you, no matter where you are in the world. That's the reason I don't recommend carrying cash with you. Credit card payment would be your best choice. However, most international students are not allowed to work, and they don't have taxable income unless they are granted with scholarships. How could international students apply for credit cards?

> 　　身上帶大量現金，在世界上任何地方都不安全，所以我不建議帶現金。在這情形下，用信用卡是最好的選擇。但多數國際學生都無法在美國工作，當然也沒有綜合所得，那國際學生應該怎麼申請信用卡呢？

♥ It's always difficult to get the first credit card, especially without a regular paycheck. The easiest way would be talking to the local banks and see if they provide credit cards to whoever opens a CD account. If not, maybe you can talk to Taiwanese Student Association and let them negotiate with the bank for a similar deal. For example, opening a $2,000 CD account and get you a credit card with credit limit of $2,000 or $1,000. Once you get the first card and **establish** some credit history, it would be easier to get other ones. If you don't get any scholarship, you can try to get a job like working as a tutor or grader to get some income. US banks know it is tough for students to get a job, so they would ease the condition for students. In that case,any kind of taxable income is helpful.

> 拿到第一張信用卡總是最困難的,尤其是在你沒有正常薪資的情況下。最簡單的方式,是到當地銀行看看,有沒有開定存送信用卡的情形。如果沒有,你可以跟台灣同學會談談,請他們跟銀行協商一下,看能不能有類似的方案。例如開一個 $2000 的定存的帳戶,就可以有張 $2000 或是 $1000 額度的信用卡。只要你有了一張信用卡,建立起信用紀錄,以後就比較容易拿到其他信用卡。如果你沒有獎學金,你也可以試試家教,或改作業的工作,藉此拿到一些收入。美國銀行知道學生比較難找工作,在這種情況下,任何的收入都有幫助。

❤ There are all kinds of credits cards, and the best credit cards for you would be the cash reward cards. On average, US cash reward cards pay 1 to 2% of your purchase. It may go higher with some special cash reward programs. For some of the purchases like gas or restaurant, you may get 5% or even higher rewards. If you pay your **balance** in full every month, you don't have to worry about any financial charges and you get to earn that one percent month interest, since you don't pay the money until one month later. With the added bonus of cash **rebate**, what better deal can you get?Once you have the crcdit history established, look for a better credit card, especially the cash reward ones.

> 信用卡有很多種,對我們而言,最好的是現金回饋卡。平均下來,美國現金回饋會給到 1 到 2%,某些特殊的信用卡甚至會更高。一些特定的消費,例如加油或餐廳,可能會給到 5%,甚至更高。如果你每個月都付清你的應付款,你根本不需要擔心任何費用,且你可以因此賺到一個月的利息－因為在一個月後才需要付款。如果還有現金回饋的話,那就更好了。在建立信用紀錄後,你可以找一些更好的信用卡,尤其是現金回饋的信用卡

3 單字與例句

booth *n.* 貨攤、攤位

We can setup a booth selling hot dogs in the Music and Art Festival.
我們在音樂與藝術節慶裡可以設立一個攤位來賣熱狗。

occupation *n.* 工作、職業、佔領、占用

The Japanese occupation of Taiwan lasted 50 years.
日本佔領台灣歷時 50 年。

rebate *n.* 折扣、退現 *v.* 退還

This credit card gives a 1.5% cash rebate.
這張信用卡提供 1.5% 的現金回饋。

establish *v.* 建立、創辦、安置

After years of negotiation, the two countries finally established a mutual trade agreement.
在幾年的協商後，這兩的國家終於建立了雙邊交易條款。

balance *n.* 平衡、結存、結餘 *v.* 使平衡、抵銷、補償

The gymnast lost her balance and fell down.
那位體操選手失去平衡而摔下來。

知識備忘錄

　　在美國，一開始多半是以支票付帳，不過只要有機會，還是要記得去申請信用卡。在大學的各種學生活動裡，少不了信用卡的申請攤位，試著申請看看。因為這類的攤位，一般都會提供小禮物給信用卡申請者，只要你填表，就可以拿到衣服或保溫杯之類的東西。申請時稍稍注意一下，看看有沒有年費？美國信用卡因為銀行間激烈的競爭，一般都是不收年費，不過還是要確認一下。

　　比較麻煩的是，到外州時，幾乎沒有店家會收支票，除了付現外，信用卡可說是唯一的付款方式。而它也是最方便、最划算的付款方式，幾乎所有商家都收信用卡，不受金額大小的限制。我們就曾經在超市，用信用卡付了不到三塊錢的帳。用信用卡最重要的一點就是，準時付帳，千萬不要拖欠，信用卡的高利率完全不划算。只要你準時付帳，免年費的信用卡一定划得來。因為你至少能方便的進行付款。如果又是現金回饋卡，那更是利上加利。

　　當然在沒有收入的狀況下，第一張信用卡總是最難拿到的。如果沒有銀行提供定存開戶就附信用卡的優惠，找台灣同學會，甚至跟中國同學會一起合作，找當地的銀行談談看，應該會有機會。

　　或許有人會問，在台灣也有信用卡，為什麼要在美國另外申請？其實只要你比較一下，美國的信用卡比台灣的好多了。現金回饋從 1% 起跳，有些加油和餐飲的回饋甚至高達 5% 到 10%。美國的絕對比較好！有機會就申請一張，記得準時付帳，不要讓銀行賺那些利率。

Part II

Unit 38 付小費文化

1 主題對話

Michael is having a dinner with David at an all you can eat restaurant.
Michael 和 David 在一家吃到飽餐廳吃晚餐。

Michael	I am almost full. It is dessert time for me.	我快飽了,該是甜點時間了。
David	I am almost full too, but the **appetizers** are pretty good. I'll try one more round before hitting the fruit and sweet stands.	我也差不多飽了,但是開胃點心很棒,我要再來一輪然後才吃水果和甜點。
Michael	Cheese cakes and pumpkin pies are delicious. You should try it.	起司蛋糕和南瓜派很可口,你該試試看。
David	I prefer the spicy chicken drumsticks and chicken wings. I am not a dessert lover, but I do love ice cream.	我比較喜歡辣雞腿和雞翅,我不是那麼喜歡甜點,不過我愛吃冰淇淋。
Michael	There are several flavors in the ice cream section. Let's take a look.	冰淇淋有好幾種口味,去看看吧!
David	Let me see, vanilla, strawberry, **cinnamon** and mango. Wow, I haven't had mango for quite some time. I got to have it.	我看看,香草、草莓、肉桂和芒果,哇!我好久沒吃芒果了,我一定要吃看看。

Michael	I'll get the newest flavor, the cappuccino delight.	我要選最新的口味，歡欣卡布奇諾。
David	The dirty dishes are piling up. Where are the **servants**? (Talking to a waiter) Excuse me, can you take away all the dishes here.	髒盤子都堆一堆了，服務生在那裡？（跟服務生說）抱歉，能不能收一下盤子？
Waiter A	Let me clean this table and I'll be right back with you for all dishes.	等我清完這，我立刻到你那裏收盤子。
Michael	I know it is Friday night. They must be super busy, but this is ridiculous.	我知道今天是週五，他們一定很忙，不過這也太誇張了！
David	The food is pretty good though. The appetizers, the main courses, the dessert and the ice cream are super. It's too bad that the service leave much too be desired.	食物是很好吃，不管是開胃菜、主食、甜點和冰淇淋都很棒，可惜的是服務真的有待加強。
Michael	Let's just enjoy the food and keep piling up the dishes. I'll get some fruit and one more piece of **pecan** pie.	我們就享受食物，繼續堆盤子吧。我要去拿些水果，再加一塊胡桃果派。
David	Get extra fruits for me. I am going to refill the drinks for both of us.	幫我多拿一些水果，我去拿飲料。
Michael	Sure.	好的。
David	Now that we are really full, it's time to pay the bill. What do you think about the tip?	現在可真是吃飽了，該付帳了。你覺得小費該給多少？
Michael	The service isn't good at all. Let's just leave one dollar.	服務又不好，給一塊錢好了。

② 心情小語

💗 Tips are part of American culture. You need to pay tips at hotel for room cleaning, baggage carrying, and other services. You need to pay tips in a sit-down restaurant. You need to pay tips for taxi and hair cut. Tips are needed for all services.

> 小費是美國文化之一，清掃房間、提拿行李，還有其他的旅館服務都要給小費。搭計程車、剪頭髮也要給小費，只要有服務幾乎都要給小費。

💗 For a casual or family style restaurant such as Applebee's, Buffalo Wild Wings, Chili's, Chipotle Mexican Grill, Denny's, IHOP, Outback Steakhouse and T.G.I. Friday, the standard tips is around 10 to 15%. For fine dining or luxurious ones, it may be to 15% to 20%. The waiters are paid with minimum wages, and they depend on the tips as their primary income source.

> 家庭或是休閒餐廳標準的小費是 10% 到 15%，例如蘋果蜂、水牛雞翅、紅辣椒、胡椒墨西哥燒烤、丹尼、國際鬆餅屋、澳美客牛排館和星期五餐廳等。在正式餐廳或高級餐廳給的小費就要 15 到 20%。服務生的薪水是最低薪資，所以他們的收入基本上就是靠小費。

💗 Talking about restaurants, if you like pancakes, French toast, or omelets, I would recommend International House of Pancakes (IHOP). They are famous for their pancakes, and they have all kinds of syrup for you to choose from. Founded in 1982 and 1993, respectively, Buffalo Wild Wings and Chipotle Mexican Grill are new kids on the block. Both of them are expanding quickly. Again, for casual restaurants, 10% to 15% tips are usually enough.

> 　　說到餐廳，如果你喜歡吃鬆餅、法國吐司和煎蛋捲，我會推薦國際鬆餅屋。他們的鬆餅很有名，連它的糖漿都有好幾種口味供你選擇。水牛雞翅和胡椒墨西哥燒烤分別開創於 1982 年和 1993 年，算是比較新的餐廳，這兩家都在迅速擴展中。再次強調，對於這類的休閒餐廳，通常 10% 到 15% 的小費就可以了。

❤ We usually leave on dollar in the hotel for their room services each day. For Mongolian barbeque and omelet stations, I'll also leave a dollar for their services. There was once I stayed in a hotel for six months for a business trip. Since I don't need room service every day, I would put up the "DO NOT DISTURB" sign to avoid room services. Of course, I can have them cleaning the room every day, and leave the tips every other day, but that won't be fair to the cleaning ladies.

> 　　住旅館時，我們通常每天留一塊錢給清潔人員。在餐廳，我也會留一塊錢給蒙古烤肉和煎蛋捲的師傅。我曾經因為出差，整整六個月住在旅館；當時時再也不用天天打掃，因此我會放上「請勿打擾」的牌子，以避免不必要的清潔工作。當然我可以每天讓他們打掃，然後隔日給小費，但這樣對清潔人員並不公平。

❤ You may not like to pay tips in US, but once you get use to it, you will realize it is actually fair to us. You pay for the services accordingly. Unlike in US, restaurants in Taiwan which add a fixed 10% surcharge to the bill, at least in US you get to decide how much you want to pay for the services. In addition, I'm pretty sure about that in Taiwan the surcharge goes straight to the restaurant owner's pocket. Even some Chinese tour guides and travel agencies copy the fixed surcharge system in US. You are told to pay whatever amount of money per day to the bus driver and the tour guide. In my opinion, that is not how tips work.

Part II

> 　　或許你不喜歡付小費，但等你習慣後，會發現這其實還蠻公平的。你可以依服務的品質決定小費的多寡。很多台灣餐廳會在帳單上加個 10% 的小費，而且我很確定這部分的費用是直接進了餐廳老闆的口袋中。但在美國，至少我可以決定服務值多少錢。很多在美國的華人旅行社學了台灣的做法，要求給司機和導遊定額的小費。而在我看來，小費不應該是這樣的。

3　單字與例句

appetizer　*n.* 餐前點心、開胃小吃

This dish can be served as a main course or as an appetizer.
這道菜可以做為主餐或是餐前點心。

cinnamon　*n.* 肉桂

She sprinkled cinnamon on the French toast.
她在法國吐司上面撒了些肉桂。

servant　*n.* 僱工、服務生、員工

A public servant is a person hired by the government for public service.
公務人員就是政府部門雇來服務大眾的人員。

pecan　*n.* 胡桃果

This restaurant bakes the best pecan pie.
這家餐廳烤的胡桃果派最美味。

知識備忘錄

　　美國真的是小費王國，基本上只要接受服務，你就應該給小費。就連剪頭髮也要給小費。一開始大家一定會不習慣，會覺得為什麼沒事就要給小費？不過基本上小費是由你決定，雖然有些公認的範圍，但如果你覺得服務不好，你絕對有權力決定要給多少。如果你看開一點，應該就會覺得好一些。

　　我有一次吃飯時，對服務非常不滿意，雖然當天餐廳生意確實很好，服務生也有點忙不過來，但基本上幾乎所有服務都要三催四請。當時我就很不想給小費，不過在場的老學生提了一個很棒的建議，那就是只給一個 quarter，也就是兩毛五。老學生解釋說，這比完全不給小費的意義還要大。完全不給只會顯得你很小氣，而給兩毛五則表示我原先是會給小費，只是你的服務太爛，只給兩毛五以施懲戒，這樣不會讓美國服務生認為中國人就是小氣不給小費。

　　說起小費，還真是服務生的主要收入。美國餐廳服務生一般都是領最低薪資，其他則由小費來賺。在美國當服務生，尤其是高級餐廳的服務生，可是可以養家的。想想這些高級餐廳的營業額，然後乘以 15% 或 20%，就是所有服務生的收入，其實還真不少！

　　在美國接受服務，該給的小費還是要給。當然只要你覺得服務真的不好，給一點點絕對沒問題，只是如果服務真的很棒，那就應該給多一點。

Part II

Unit 39 社交禮儀與社團活動

1 主題對話

Michael is having a conversation about fraternities and sororities with Lucas.
Michael 和 Lucas 聊到了兄弟會和姐妹會。

Michael	I am interested in fraternities. Can I join one?	我對兄弟會還蠻有興趣的，可以參加嗎？
Lucas	Sorry, fraternities are mostly for undergraduate students. From what I know, they don't accept graduate students.	抱歉，兄弟會基本上是給大學部的學生，就我所知，他們不收研究生。
Michael	I also heard about sororities. What are they?	我聽說也有姐妹會，是什麼樣的組織？
Lucas	Fraternities and sororities come from the Latin words frater and soror, meaning "brother" and "sister" respectively. So basically, fraternities are for males while sororities are for females.	兄弟會和姐妹會的名稱是由拉丁文的 frater 和 soror 而來的，相對的意思是兄弟和姊妹。所以基本上 fraternities 是男士組織，而 sororities 是女士組織。
Michael	Really? That is interesting.	真的啊，還蠻有趣的！

Lucas	However, the use of "fraternity" may have sexist meaning, and the description of "fraternity" and "sorority" is **ambiguous**, some people start to call these groups "Greek letter organizations". This is because most of these groups were named themselves with Greek letters. However, most of its members still use the term "fraternity" and "sorority" to refer to their groups.	但是最近因為 fraternity 這個字有性別歧視的疑慮，"fraternity" 和 "sorority" 這兩個字的含意也不清楚，因此有些人就用『希臘字母組織』來稱呼這些組織，因為這類的組織多半是以希臘字母命名。儘管如此，許多會員還是用兄弟會和姐妹會的名稱，來分別這些團體。
Michael	What are the purposes of these organizations?	這些團體的宗旨是什麼？
Lucas	Most of them are considered mutual groups, hosting academic and social activities. Some of them even maintain a chapter house, providing residential facilities for its members.	他們大部分是互助團體，舉行學術和社交活動。有些團體還有會員之家，為會員提供住宿。
Michael	Is that all?	還有嗎？
Lucas	Some groups **distinguish** themselves by function. They can be specifically **orchestrated** as community services, professional advancements, and academic achievement.	有些組織以功能來區分，可以分為社區服務、專業發展或是學業成就。
Michael	It sounds good, but is there any negative impact to the members?	聽來不錯，但是對會員會有不良影響嗎？

Lucas	According to some research, fraternity and sorority members have generally lower GPA than non-**affiliated** students. However, there are some evidences showing that affiliated students have significantly higher **self-esteem** than their non-affiliated counterparts.	根據一些研究，兄弟會和姐妹會會員，一般成績比非會員差。但也有證據顯示，比起非會員，會員比非會員更有自信。
Michael	Thanks for your information.	謝謝你的訊息。
Lucas	Sure thing.	不客氣。

❤ If you are an undergraduate student in a US college, I would suggest you to join a fraternity. However, you have to be careful when choosing a fraternity. Some fraternities do have alcohol related problems or **hazing** issues. You need to do some research first and then decide which one is more suitable to you. Obviously, you need to avoid those with **alcohol** problems. Also, make sure you consider the time needs to be **committed** to the fraternity that you are interested in. If time is at a minimum for you, you better think twice before signing out.

> 如果你是美國大學學生，我會建議你參加兄弟會或姐妹會。不過在選擇時要小心，有些組織確實有酗酒問題或是霸凌問題，你先要做些研究，然後決定哪一個比較適合你。很明顯地，盡量避免有酗酒問題的組織。同時也確認每個組織所需要的時間，如果你時間原本就不多，或許就該多考慮考慮。

❤ Unlike the clubs in universities in Taiwan, you have to follow and pass certain procedures before you are allowed into the fraternity. I'll take Pi Kappa Phi as an example here.

> 跟台灣的大學社團不同的是，在美國你需要先遵循並通過某些程序，才可以加入兄弟會。以下我會以 Pi Kappa Phi（pkf）為例子來說明。

❤ First, you have to be interviewed by some existing members. This is the chance for you to get to know them and figure out if your personality fits the organization. You also need to study and learn the history, tradition and rituals of the organization. You have to pass quizzes and a final exam to show that you are knowledgeable enough to join it. After that you have to finish two projects: one of them is to organize a picnic or cook out event; the other is to help painting or remodeling part of the fraternity house. After passing the requirement, you can officially join the organization.

> 首先你要先跟一些會員面談，了解他們，並搞清楚你的個性是否合適這個組織。同時你要學習這個組織的歷史、傳統和儀式，並通過測驗和考試，證明你了解並有資格加入這個組織。再來要完成兩個作業，其中一個是籌備一場野餐或是烤肉聚會，另一個則是協助裝潢或是油漆會員之家的設施。在通過這些項目之後，你才可以正式加入組織。

❤ There are usually weekly chapter meetings and **mandatory** events. They can be community services, social events, and others. You need to **allocate** your time between academic work and fraternity activities wisely.

> 　　組織裡通常有固定聚會，還有些必須參加的活動項目，像是是社區服務、社交活動或是其他活動。你需要在課業和活動間妥善分配時間。

❤ Why join a fraternity? As an overseas student, occasionally you need a place to stay when school dormitory is closed. A fraternity with a chapter house can obviously help. It will also be a group of close friends which you belong to during and after college. It will also connect you with an alumni network when you are looking for jobs.

> 　　為什麼要參加呢？作為一個海外學生，你在學校宿舍關閉時，會需要一個住處。有會員之家的兄弟會將會有很大的幫助。團體成員也將成為你大學時和畢業後的密友。透過這些團體你也可以認識畢業校友，在求職的時候提供人脈網路。

❤ With all the benefits, you should start looking for a fraternity to join which might be helpful for your college life.

> 　　加入這些社團的好處很多，你應該盡快開始找個兄弟會加入，這對你的大學生活可能將有所助益。

3 單字與例句

ambiguous *adj.* 含糊不清的

We are confused by the ambiguous wording of the message.
我們被訊息裡含糊不清的字義搞糊塗了。

distinguish *v.* 區別、辨認

It is important to distinguish between right and wrong.
如何分辨好壞真的很重要。

orchestrate *v.* 編排管弦樂曲、精心安排、協調

The government still has no idea who orchestrated the attack.
政府還是不知道是誰策劃了這次的攻擊。

affiliate *v.* 聯繫、參加

This group does not affiliate itself with any political party.
這個組織還沒跟任何政黨有關連。

self-esteem *n.* 自尊、自負、自信

Letting a child do things on their own helps build up his self-esteem.
讓個小孩自己做自己的事會幫助他建立自信。

hazing *n.* 被欺凌、被欺負

The hazing incident left him battered and bruised.
那次的欺凌事件讓他受到打擊與傷害。

Part II

alcohol *n.* 酒、酒精

He decided to keep off alcohol after the car accident.
在那次車禍後他決定不再喝酒。

commit *v.* 保證

I felt that we don't have to commit to anything.
我覺得我們不需要保證些什麼。

mandatory *adj.* 命令的、義務的、強制的

It is mandatory to wear a school uniform to school.
到學校必須要穿制服。

allocate *v.* 分派、分配

We need to determine the best way to allocate our time and resources..
我們必須決定一個最好的方式來分配時間和資源。

知識備忘錄

　　美國大學的 fraternities 和 sororities 就是一般俗稱的兄弟會和姐妹會。這類的組織基本上都是以大學生為主，如果你是研究生，那就沒有機會參加了。對於研究生，一般就是加入同學會，從同學會裡就可以問到關於學校，還有研究所的一些訊息。在這裡我就不再贅述，我想討論一下美國一般的禮儀。

　　其實在學校裡，幾乎沒有什麼機會參與美國人的社交活動，所以我就簡單的講一下，美國人一般生活上常見到、常聽到的話語。在你看完之後，你會對這些語言比較熟悉，並適時地說出一些合宜的話。

　　在美國如果聽到別人打噴嚏，立刻就會說 Bless you。其實這是由 God bless you. 所簡化而來，也就是祝福你、保佑你。如果你是打噴嚏的那個人，就要立刻接說 Thank you，謝謝你。這兩句話已經成為美國生活的一部分。

　　還有在美國記得，隨時把 excuse me 掛在嘴邊。想問問題時、請人讓路借過時、不小心做了或說了一些不好意思的舉止或言語時、禮貌性地讓對方知道你不同意時。而 I am sorry 或是 sorry，就比較像是在道歉。還有當你在聽到對方講出一些不幸的事時，要立刻說 Sorry to hear that 以表達你的遺憾之意。舉例來說，對方說他得了感冒或是他養的貓死了，你竟應該立刻說 Sorry to hear that.

　　只要你熟悉了這幾句話，一般問題就不會大了。

Unit 40　國際電話卡

1　主題對話

Michael is ordering a prepaid calling card on the phone.
Michael 在電話中跟 Natalie 訂購預付電話卡。

Natalie	This is Natalie from Low Cost Calling Cards. How may I help you?	這是低價電話卡公司的娜塔莉，有什麼可以幫忙的嗎？
Michael	I'd like to buy a prepaid calling card.	我想買張預付電話卡。
Natalie	I can certainly help you with that. Which country do you mostly call to?	沒問題，我可以幫你，請問多數打去哪個國家？
Michael	I am from Taiwan, so I always make calls to Taiwan.	我從台灣來的，都是打到台灣。
Natalie	We have a card specifically designed to make calls to Taiwan and China, and the rate is only five cents per minute. Are you interested in that?	我們有個專打台灣和中國大陸的電話卡，費率是每分鐘五分錢，你有興趣嗎？
Michael	Five cents per minute? I was told there are phone cards with a much lower rate.	每分鐘五分錢，我聽說有些電話卡比這還便宜。
Natalie	Did you check the **fine print** on that card? There are usually connection fees, and there may be only a few local access numbers. You also need to check out the **rounding** time.	你有沒有仔細看小字的說明？通常它們還有連線費，本地的聯播號碼也不多，你還要注意他們計費的單位時間。

Michael	What do those terms mean?	這些術語的意思是？
Natalie	A connection fee is a fixed fee that you have to pay to get the call connected. Once the call is answered, the fee is charged no matter how long the call is. We don't charge connection fees at all. As for the local access number, you need to call the local number first before you use the prepaid card. If you are not in the area with local numbers, you will probably need to call a toll free 1-800 number, which would make the rate much higher. We have local numbers all over US, so you don't have to worry about that.	連線費是電話連線收取的固定費用，只要對方接了電話，不管講多久，都會收定額的連線費用。而我們則不收連線費。至於本地電話號碼，是所有電話卡都會要求您先打一個當地的號碼來連接電話。如果你不住在這個電話號碼所屬的區域內，你就要使用 1-800 的免付費電話，但電話卡的費用就會被提高。我們在全美國都有本地電話，所以你不必擔心這個問題。
Michael	How about the rounding time?	那你說的計費單位時間是？
Natalie	Rounding time is the minimum time the phone card charges. If the rounding time is 3-minute, you are charged every 3 minutes. If the call lasts only 50 seconds, you will still be charged by three minutes.Our rounding time is 6 seconds, which is much better than most of the calling cards.	計費單位指的是電話卡收費用的最小時間。如果是三分鐘，就是收費以每三分鐘計算，如果你只打了50 秒，還是會收三分鐘的金額，我們的計費單位是六秒，比大多數的電話卡好多了。
Michael	Thanks for your explanation. I'd like to buy a 20-dollar phone card.	謝謝你的解釋，我要買 20塊的電話卡。

Part II

Natalie	Please give me your credit card number, and I'll give you an access code, which can be used to make international phone calls. You can also check our website with that number to take a look at your calling history.	請給我你的信用卡號碼，我會給你一個代碼用來打國際電話，你還可以到我們的網站，用那個代碼來查看你的使用紀錄。
Michael	Here it is, 1234 5678 9012 3456.	號碼是 1234 5678 9012 3456。
Natalie	Thanks, your access code is 9876 5432 1098.	謝謝，你的代碼是 9876 5432 1098。

② 心情小語

♥ There are all kinds of prepaid calling cards. They basically use internet to wire your international calls. Using internet to make phone call would cost a lot less than the traditional phone call and that is why they can offer you a much lower rate. To make a cost effective solution, I would suggest you check the detail information as explained in the previous section before deciding which one is the best for you.

> 市面上有各種電話卡，基本上都是用網路來接通你的國際電話。用網際網路來打電話，比傳統電話線便宜多了，這也是國際電話卡會便宜很多的原因。要有效的用國際電話卡省錢，我建議你先仔細看看前一段所說的訊息，然後來決定哪一種電話卡最適合你。

♥ In US, the customers pay a flat monthly fee for all local calls, so basically this local call doesn't add any extra cost. You have to then dial an access

number or a personal identification number (PIN) and finally your international phone number. The whole process is kind of **troublesome**. But with a much lower rate than that of the regular international call, customers are willing to go through it to save money.

> 在美國，本地電話只收月費，所以這個本地電話基本上不會增加你的電話費。然後你要撥一組使用代碼或稱為識別碼，最後才是撥打你的國際電話號碼，整個程序有點麻煩，不過電話費省了很多，顧客也就願意打這個麻煩的電話來省錢。

♥ For any particular prepaid phone card, the access code or PIN is the most important information for the users, since it is the only information you need from the calling card company to make the call. You are basically buying the number with your money. When making an international call, you need to dial the local number, the access number, and then the international number you are calling. There are a lot of numbers for you to dial to save money. To save the trouble, some companies use your local telephone number as the access number. Once you register your phone number, if you make the call from that particular phone, you don't have to dial the access number since the calling center can automatically identify the phone number you are calling from.

> 對任一個電話卡而言，這組使用代碼或識別碼是最重要的資訊，因為這可是你打國際電話時唯一需要的資訊。你付的錢其實只是用來買這組號碼。在打國際電話時，你要先打一組本地電話，然後是這組識別碼，然後是你所要打的國際電話，為了省錢，你可是要撥大堆號碼。為了省去這個麻煩，有些公司就用你的電話號碼作為識別碼，在你註冊你的電話號碼後，只要你是從這個電話所撥打的國際電話，你都不需要再撥識別碼，因為它們可以自動的認出你的號碼，也就確認你是它們的客戶了。

Part II

❤ Most of the calling cards have official websites from which you can check the balance and calling history, recharge your calling card, and check rate to different country. If the party you are calling doesn't have internet access, the prepaid phone call is one of the best ways for you to save money.

> 多數的電話卡都有官方網站，你可以從那裏看你的餘額、你打電話的紀錄、儲值以及查看打到各個不同國家的費率。如果你打電話的對象沒有網路，預付電話卡是個最好的省錢方法。

3 單字與例句

fine print　小號印刷字體（通常文件的限制、說明以）小號字體印出來

You need to read the fine print before signing the contract.
在簽合約之前你要先把小字說明看清楚。

rounding　*adj.* 弄成圓的、圓的、四捨五入進位

Rounding error is caused by approximating a number with fewer digits from an original one with more digits.
進位誤差是由原始多位數數字，在進位成位數比較少的數字時，所造成的誤差。

troublesome　*adj.* 令人煩惱的、討厭的

It is troublesome that there will be more cuts in the budget.
令人厭煩的是預算還會被刪減。

●○ **知識備忘錄**

　　由於網際網路的進步，對一些傳統媒體與通訊業造成了不小的影響。最明顯的就是報紙。你最後一次訂報紙是哪時候？想不起來了吧！那你最後一次買報紙是哪時候？我是前幾個星期去找我父親時，幫他買的。因為網路的衝擊，一些傳統媒體大亨紛紛陷入困境，就算開闢新聞網站也無法停止虧損。

　　電信電話也是一個受影響很深的產業，以往國際電話費高的嚇人，如非必要不會想打國際電話。網路的進步與寬頻上網的盛行，讓國際電話費用再也不是遙不可及。跟報業不同的是，電信業者的成本也相對降低，所以衝擊不像報紙那麼大。

　　說到電話溝通，其實只要有寬頻網路，利用社群網站或是 Skype，其實都可以做為免費的溝通媒介。海外學生的問題，往往是老一代的爸爸、媽媽不那麼習慣使用新一代的網路工具，往往還是要打長途電話回家。在這種狀況下，國際電話卡或是 Skype，就是一般的選擇了。比較一下，如果國際電話按每分鐘費率來看，還是比 Skype 便宜多了。更何況 Skype 還收取接通費，除非你用的是不限國家選項，不過光是十幾塊美元的月費就比較貴了。

　　如果可能的話，我會建議教一下父母使用 Skype，就算是老一輩的人，教一下應該就會了。你還可以跟他們說這還可以影音通話，比起電話好太多了，順便還可以幫他們開個 FB 帳號，讓大家都可以隨時留言、溝通，還可以藉由 FB 交換彼此的最新動態，網路好用又免費，何樂而不為。

 網路通訊無國界

1 主題對話

Michael is video chatting to his sister Amelia in Taiwan, via Skype.

Michael 用 Skype 跟他的妹妹 Amelia 影音聊天。

Amelia	Hi, Michael, haven't talk to you for a while. Where have you been?	老哥，有一陣子沒跟你聊天了，你都到哪兒去了？
Michael	I've been busy preparing the finals, and I also have to work on some term projects, including final reports and presentations. It's been a **hectic** month. How about you? How is the life in Taiwan?	我忙著準備期末考，而且還要準備期末的報告和演講。這個月我可是忙翻了。妳呢？台灣的生活如何？
Amelia	Being the president of the Pop Dance Club, I am really busy, trying to balance between **academic** study, dancing, and my own leisure activity.	身為熱舞社社長的我也很忙，正試著在功課、跳舞和休閒之間找到平衡。
Michael	How is your grade?	成績如何？
Amelia	Just surviving. I barely pass it.	僥倖過關，可以説是低空飛過。
Michael	Are you still interested in coming to US for your graduate study?	妳還想到美國來唸研究所嗎？

Amelia	Sure, I am. Improving my English while getting a graduate degree in US is one of the most important goals of my life.	當然，到美國念研究所並增進英文，一直都是我人生中最重要的目標之一。
Michael	Then the most important thing for you is to get good grades. Your college grade is the first thing US graduate school would be looking at.	那妳最重要的事就是拿到好的成績。
Amelia	I thought extracurricular activities count as part of application credit, especially in US.	課外活動不是也算在申請資格裡嗎？尤其是在美國。
Michael	Yes, but they look at your grade first. No extracurricular activities could save your terrible grades. You are only a freshman, so you still have plenty of time to **right your ship**.	是沒錯，不過美國大學還是先看成績，成績不好的話，再好的課外活動也救不了妳。妳只是個大一新鮮人，還有很多時間補救。
Amelia	I am surprised by the information. I'll focus on my study and cut down my time on all the other activities.	我真的很訝異，我會在認真在課業上，並減少其他活動的時間。
Michael	By the way, remember to teach mom and dad about Skype. I'd like to video chat with them.	對了，記得教爸媽 Skype 我想跟他們用影音聊天。
Amelia	Sure, I'll do that when I go home in summer vacation.	沒問題，暑假回家我就教。
Michael	Thanks, and get your school works in order.	謝謝，記得學校成績啊。
Amelia	I will. Thanks and bye.	我會的。謝謝。

Part II

2 心情小語

❤ As I said numerous times in this book, internet basically changes almost everything. Communicating with friends and relatives is a lot easier, cheaper, and more convenient than ever. You can video chat with Skype, leave a personal message and update your status on FB, share your pictures and videos on Instagram, post your article on Tumblr, and let your friends know what you are thinking on Twitter. The best thing is that you can do all of these for free.

> 就像我在這本書裡已說過無數次的，網路基本上幾乎改變了所有事物。跟朋友或親戚溝通比以前更簡單、便宜、也方便多了。你可以用 Skype 影音對談、在 FB 上留私人訊息並更新你的狀況、在 Instagram（一個影音照片分享的社群網站）上面分享你的影音和照片、在 Tumblr（一個微網誌網站）上發表你的部落格文章、在推特上讓朋友知道你的想法、看法。最棒的是這一切都是免費的。

❤ One thing you need to keep in mind when communicating through internet is to know how those applications or web sites work. For example, Skype message only pops up when both users are online, but FB personal message is posted to the other user immediately when the message is sent. So, I use FB for message and chat on Skype. You don't want to send an important message on Skype and then find out both of you were never online at the same time when it is already too late.

> 在用網路溝通時，有件事你要注意，就是要知道這些應用程式或網站是如何運作的。例如 Skype 簡訊只有在兩人都上 Skype 時才會傳遞，而 FB 只要你在傳送以後，另一方一上線時就會看到。所以我都是用 FB 傳簡訊，而用 Skype 聊天。你可不要用 Skype 送緊急的簡訊，等到出問題後，才發現兩人很少同時上線！

♥ I still remember back in the days of my graduate study while World Wide Web was still in its **infancy**, and Web 1.0 was still taking shape. The WWW was a one way street, and the user could not conveniently get their thoughts posted to the web sites. Before we know it, the dot-com bubble came along and wiped out countless companies. Yet, while the turbulence was still raging, Web 2.0 was quietly **materializing**. Social networking sites, blogs, wikis, web applications and video sharing sites were developing and **thriving**.

> 　　我還記得在我念研究所時，全球資訊網還在嬰兒期，網路 1.0 才剛剛開始。當時的全球資訊網只是個單行道，使用者不是那麼容易的能讓在網站上發表他們的看法。一不注意，網路泡沫來臨，許多公司倒閉。但是還在混亂之中，網路 2.0 也開始成形。社群網站、部落格、維基、網路應用程式、影音分享網站，一路發展大行其道。

♥ With the forming and developing of Web 3.0, I can't imagine what the future communication would become, and how our future life would shape up.

> 　　目前正在形成與發展中的網路 3.0，令我無法想像未來的通訊會變成怎樣？未來的生活又會如何的改變？

③ 單字與例句

hectic　*adj.* 忙亂的、鬧哄哄的

As a journalist and a mother, she regularly maintains a hectic schedule.
作為一個新聞人員和媽媽，她的行程通常都很繁忙。

academic　*adj.* 學校的、學術的

Professor Lee is leaving the academic world to take an industrial job.
李教授要離開學術界去業界服務。

right the ship　導向正軌

The latest company financial result isn't good at all and we need to right the ship or we are going to be looking for new jobs.
最新的公司財報很不好，我們需要導正，要不然我們都得找新工作。

infancy　*n.* 初期、嬰兒期、幼年

Until a child can walk on his own, it is consider infancy.
在小孩可以獨自走路前，都被認為是嬰兒期。

materialize　*v.* 成形、實現

Dark clouds materialize on the horizon and it looks like it's going to rain soon.
烏雲正在地平線上成形，看來即將要下雨。

thrive　*v.* 詞 繁榮、興盛

Plants would thrive with the proper amount of sunlight and water.
植物在適量的陽光與雨水下，會繁茂的生長。

知識備忘錄

　　網際網路與寬頻上網，基本上已經改變了人們溝通的方式，也真的變成了網路通訊無國界。十幾年前根本不可能的影音通話，現在變成家常便飯，更棒的是還完全免費！你可以把你小孩的照片、生活影音放到 YouTube 或是 FB，讓遠在台灣的阿公、阿媽觀賞。上 FB 或是利用 Google 搜尋，可以找到多年沒有聯絡的老友，回台灣想跟眾親友相聚，上 FB 宣布回台訊息，相關人等立刻知悉。

　　如果老一代的爸爸媽媽不習慣用網路溝通，智慧型手機或觸控平板則是個很好的開始。我就有好幾位朋友買了 iPad 給爸媽，花點時間教一下如何使用，在他們面前打開並使用 Apps 應用軟體，幫他們建立並使用 FB 帳號，然後引導他們親自操作，不用多久他們就會開始使用網路，甚至愛上網路。如果你不在台灣，請個年輕的家人、朋友教一下，真的很容易就能讓他們上手。

　　最後我想提醒一下，方便之餘有個問題也必須注意，那就是你的隱私。要注意各個網站的隱私設定，哪些人可以看到你的資訊，哪些人就算找也找不到，哪些私密資訊只想被親人知悉。說句實話，只要是真正的個人隱私，只許最親近的人清楚的事情，就不要放到網路上。記得一句話，凡走過必留痕跡。當然網路上也有許多人不計一切代價，只想出名！如果你也想如此，先想好萬一之時，你該如何應對？簡單的說，在你真的在不計代價確實出名以後，以往不計代價的東西，會不會造成成名後的困擾？如果真的如此，是不是該先想好應對之策？

時差調適

 **主題對話**

Michael is talking to his roommate Gabriel.
Michael 跟他的室友 Gabriel 聊天。

Gabriel	Hi, Michael, you look really sleepy.	嗨，麥克，你看起來累垮了。
Michael	The jet lag is killing me. After three days I still have problem sleeping at night and that makes me tired and sleepy during day time.	時差把我搞得累翻了，都三天了，我晚上還是睡不著，也讓我在白天又累、又想睡。
Gabriel	Jet lag? Have you try melatonin?	時差？你試過褪黑激素嗎？
Michael	Melatonin? What is it? I have never heard of it.	褪黑激素？是什麼東西我從沒聽過？
Gabriel	It's basically a hormone found in animals, plants, and **microbes**. The production of melatonin is inhibited by light and permitted by darkness. If you use it several hours before sleeping, it would help improving the sleeping problems.	基本上它是種荷爾蒙，在動物、植物和微生物裡都有，褪黑激素會被光線抑制，在夜晚則會增加。如果在睡前幾小時服用的話，有助於你的睡眠問題。
Michael	Really, I don't know that. How can I buy it? Do I need a prescription?	真的嗎？我完全不知道耶。怎麼買？需要醫生處方嗎？

Gabriel	Prescription is not needed. Actually, it is categorized by the Food and Drug Administration (FDA) as a **dietary** supplement, not a drug. You can find it in any local pharmacy.	不需要，這東西歸食品暨藥物管理局管，是日常保健品而不是藥物，在任何藥房專櫃上都可找到。
Michael	Have you used it before? Did it help?	你試過嗎？有幫助嗎？
Gabriel	Based on my own experience, it helps a bit with jet lag adjustment. Somebody claims it really helps a lot, but others say it is not effective at all. It's more like a "he said, she said." It won't hurt to give it a try.	根據我的經驗，對時差是有些幫助。有人說幫助很大，也有人說沒什麼用，有點像各說各話。試看看也沒差就是了。
Michael	I should just try it and see how it goes.	我該試試，看作用如何。
Gabriel	Also, if you are really tired at day time, take a brief snap but not a long sleep. Try some outside activity when you are tired. Don't stay home and do nothing but watch TV.	同時如果白天很累，可以短短的午睡一下，但是不要睡太久。如果累了就到戶外活動 下，不要只待在家裡看電視。
Michael	I'll remember that and please wake me up if my nap is over one hour.	我會記住，還有如果我睡超過一小時記得叫醒我。
Gabriel	No problem, I can do that.	沒問題，我會的。
Michael	Thank you. I really appreciate it.	謝謝。感恩。
Gabriel	Don't mention it.	不客氣。

Part II

2 心情小語

♥ Jet lag is basically caused by long-distance trans-**meridian** (east–west or west–east) travel. Maybe you are wondering why it is named jet lag. The term jet lag is used because before jet airplanes, people were not able to travel far and fast enough to cause jet lag. Propeller airplanes were slower and much shorter on travel distance, therefore it wouldn't cause jetlag.

> 時差基本上是因為長途的東西向旅程所造成的。或許你在想為什麼時差被稱為 jet lag？這個名字的由來是因為在噴射客機之前，人們無法進行這種快速長途旅行，也不會造成時差；螺旋槳飛機飛得慢，也飛不了多遠，也就不至於造成時差問題。

♥ It usually takes a few days to adjust jet lag, and it may disrupt your daily routine during that time. When you travel across several time zones, your body clock will be out of **synchronization** with the destination time. The natural pattern of your body is disturbed and it no longer corresponds to the new environment. The speed of the adjustment to the new schedule depends on each individual. Some people may take a few days while other experience little disruption.

> 時差的調整，往往需要幾天的時間，而且會打亂你的生活步調。當你穿越時區時，你的生理時鐘無法跟當地的時間同步，你身體的自然步調被打亂，無法跟現有環境一致。時差調整的快慢跟個人有關，有些人要好幾天，有些人則沒什麼太大的影響。

♥ There are a few strategies that can be used to **cope** with jet lag or travel **fatigue**. Try arrival at night if possible. Nothing beats a good night's sleep after a long international flight and nothing helps jet lag better than a good night's sleep. Drink water or fruit juice rather than tea, coffee, or alcohol during the flight. Sleep on the plane only when it is within the destination's sleep time. Upon arriving at the destination, try outdoor activities or simply talk to friends and family when you feel tired during day hours. Basically keep yourself busy and have your body properly exposed to light. Take a short snap only if need, and make sure there is an alarm clock or somebody who will wake you up. Try some melatonin if it helps.

> 有些方法可以用來調適時差和旅遊疲勞。如果可能的話,試著在晚上抵達目的地。在長途的國際航班後,沒什麼會比一夜好眠更棒,而且一夜好眠也最能幫助時差的調整。在飛機上多喝開水或是果汁,避免喝茶、咖啡或酒精類飲料。在飛機上,只有在是目的地的睡眠時間時才睡覺。在抵達後,到戶外活動一下,或是和朋友、家人聊天。基本上讓自己忙碌點,並讓自己曬曬陽光。只有在有必要時小睡一下,而且要確認有鬧鐘或旁人能把你叫醒。如果你覺得有幫助的話,也可以吃一點褪黑激素。

❤ To be honest, I believe a strong will may be the best practice for jet lag adjustment. If you just take a nap whenever feeling tired, and rcfuse to get up whenever the alarm sounds, it may take forever for you to adjust to the new time zone. If you can will yourself through the sleepiest time by going outside and enjoying yourself to sunlight, your body will be able to regulate itself to the new environment in no time. It is all up to you and your will.

> 老實説,我相信堅強的信念是時差調整時最好的方法。如果只要覺得疲累時就睡覺,而且在鬧鐘響了還拒絕起床,那可能永遠也調不了。如果你能以到戶外享受陽光堅定地撐過疲累時光,短時間內就可以把自己調到新環境了。這完全看你和你的意志。

Part II

3 單字與例句

microbe　*n.* 微生物、細菌

You have to use a microscope to see microbes that cause the disease.
你需要用顯微鏡，才能看到造成這種疾病的細菌。

dietary　*adj.* 飲食的

Elder people usually have special dietary needs.
老年人通常都有特殊的飲食需求。

meridian　*n.* 經線、子午線

The Prime Meridian is an invisible line which runs from the North Pole to the South Pole.
初始子午線是條由北極到南極的無形線。

synchronization　*n.* 同步、同時性

The audio is out of synchronization with the video.
聲音跟影像不同步了。

cope　*n.* 處理、對付、解決

After being appointed as the CEO of the company, she is learning to cope with the demands of her busy schedule.
被指派為公司的總裁後，她學著處理她的忙碌行程。

fatigue　*n.* 疲乏、勞累

His health is deteriorating from fatigue caused by his busy schedule.
他的健康，正因為忙碌行程所造成的疲累而惡化。

知識備忘錄

　　不管是去美國或是回台灣，時差永遠是最大的難題。剛剛抵達目的地的兩三天，白天總是昏沉沉的，而每到夜晚卻又精神奕奕。這種日夜顛倒的狀態總要幾天才能恢復。

　　如何加速調適時差？一般而言，如果可能的話，把抵達時間安排成晚上，也就是說一抵達目的地就接近睡覺時間。搭飛機一定不好睡，一到達就睡覺，正好適應時差。還有在搭飛機時，把時間調成目的地的時區，然後按照目的地的時間做事，該吃飯就吃飯，該睡覺就睡覺。如果不是睡覺時間，強迫自己撐過去。看電影、聊天，真的累了起來上個洗手間，走動一下都可以。

　　根據網路上的說法，由西往東（美國到台灣）的時差，比起由東往西（台灣到美國）的時差，要難調適。其實我的經驗倒不是如此，我覺得兩地間的時間差距影響比較大。我比較常在加州、台灣間搭飛機。由加州到台灣的時差容易適應多了，最難的是從台灣到加州。我曾想過其中的原因，以下就是我的看法。

　　如果把人一天的行程攤開，並假設由晚上十一點睡到七點，而且假設不是美國日光節約時間，台灣的晚上十一點到七點是美國加州的下午三點到晚上十一點，而加州的晚上十一點到七點是台灣的早上七點到下午三點。仔細想想台灣人睡醒之時，加州人正準備睡覺，也就是說由台灣抵達加州撐了八小時不睡覺（原先的睡覺時間）後，就是睡覺時間。但是加州睡醒之後，卻是台灣下午三點，還要再撐八小時才能睡覺。簡單的說，就是要撐過十六小時，這可是最難調適的時差。如果網路的說法正確，那由西往東時差八小時，應該是最難調適的！還好實際生活上我不需要這樣的經驗。

Unit 43 打工常識

1 主題對話

Michael is talking to his roommate Daniel.
Michael 跟他的室友 Daniel 聊天。

Daniel	Hi, Michael. Haven't seen you lately, what have you been up to?	嗨，麥克，近來都沒看到你，都在做什麼？
Michael	The semester is ending. I am trying to get a part time job.	學期快結束了，我試著找打工的機會。
Daniel	Really? Do you have a green card?	真的嗎？你有綠卡嗎？
Michael	Yes, I have one. Does it matter?	我有，這有差別嗎？
Daniel	It does matter. Without the green card, you are not allowed to legally work in the US. You can only take a job in the school, for example, as a grader or a tutor. Since you have one, you can take a job without getting into any legal trouble.	有啊，差很多。沒有綠卡就不能合法的在美國工作，只能在學校裡面打工例如改作業或家教。既然你有綠卡，就可以安心找工作不用擔心。
Michael	Having a green card does help, I guess.	看來有綠卡真的有幫助。
Daniel	What kind of jobs are you looking at?	你想找什麼樣的工作？

| Michael | Any part time jobs would help. | 任何打工機會都可以。 |

| Daniel | You majored in Computer Science in your undergraduate study, right? | 你大學主修電腦對吧！ |

| Michael | Yes, I did. | 是啊。 |

| Daniel | How about getting a real job? Go to Silicon Valley and try getting a programmer job there. Programmers are in great demand there. | 那何不找個實際的工作？到矽谷去找個程式設計師的工作，那裏需要很多程式設計師。 |

| Michael | Can I? | 我可以嗎？ |

| Daniel | Sure you can. Based on your undergraduate degree plus your graduate study, you can easily get a job and work there for a couple of years, getting to know the latest industrial trend in computer science. Then, you can come back to finish your master degree. | 當然可以，根據你的大學學歷和你的碩士課程，你可以很輕易地找到並工作個一兩年，清楚業界最新的電腦趨勢，然後再回來修完你的碩士。 |

| Michael | Thank you. I'll seriously consider it. | 謝謝，我會慎重考慮。 |

| Daniel | Sure thing. | 不客氣。 |

Part II

2 心情小語

💜 Getting a job in US while you are in college would not be easy unless you are a US citizen or have a green card. Without either of them, it would be illegal for you to work in US, not even part time jobs. You can however, take an on-campus job because it is **permitted** by the United States Citizenship and **Immigration** Service (USCIS).

> 　　在學校裡想在美國找到工作很不容易，除非你是美國公民或有綠卡，兩者都沒有的話，在美國工作就不合法，連打工也是。但是你可以在學校裡打工，因為這是美國移民局准許的。

💜 The following are the rules for you to take the on-campus jobs. You must maintain valid F-1 status. You can work up to 20 hours per week while school is in **session**. You can work full time (40 hours per week) during holidays and vacation periods if you intend to register for the next semester. The employment may not displace (take a job away from) a U.S. resident. The problem is on-campus employment opportunities are limited. Even if you get an on-campus job, it would not provide enough financial support, and the worst of all, those jobs are probably not related to your studies, and would not be helpful when you are looking for a real job after getting a degree. Based on the rules and the actual situation, I would not suggest getting an on-campus job unless it is closely related to your major, or it can beef up your resume when you graduate.

以下是你要找校園工作的規定：你必須持續保有 F-1 學生簽證。學校上課期間每周可以工作到 20 小時，在假日和假期間你可以全職工作（一周 40 小時），前提是你下學期要註冊。這個工作不能搶走美國居民的工作。問題是，學校的工作機會原本就不多，就算你找到工作，賺的錢也不足以支付你的開銷，最壞的是，這些工作很可能跟你的學業無關，而且對你畢業後找工作也沒有幫助。根據規則與實際狀況，我不會建議你找學校的工作，除非跟你的主修相關，或是能讓你在畢業後的履歷加分。

❤ Off-campus employment is not entirely impossible, and actually there are four categories for off campus employment: optional practical training (OPT), **curricular** practical training (CPT), severe economic hardship, and approved international organizations. The later three cases are rare so I would not discuss them here. As for the first one, international students in U.S. holding valid F-1 immigration status are permitted to work off-campus in optional practical training (OPT) status both during and after completion of their degree.

校園外的工作並非完全不可能，實際上有四種種類的校園外工作機會：OPT 工作許可、CPT 學業相關工作許可、嚴重的經濟困難，以及受核可的國際組織。後三者機會渺茫，我就不討論了。至於第一類，在美國擁有合法學生簽證的學生，可以用工作許可在校外合法工作，不論是在學中或畢業後都可以。

❤ The rules for OPT before completing a degree:

- Students must be **enrolled** in school full-time
- Students may only work 20 hours per week while school is in session
- Students may work full-time during summer and other breaks (as long as the student will return to school after the break)
- Student may work full-time after completion of all coursework, if a thesis or dissertation is still required and student is making normal progress towards the degree

> 在學中的工作許可規定：
>
> ● 學生必須在學校全時註冊。
>
> ● 學生在上課期間，每週只可以工作 20 小時。
>
> ● 在暑假或其他假期可以全職工作（只要學生在假期結束後會回學校上課）。
>
> ● 學生可以在完成課業後，可以全時工作，如果還需要碩、博士論文而且學生在取得學位上也有適當的進度就可以。

❤ The rules for OPT after completing a degree:

- After completion of your degree, OPT work must be full time (40 hours/week)
- All OPT must be completed within 14 months after completion of your degree
- Applications for post-completion OPT must be received by USCIS before the completion of the degree

> 畢業後的工作許可規定：
>
> ● 在完成學位後可以全職工作（每周 40 小時）。
>
> ● 所有的工作許可，要在拿到學位後 14 個月之內完成。
>
> ● 工作許可的申請，必須在完成學位前交到移民局。

♥ OPT is permitted for up to 12 months, and the clock starts **ticking** once you apply for it. It should be noticed that both before and after completing a degree are counted into that duration. Thus, I would not suggest you taking OPT before getting your degree because it would only reduce your time to look for a job after graduation.

> 工作許可最多容許時間是 12 個月,而且只要你申請之後就開始計算。要注意到,不管是在學中或是畢業後的時間,都算在這個期限內。因此我不建議還在就學中就申請工作許可,因為這只會減少你畢業後可以找工作的時間。

Part II

3 單字與例句

permit *v./n.* 允許、許可

We'll discuss all questions if time permits.
時間容許的話，我們會討論所有問題。

immigration *n.* 移居、移民

There was a huge immigration of Chinese citizens to the USA to help with the railroad construction.
許多中國移民到美國幫助鐵路建設。

session *n.* 會期、開會、會議

At the end of the session, we all exited out of the meeting room and went out to have lunch.
會議結束後，我們都離開會議室到外面吃午餐。

curricular（單數） curriculum（複數） *n.* 課程

Studying topics outside of the curriculum, the student is very knowledgeable.
研究課外主題，這個學生很有知識。

enroll *v.* 註冊

He enrolled in an online college for the convenience.
因為方便，所以他到網路大學註冊。

tick *v.* 發出滴答聲（計時）、起作用

The clock is ticking and we don't have much time.
時鐘開始滴答響了，我們沒時間了。

知識備忘錄

　　說到在美國打工，美國移民局對 F-1（學生）簽證的學生有很嚴格的限制，基本上除了學校內的工作外，其他的工作可說是一律不准。除非你是公民或是有綠卡（永久居留證），合法的打工幾乎是不可能！或許你會說，前面不是講了有所謂的 OPT 工作許可，可以讓你找工作。問題是工作許可期限總共一年，你在學期中所使用的 OPT 時間，都會降低你日後畢業的 OPT 限額，也就限制了你在畢業後留在美國找工作的時間。我還是強烈建議把這十二個月都用在畢業後，比較實際。

　　我不建議在校內打工，除非工作內容和你的專業有關。就算每個小時有個十幾塊美金，對經濟幫助並不大。但是如果跟你的主修有關，或是對日後找工作有幫助，那就去爭取吧！說不定這會成為你一生的轉捩點。

　　在美國工作時，認識了一位大陸來的同事，他當時在公司裡管電腦。有次在閒聊中，才發現他的碩士學位和機械電腦完全無關。我問他怎麼會找到這個工作？原來他在學校裡聽到機械系的電腦教室在徵助理，於是臨時找了一些電腦書籍來看，也問了幾個主修電腦的朋友，做了些事前的準備，結果真的讓他應徵上。當時他知道機械碩士在美國比較不容易找工作，於是在得到這個機會後，他認真學習，有機會就看書，並藉由自己的工作，學會管理電腦網路。他的認真態度也贏得了系上教授的讚揚，日後到矽谷就靠這個經驗，以及他系上教授的強力推薦，找到了第一份網路管理的工作，從此變成矽谷的電腦網路工程師。

　　看了以上實際的例子，是不是給了你一點啟發與激勵？

Part II

Part III
留在國外
找工作

Unit 44　履歷如何寫

1　主題對話

Michael is talking to his roommate Daniel about preparing a résumé.

Michael 跟他的室友 Daniel 聊到了如何準備履歷。

Michael	Congratulations on passing your thesis defense and getting the degree.	恭喜你通過論文答辯獲得學位。
Daniel	Thanks, but now I am facing an even tougher task, finding a job.	謝謝，但是我目前面對一個更大的問題：找工作。
Michael	How do you proceed?	你要怎麼進行？
Daniel	The first thing I need to do is to prepare a résumé.	第一件要處理的當然是準備履歷。
Michael	Is there anything that I can learn from you?	有什麼可以跟你學習的嗎？
Daniel	I can share with you my experience in working on my résumé.	我可以跟你分享我準備履歷的經驗。
Michael	That would be really helpful to me.	那會對我有很大的幫助。
Daniel	The first and the most important rule that you have to remember is 10 seconds and counting.	首先也是最重要、需要記住的，就是十秒鐘，計時開始。
Michael	What does that mean?	意思是？

Daniel	Recruiters spend an average of 10 seconds glancing over each résumé, so you have to **seize** their attention in the brief but precious 10 seconds. If you fail to let them feel like taking a second look at your résumé, you have no chance of getting an interview.	徵聘人員平均花十秒鐘看每份履歷，所以你必須在寶貴的十秒內抓住他們的注意力。如果你沒法讓他們覺得這份履歷值得再看一次，你永遠不會有面試的機會。
Michael	Wow, that sure is critical. I need to keep that in mind.	哇！這可真嚴重。我會好好記住。
Daniel	You need to keep it **concise**, structured and specific, and customize your résumé for each job opening. Also, in this internet age, you absolutely need to include some keywords in your résumé.	履歷需要簡短、架構化、特定化並對每份工作客製化，同時在這個網路時代，履歷裡面一定要包含一些關鍵字。
Michael	What do you mean by that?	你的意思是？
Daniel	A lot of big companies are using computer software to screen through all the résumé, and those keywords would help yours stand out from others'. You can use Google and search the keywords in your profession.	很多大公司用電腦軟體來篩選所有的履歷，而這些關鍵字可以凸顯你的履歷，你可以用谷歌來搜尋出你這個行業的關鍵字。
Michael	Thanks, and I learned a lot today.	感謝，我學了很多。
Daniel	Sure thing.	不客氣。

Part III

2 心情小語

❤ If you want to have a better chance of getting jobs in US, a well prepared résumé is a must. As stated in the previous section, recruiters or hiring managers only have 10 seconds or less to take a peek at your résumé and decide if it deserves a second look. You need to get their attention immediately just to pass the first round of screening.

> 如果你想要在美國找到更好的工作機會，一份俐落實用的履歷可是必備的。如同在前一節裡所提的，徵聘人員或是人事經理只有不到十秒的時間來看你的履歷，並決定是否值得再看一次；要通過第一輪的篩選，你需要立刻抓住他們的注意。

❤ To grab their attentions in 10 seconds or less, you really need to work on your qualifications and career objectives. List 3 to 4 key qualifications and be specific with regards to what you can offer pertaining to those qualifications. Those items should clearly identify your strength and capability for the job, plus what you can bring to the table for the company. It needs to be concise, **distinct**, and eye-catching.

> 要在不到十秒的時間裡引起別人的注意，你需要好好地寫你的適任資格和生涯目標。列出三到四項你符合工作需求的優點，標出你能為工作貢獻的特色，以及跟這些資格相符的特質。你必須把你的長處、能力以及能為公司帶來的價值清楚的顯現在履歷中，而且必須要簡潔、有特色、引人注目。

❤ For a new college graduate with little work experience, you need to have a couple sentences for objective statement. Again, it needs to be short, notable, and to the point. The qualifications and objectives should be customized to fit the specific position that you are applying. Research on the position and the company, talk to current or formal employees if you can, do whatever you can to find out the goals and culture of the company, and adapt the qualifications and objectives to reflect the priority emphasized for the position.

> 對一個沒什麼工作經驗的大學畢業生而言，你需要一到兩句的生涯目標。再強調一次：簡潔、引人注意、扼要。針對你所申請的每個工作，客製你的能力資格與生涯目標。對你要申請的公司和職位做一些研究，或是可能的話，跟現任或過去的員工聊聊，盡可能地找出公司的目標與文化。修改你的能力資格與生涯目標，來反映這個位置上所強調的優先項目。

♥ With the carefully scripted qualifications and objectives to get you into second round of résumé review, you now need to beef up the content to get them into calling you. Again, customization is the absolutely top priority. First and foremost, resist the **temptation** of telling them everything you have done and you can do. Look at your résumé from the hiring manager's point of view. What they need to know to get them into contacting you? Select the skills, capabilities, achievements, and experience that point directly to their suggested and implied needs. Add some of the related courses you took if necessary. Focus on making the description listed on the résumé as a summary of what you accomplished at school and what you can contribute to the job and the company. Please remember that a résumé is a marketing document, not a laundry list of the jobs you've done. Before writing a résumé, you should carefully study the job description and get as much information as possible. Then you can make a much better presentation of you, being the perfect person for the job.

Part III

有了細心準備的能力資格與生涯目標讓你進入第二輪的履歷評估後,你需要加強內容,設法讓他們打電話給你。再強調一次:客製化是最重要的項目。最重要的,就是要克制那種想要把你所有做過的及能做的事情一吐而快的衝動。試著從人事經理的觀點來看你的履歷:什麼樣的能力和特點會讓他們想和你聯絡?用這個方式推出一個目標,把和這個目標相符合的技術、能力、成就與經驗列出來;甚至加上你曾修讀過的相關課程。把你選擇列出來的資料,統整成你可以對公司做出貢獻的結論。請記住:履歷是一份行銷文件,不是你所完成的工作清單。在寫履歷之前,你應該要仔細研究職位的細節,試著得到任何可得到的資訊,然後你才可以有個更好的機會,來陳述你是這個工作的最佳人選。

3 單字與例句

seize　*v.* 抓住、捉住

Seizing the opportunity, she introduced herself to the famous movie director.
捉住機會,她跟那位知名的電影導演自我介紹。

concise　*adj.* 簡潔的、簡要的

The summary needs to be concise, to the point and convincing.
結論需要簡潔、扼要、有說服力。

distinct　*adj.* 有特色的、特殊的

Coming from Eastern Europe, he has a distinct accent.
由東歐而來,他有個特殊的口音。

temptation　*n.* 引誘、誘惑

The chocolate cake was too much of a temptation to the kids.
這巧克力蛋糕對小孩而言,是個太大的誘惑。

談到準備履歷，美國和台灣還真有些不同。首先美國履歷沒有照片，而美國公司的大小也有很大的不同。從橫跨全球員工幾十萬人的國際公司，到只有幾個人的超小公司都有。針對大小不同的公司，當然你的履歷也要有所不同。對於大型的美國公司，許多已經會事先用電腦來篩選履歷，而電腦最優先挑選的，多半是跟每個工作有關的關鍵字，這也是我在前面再三強調的履歷表裡一定要有關鍵字的原因。如果你的履歷裡關鍵字不夠多，電腦就直接把它給擺在一邊，連給人看的機會都沒有。當然如果是小公司，那關鍵字就不是那麼重要。

　　準備履歷上一定要注意的就是：十秒鐘。美國公司不管大小，多半都有一堆履歷要篩選、審核。在第一輪時，每份履歷確實只有十秒不到的時間，來決定去或留。如果一眼之間沒法讓人覺得留，你基本上就玩完了。

　　我還記得當年為了吸引目光，我把我的名字寫成：TC（Circuit Designer）Hung，子健（線路設計師）洪。當時雇用我的經理後來跟我說，當她看到這個括號線路設計師時，就決定一定要跟這個人聊聊。我的能力資格裡列出三大項：Good at（專長）、Familiar with（熟悉）、Worked with（曾經做過），另一家公司的雇用經理跟我說，這三項簡單、明瞭一眼就看出我擅長的項目和會執行的技能。

　　當然這兩個項目並不適用於電腦篩選，這也是我一直強調的，要根據公司型態、工作項目來客製化你的履歷，這是最重要的一點！

Part III

Unit 45　如何找工作

1　主題對話

Michael is talking to his roommate Daniel about looking for a job.
Michael 跟他的室友 Daniel 聊到了如何找工作。

Michael	You prepared the résumé, right? So, how is your job hunting?	履歷準備好了吧！工作找得如何？
Daniel	It's going well, I think. I got several telephone interviews and I am going to have some on-site interview next week.	看來還不錯。有幾次的電話面試，下禮拜也會有幾次的面對面的面試。
Michael	Wow, that is great. Could you tell me some details about job hunting?	哇，這太好了！能不能告訴我相關的細節？
Daniel	Sure, in terms of getting a job, the first step is, not surprisingly, preparing a résumé as we talked before. After that, you need to find the companies and the jobs that you are more qualified and interested in.	當然，說到找工作第一件事，毫不意外的就是，上次說過的準備履歷，然後要找到你可以勝任又有興趣的公司和工作。
Michael	How or where can I find the information?	我該怎麼找、到哪裡找相關的資訊呢？
Daniel	Get on the internet. Previously monster.com is one of the most popular recruiting website, but now LinkedIn is getting more and more popular.	上網去找，早先巨獸公司 (monter.com) 就是個很受歡迎的就業網站，但是現在則是鄰客音 (LinkedIn) 越來越受歡迎了。

Michael	LinkedIn? What is that?	鄰客音？是什麼啊？
Daniel	LinkedIn is a social networking website for people in professional occupations. You can also join LinkedIn's professional groups that are related to your major and learn the latest trend in your field. You can further expand your reach and even find some tips in how to prepare a résumé.	鄰客音是個專業人士的社群網站，你也可以加入裡面跟你主修有關的專業群組，並可以得知你專業上的最新趨勢，你可以擴展你的社交圈，甚至找到一些準備履歷的小撇步。
Michael	I would definitely take a look and possibly sign up.	我一定會去看看，也很可能會加入。
Daniel	You can also go to the websites of the companies which you are interested in, and search for any opening that fits your major. There is one more important tip for you. Contact those friends or alumni who are working for those companies to send your résumé for you, directly to the hiring manager if possible.	你也可以到你有興趣的公司網站，去找找看有沒有相關適合你主修的職缺。告訴你一個很重要的技巧：跟已經在那些公司裡工作的朋友或校友聯絡，並請他們幫你送履歷，可能的話，直接給雇用經理。
Michael	Isn't it kind of troublesome to them?	對他們是不是有點麻煩？
Daniel	Not at all. In fact, almost all companies provide **referral** bonus to the persons who submit the résumés of those who get hired. In most cases, they would love to submit your résumé.	完全不會，事實上幾乎所有公司都有提供介紹獎金，給那些成功介紹就職員工的人。他們會很高興幫你送履歷。

Part III

| Michael | I didn't know that. Thanks for all the information. | 我還不知道這件事,謝謝你告訴我這些資訊。 |
| Daniel | My pleasure. | 我的榮幸。 |

❤ For an international student without a green card, finding a job in US is surely more difficult than the students with one. However, with determination, **persistence**, good preparation and sufficient skill sets, you could still get a job that you like, especially if you are majoring in Computer Science. In my opinion, today's job hunting started from the day you stepped into the classroom. Getting a good grade would help you enormously.

> 對於一個沒有綠卡的國際學生,在美國找工作是比起有綠卡的更難。但只要有決心、做好良好的準備,並具有足夠的專業技能,你還是可以找到你喜歡的工作,特別當你主修的是電腦。在我看來,現代找工作的程序,其實從你踏進教室的那天就開始了。拿到好成績會對你有極大的幫助。

❤ As soon as you started your student life, join LinkedIn, the number one social networking website for professionals. Get connected to those who are in the similar majors and expand your reach and connection. While in school, get to know more friends and those who are more senior than you. Those friends and extra connections could be the ticket for you to get a job in the future.

學生生活開始後，盡快加入鄰客音，那是美國最大的專業人士社群網站。跟那些有類似主修的人打上關係，同時擴展你的社交圈。在學校裡，多認識些朋友，以及比你資歷深的學生，這些朋友和額外的關係，可能就是你未來找到工作的門票。

❤ In previous sections, we talked about preparing a résumé and how to get in touch with the companies with opening position. Now, I like to talk about the next step: the interview.

在前面章節，我們已經提到了如何準備履歷，以及如何和有職缺的公司聯絡。現在我想談談下一個步驟：面試。

❤ For most US companies, the interview is a long and enduring process. It would take at least half a day and sometimes a full day. If you don't live nearby, the company would start out with telephone interview, sometimes twice or even three times. Remember one thing: talking on the phone is way different from talking in person. Write down every question you have been asked in every telephone interview, and look for the best answers to those questions. Write down those answers and have it ready next to the phone. Talk to your friends who are also looking for jobs, exchange the questions being asked. Helping each other is the best way for all of you to get offers.

對多數美國公司來說，面試是個漫長、持久的過程，最少半天，有時則要一整天。如果不住在附近，公司往往會先進行電話面試，有時甚至多達二、三次。首先要記得，在電話中交談跟面對面對談有很大的不同。寫下每次電話面談所提到的問題，找出最好的答案，並放在電話旁邊隨時準備使用。跟一樣也在找工作的朋友聊聊，互相交換一下被問到的問題。互相幫助是找到工作的最好方法。

Part III

♥ The onsite interview usually has three to four people asking questions related to the position. Before the interview, make sure you **assemble** and **compile** all the questions being previously **inquired**, and be well prepared for those questions. If you **encounter** questions you don't know, try to find out more information about it and see if you can come out with possible solution. Some questions are not meant to be correctly answered but are used to see your reaction and **sentiment** when you try to overcome an **obstruction**. Don't just give up when you face a tough question. Sometimes these questions are given to see your **tenacity**.

> 　　現場面試通常會有三到四位考官，向你提問和工作職位相關的問題。面試前，先收集並編輯先前被詢問過的問題，做好準備。如果碰到一些毫無頭緒的問題，試著找出相關的資訊，並試著找出解決方案。有些問題並不一定要有正確答案，而只是用來測試你在解決難題時的反應與情緒。碰到難題時，不要放棄，這些難題可能只是用來測試你的韌性。

♥ Take my advises and prepare well for the interview. Getting a job isn't as tough as you think it would be.

> 　　參考我的建議，為面試做好準備。找個工作並沒有你想像的那麼難。

 **單字與例句**

referral *n.* 推薦、介紹

If you need to see a specialist, you need a referral from your family doctor.
如果你需要見一個專業醫師，你需要家庭醫師的轉薦。

persistence *n.* 堅持、持久、固執

The hunter showed great persistence in pursuing the deer.
在追尋那頭鹿上面，那位獵人展現了超強的持久力。

assemble *v.* 招集、聚集、裝配

Their father helped the kids assemble the new bikes.
孩子們的老爸幫忙小孩裝配了些腳踏車。

compile *v.* 收集、編輯、編譯

They assembled the best poems and compiled them into a book.
他們收集了最好的詩編輯成一本書。

inquire *v.* 詢問、調查

At the front lobby, we inquired about the holiday rates.
在前門大廳，我們詢問了假日的價錢。

encounter *v.* 遭遇、遇到

The hotel staff would do their best to help you when you encounter problems.
在你遭遇任何問題時，旅館員工會盡力幫你。

Part III

sentiment *n.* 心情、情緒、觀點

The editor's criticism of the government's decision expressed a sentiment shared by many citizens.
那位編輯對政府的指責,表達了許多市民的情緒。

obstruction *n.* 阻礙、妨礙、阻塞

After the typhoon, they removed trees and other obstruction from the streets.
颱風過後,他們移開了許多樹以及其他街上的障礙物。

tenacity *n.* 固執、堅持、韌性

Showing her tenacity, she finally overcame the obstacles and obstruction.
展現了她的韌性,她終於克服了所有的障礙與阻礙。

知識備忘錄

　　說到找工作，我還真可以分享一下我的經驗。我開始找工作時正碰上電腦產業起飛的年代，慢慢就有越來越多電話面試的機會。當時我就發現，電話裡交談，跟面對面交談真是差太多了！因為看不到對方的表情，你完全不知道對方聽到你回答時的反應。我當時的英文還不是很順暢，電話裡溝通是一大難題，所以更需要好好準備。但是電話面談也有好處，就是對方看不到你，所以你可以把答案寫在電話邊，方便你回答。

　　後來有了幾次實際面談，去過奧斯汀兩次、達拉斯和矽谷一次，早上去，下午才結束，一般大概都超過半天。不過說實話，時間越長越好。我就曾聽說過有人面試了第一位之後，人事就出面說：謝謝光臨，有空再連絡，連午餐都沒得吃！還有一件事很有意思，看對方請你吃的午餐，就約略知道你的面試結果。如果吃的是很不錯的餐廳，你就知道一切順利，奧斯汀的一次和矽谷那次，一進餐廳看那個排場，就知道工作大概拿到了。

　　最後我想提一下談薪水，如果沒把握的話，你就直接說按市場行情。如果你已經有工作了，可以提出來哪些公司已經要你了，有數字把數字說出來也沒關係。如果你說了個數字，對方也答應了，那就不要再提高了。除非你事後又想拿到更好的價錢。如果你真想為這家公司工作，可以再提一次，只要差價不高，是有機會拉高一點，不過最多一次。美國薪水不像台灣有固定的範圍，只要有能力，以後不怕拿不到高薪。

Part III

Part IV
返國後

同校同學會

1 主題對話

Daniel Chen is talking to Hudson Lin about a possible gathering.
Daniel 跟 Hudson 談到一場可能的聚會。

Daniel	I was told you are from UCLA, right?	我聽說你從洛杉磯加大來的。
Hudson	Yes, I got my Master degree there couples of years ago. I've been working here ever since I graduated there.	是，幾年前我從那裡拿到碩士，畢業後就來這裡了。
Daniel	I just got a job and moved here a few months ago. Do you know anyone who is also from Los Angeles?	我剛找到工作，幾個月前搬來的，你認識其他從洛杉磯來的人嗎？
Hudson	Yes, I do know some people from there, and actually, we get together from time to time.	我是認識幾個，事實上我們偶而會聚一下。
Daniel	I'd like to have a chance to know them if possible. Is there any FB group for this purpose?	有機會的話我想認識他們，有任何這類目的的臉書團體嗎？
Hudson	Actually, there is Facebook group created by us. You can join it and get the latest news.	我們有一個臉書社團你可以參加，還可以從上面看到大家得最新消息。

Daniel	Great. Since I just came here, I'd like to know friends from Taiwan, especially those from the same school. By the way, you just mentioned that you guys occasionally have gatherings. Do you know when the next one is?	太棒了，自從來到這裡後，我就想多認識一些台灣同學，尤其是同校的朋友。還有你剛剛提到偶而會有聚會，你知道下一次會是什麼時候嗎？
Hudson	I have no idea, but we haven't had one in probably more than a year. Maybe it's time for another one.	我不知道，不過也差不多一年多沒聚過了，或許該再辦一次了。
Daniel	That would be great.	那很棒。
Hudson	I'll call a couple of guys and set up the time and a place. I'll let you know when I have more information.	我會先連絡幾個朋友，商定時間、地點，等有更多消息時再通知你。
Daniel	You can also post the gathering information on Facebook group, right?	你也會把聚會訊息放到臉書社團裡，對吧。
Hudson	Yes, can you do that for me?	沒錯，你能幫我嗎？
Daniel	Sure, right after I am accepted into the group.	當然，等我加入以後立刻會做。
Hudson	Thanks.	謝謝。
Daniel	I should thank you.	應該是我謝謝你啦。

Part IV

2 心情小語

♥ Before the internet age, it is much more challenging to stay in touch with old classmates, friends and alumni. Even if you carefully **preserve** their addresses and phone numbers, it can become useless when they move and change their numbers. That is what happens to me, and I lost contact with almost all of my college and grad school classmates. Luckily, as I mentioned several times in this book, the internet changed everything.

在網路時代前,要和老同學、老朋友和校友保持聯絡,可真是個大挑戰。就算你小心的保存了他們地址、電話,在他們搬家、換號碼以後,還是一無所用。這正是發生在我身上的情況,我幾乎失去所有大學和研究所同學的聯絡資料。幸運的是,如同我在書裡所說的,網路改變了每件事情。

♥ Social network websites are more popular each day, and with them, it is a lot easier to get in touch with your friends, alumni and former colleagues. By joining FB, twitter, Instagram and **myriads** of other social networking sites, you can easily **establish** connection and stay in touch with them. Also, try to find the FB or LinkedIn groups that are of interest to you and join them. If there isn't any FB group for the particular one you are interested in, you can start a new one **proactively** and invite your friends to join.

社群網路越來越普及,透過這些網路,也更容易和朋友、校友和以前的同事保持聯絡,經由加入臉書、推特、即時影音,還有其他無數的社群網站,你可以輕鬆的建立管道,並跟親友們保持聯絡。同時在臉書或是鄰客音裡,尋找你有興趣的團體加入。如果在臉書沒找到有興趣的團體,你可以自己創設一個社團,並邀請你的朋友加入。

💜 I joined FB in 2009, and it didn't take long for me to find my Aggies friends and classmates from high school and college in **cyber** space. Through these friends, I get in touch with more friends and classmates. I even get to know some senior Aggies I never would have a chance of getting **acquaintance**. I joined several groups in FB and really enjoy the convenience.

> 我在 2009 年加入臉書，沒多久就在網絡空間中找到些高中、大學同學，還有台灣的德州農工校友。經由這些人，我和更多的朋友和同學取得連絡，我甚至認識了幾位我原先不可能認識的資深校友。我也加入了幾個臉書社團，享受臉書社團帶來的便利。

💜 Planning a reunion is easier with the help of social networking websites. Instead of the conventional phone calls, you can post a reunion message on FB or twitter, and easily spread the words. I know some people who don't use FB in Taiwan, but it is still a simple and straightforward alternative, especially if you can post the messages on the group page.

> 在社群網站的幫助下，舉辦同學會變得更簡單了。你不用像以前一樣用電話聯絡，而可以將相關訊息放在臉書或推特上，用網路把訊息散布出去。我知道在台灣還有些人沒用臉書，但這確實是個簡單、直接的替代方案，尤其是當你可以透過社團張貼資訊的時候。

💜 Finally, I would like to mention that I have a fan page on FB, which is learn English with TC. You are more than welcome to join the fan page and start learning English with mc.

> 最後我想提一下，我在臉書也有個粉絲專頁就是「跟 TC 學英文」。歡迎你加入這個粉絲團，並開始跟我學英文。

Part Ⅳ

3 單字與例句

preserve　*v.* 保存、保藏

We need to take effective measures to preserve our natural resources.
我們需要採取有效的方法，來保存我們的天然資源。

myriad　*adj.* 無數的、大量的

I was surrounded by myriad of trees in the forest.
我在森林裡被大量的樹所包圍。

establish　*v.* 建立、設立、確立

The company has established itself as a leader in the computer industry.
這公司已經將自己建立成為電腦工業的領導者。

proactively　*adv.* 主動地、積極地

Let's move forward and proactively work on the solutions.
我們往前進並主動地尋找解決方法。

cyber　*adj.* 電腦的、網路的

In this internet age, there are more and more cyber-crimes.
在這網路時代，電腦犯罪越來越多。

acquaintance　*n.* 相識、了解

To me, David is more of an acquaintance than a friend.
我跟 David 只是認識，不算是朋友。

知識備忘錄

　　還記得我剛回台灣工作的第一個星期，就接到高中同班同學的電話。我當時我真的很驚訝，因為除了家人之外，我還沒通知其他台灣朋友我回國了。當時他就說，因為他曾在工研院待過，透過 Google 就搜尋到剛回工研院上班的我。我也因此和其他高中同學取得聯繫，兩個月內就參加了回台後第一次的高中同學會。說真的，這還真得感謝網路和 Google。

　　在加入 FB 之後，就跟越來越多的往日同學朋友連絡上，也參加了好幾次的高中同學會，也和一些朋友、昔日同學聚會。不過說實話，就算社群網路提供這些便利的方式讓大家互相聯絡，還是要有個熱心的人把大家隨時的串在一起。如果你懷念當年的相處時光，而又沒人自告奮勇地做這件事時，或許就是你主動擔起責任的時候了！到 FB 籌組個新群組，邀請大家加入就可以了。

　　在參加過幾次的同學會和聚會之後，也發現了一些是有些人真的很忙，沒什麼時間參加。有些人就是從不出現，我不知道為什麼？或許有人愛面子，覺得沒什麼成就，不好意思參加也說不定！但是我相信友誼是永久的，真正的朋友不會計較榮華富貴，不論你在學校時成績如何，不論你出社會後狀況怎麼樣，同學、朋友是一輩子的。跟老朋友見面聊聊才是真的。更何況人生沒有永遠的順遂，也不會有永久的低潮，有需要時，同學會永遠會是最好的管道，有機會就參加吧！

Part IV

Unit 47 聯絡國外友人

1 主題對話

Michael is talking on the phone with his American friend, Cameron Taylor.

Michael 跟他的美國朋友 Cameron Taylor 在電話裡聊天。

Michael	I just passed my thesis defense and I am going to graduate this semester.	我剛剛通過論文口試，會在這學期會畢業。
Cameron	Congratulations, You finally get the credit you deserve. What's your next plan?	恭喜，你終於得到你應有的榮譽，你的下一步呢？
Michael	Thanks. I am starting to look for a job and take on the next step of my life.	謝謝，我正開始找工作，進行我人生的下一階段。
Cameron	Are you going to look at any local company?	找過本地的公司嗎？
Michael	Yes, but there are more opportunities in Silicon Valley. Given a chance, I would like to stay here though.	有，不過矽谷機會比較多，只是如果可以的話，我還是想待在這裡。
Cameron	Good for you. Anything I can help?	很棒，有什麼我可以幫忙的嗎？
Michael	Not really, but thanks for the offering. I am calling to thank you for the great dinner we had last Thanksgiving. I had a great time and learned a lot of American traditions.	應該沒有，不過謝謝你。我打來是要感謝你上個感恩節準備的豐富晚餐，那是段愉快的時光，而且我也學到了許多美國傳統。

Cameron	We really enjoyed it too, and we got to learn more about Taiwan, and we'd like to visit Taiwan in the next couple of years. Taking a tour of National Palace Museum, the night market, street vendors, Taipei 101, and the Love River. We would definitely have fun there.	我們也很高興啊！而且我們也更加認識台灣，過幾年我們想去台灣看看，去故宮博物院、夜市、攤販、台北 101、還有愛河，一定會很好玩。
Michael	Don't forget Mount Ali and Taroko National Park. Do you have a Facebook account? I'd like to add you to my friend list and be your tour guide when you visit there.	不要忘了阿里山和太魯閣。你有臉書嗎？我想把你加入朋友，等你去台灣時當你的導遊。
Cameron	Sure, just search by my email address. Please let me know if you need any help in your job hunting.	當然有，用我的電子郵件地址可以找到。如果找工作上需要幫忙的話讓我知道。
Michael	I will, and please accept my friend invitation. It's a lot more convenient and easier for us to get in touch.	我會的，請接受我的臉書朋友邀請，會更方便、更容易的讓我們保持聯絡。
Cameron	Let me check. OK, it's done. Good luckin looking for a job.	讓我看看，OK，好了。祝你找工作好運。
Michael	Thanks, I need it. Nice talking to you, bye.	謝謝，我需要這好運，很高興跟你聊，再見。
Cameron	Bye.	再見。

Part IV

② 心情小語

💙 Have you heard of Myspace? Never? Don't worry, because most Taiwanese have not heard of it either. **Launched** in 2003, Myspace quickly became **ubiquitous** among teenagers and young adults. IIn February 2005, it was in talk of acquiring FB. News Corporation purchased Myspace for $580 million in July 2005. In June 2006, it overtook Google as the most visited website in US. From 2005 to early 2008, it was the most visited social networking site. During that time, it was more like Myspace in the West Coast and FB in the East, but actually Myspace was considered the most prominent social networking site and the emerging FB did not diminish Myspace's popularity. In 2007, Myspace was valued at $12 billion.

> 聽說過聚友網嗎？從沒聽說過？不用擔心，因為多數的台灣人也沒聽說過。2003 年創立後，聚友網很快地受到青少年和年輕人的歡迎，實際上，在 2005 年 5 月，聚友網一度曾談過要收購臉書。新聞集團在 2005 年 7 月以五億八千萬美元收購聚友網。在 2008 年 6 月，它超越谷歌成為美國最多人拜訪的網站。從 2005 到 2008 早期，它是最多人拜訪的社群網站。在那時候，西岸流行的是聚友網，而東岸流行的是臉書。不過實際上，聚友網被認為是最受歡迎的社群網站，當時興起的臉書還無法對它造成威脅。在 2007 年，聚友網的估計價值是 120 億美金。

💙 FB eclipse Myspace as the number one social networking site in 2008, and since then, Myspace has been in a downward **spiral** and kept losing membership. There are several suggestions and theories for its **demise**. In my opinion, one of the most important factors was while FB concentrated and still is focusing on creating a clean and an effective social networking platform, Myspace was more concerned about making money. Myspace was sold for only $35 million in June 2009.

在 2008，臉書超越聚友網，成為第一名的社群網站。從此之後，聚友網就盤旋而下，持續失去會員。對於它的垮台，各界有許多見解和理論，在我看來，最重要的因素之一，就是臉書持續的專注在建立一個簡潔、有效的社群網路平台，而聚友網更關心於如何賺錢。在 2009 年 6 月，聚友網僅僅以三千五百萬美元出售。

❤ Why am I telling you this? Myspace crashed partly because of its **misdeeds**, but it's more related to the rising of the FB. If FB **dwindles**, it would be caused by the emerging of a more popular and simpler social networking site. You and your friends would have plenty of time to move from FB to the better site. Just enjoy the convenience of FB for now and let the general public decide if there is a better alternative.

　　我為什麼説這個故事？聚友網垮台，有些原因是因為它的一些錯誤，但是跟臉書的興起更有關係。如果用臉書的人數減少了，多半會是因為另一個更受歡迎、更簡單使用的社群網站的興起。你和你的朋友，會有很多時間從臉書搬到更好的網站。目前只管享受臉書的便利，並讓一般老百姓來決定，是否有個更好的選擇。

Part IV

3 單字與例句

launch　*v.* 招集、裝配、發射、開辦

iPhone one was launched on June 29, 2007.
第一代 iPhone 在 2007 年發表的。

ubiquitous　*adj.* 到處存在的、普遍存在的

The smart phone has become ubiquitous around the world, as it is seen everywhere.
智慧型手機已經遍布世界，到處都看的到。

spiral　*n.* 螺旋、盤旋 形容詞：盤旋的、螺旋的 動詞：螺旋、盤旋

With one of the blades hitting the tree, the helicopter spiraled out of control.
其中的一個螺旋槳打到了一棵樹，直升機就失去控制。

demise　*n.* 死亡、終止

His demise happened so sudden that it caught everyone off guard.
他的死亡太快了，讓大家完全沒有（心理）準備。

misdeed　*n.* 不端行為、錯誤、罪刑

You have to pay for the consequence whenever you commit a misdeed.
對你所犯的錯誤都要付出代價。

dwindle　*v.* 變小、縮小

With the economy getting worse, the company's revenue is dwindling.
經濟越來越差，公司的營收也變小了。

知識備忘錄

　　如果説跟台灣的同學、朋友保持連絡的最好方式是臉書，那跟美國朋友更需要臉書。臉書在美國受歡迎的程度比台灣高多了。問問你的老外朋友，應該都有臉書帳號，記得先把他們加入朋友。有了這個關係，就很容易持續保持聯絡了。如果你不相信臉書在美國更流行，2009 牛津字典年度最夯單字就是臉書裡的 unfriend：刪除好友。以下是牛津字典對 unfriend 的定義：

unfriend - verb - To remove someone as a 'friend' on a social networking site such as Facebook. As in, "I decided to unfriend my roommate on Facebook after we had a fight."

　　刪除好友 - 動詞 - 將原先是諸如臉書的社群網站裡的某人，由朋友名單移除。例如：在我們吵架以後，我決定把我的室友在臉書上移除好友。

　　我在 2009 加入臉書，而當時刪除好友已經成為牛津字典的年度風雲字，就知道臉書當時有多受歡迎，更何況是四、五年後的今天。另外如果你的朋友是年輕的大學生，或許要加上推特（twitter）或是即時影音（Instagram），基本上就把多數美國人涵蓋在內了。可能的話問問你的朋友，看看臉書裡有沒有相關的團體，直接加入會更方便。

　　當然加入臉書朋友後，有空就跟朋友打打招呼、熱絡一下保持關係。不要沒事都不連絡，有事才找人幫忙，這感覺總是不好。至少偶爾上上社群網站，聯絡感情。

Part IV

留學達人英語通 Here I Come! USA

作者	洪子健◎著
特約編輯	焦家洵
封面設計	高鍾琪
內頁構成	華漢電腦排版有限公司
發行人	周瑞德
企劃編輯	丁筠馨
執行編輯	陳欣慧
校對	徐瑞璞、劉俞青
印製	大亞彩色印刷製版股份有限公司
初版	2014 年 04 月
定價	新台幣 329 元
出版	倍斯特出版事業有限公司
	電話／（02）2351-2007 傳真／（02）2351-0887
	地址／ 100 台北市中正區福州街 1 號 10 樓之 2
	Email ／ best.books.service@gmail.com
總經銷	商流文化事業有限公司
	地址／新北市中和區中正路 752 號 7 樓
	電話／（02）2228-8841 傳真／（02）2228-6939
港澳地區總經銷	泛華發行代理有限公司
	地址／香港筲箕灣東旺道 3 號星島新聞集團大廈 3 樓
	電話／（852）2798-2323 傳真／（852）2796-5471

版權所有　翻印必究